ONCE UPON A WAVE OF WITCHES

ELI BELT & HELEN WHISTBERRY
ONCE UPON A WAVE OF WITCHES
A BEATRICE & AMELIA ADVENTURE
ILLUSTRATED BY HELEN WHISTBERRY

From Eli:

To Angelia, who inspired Coral, I only wish I could have made you immortal too
To my cousin Gabbi, who loved the tale
And to my coauthor Helen, who insisted we should share this with the world and
not just a story we told ourselves

From Helen:

Most anything that astounds the reader in this volume can be attributed to my
coauthor Eli, who has the most amazing imagination in all the world
And as always, to my sister, who inspired my writing and art journey

CONTENTS

CONTENT WARNING

Content warning for limb loss/amputation, brief violence, depression and trauma

Welcome

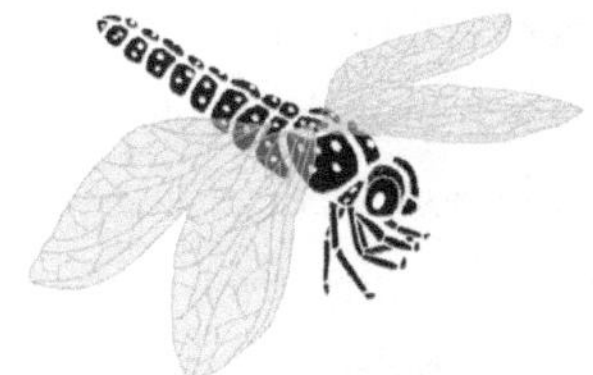

CHAPTER 1

MOVING HOUSE

B EATRICE BUTTONS FELT AN itch, followed by a twitch. Her toes wiggled and jiggled and implored her to wake up and get going. It was the morning of her fifty-seventh birthday, which could mean only one thing: Moving Day!

The owner of an adventurous and restless spirit, she was filled with a yearning to experience as many different places and meet as many different folks as was possible in one lifetime. So, every year on her birthday, she packed up the few things she wanted to keep into a pair of saddlebags and rode off on her trusty companion, Sir Walks-a-lot.

Sir Walks-a-lot was a nuff, a sloth-like creature that walked on its stupendously long front legs while its hind legs had great sails like a bat's wings that enabled it to fly shorter distances by catching the passing breezes. Their soft, fur-covered backs bent into a shape not unlike a plush wingback chair, allowing a rider to travel in comfort. They also had happy and affectionate natures, making them the perfect traveling companion.

As for Beatrice, she wasn't particularly tall or wide or anything out of the ordinary for the people of Lichen. She had silver-gray skin, celadon green eyes, and dark brown curls mixed with stray white hairs sticking out like snowy twigs of straw. Her small delicate-looking hands belied their strength and cunning, and she loved to wear clothes with exuberant patterns on them so she would always have something beautiful and exciting to look upon.

Some years, Beatrice and her nuff wandered for weeks looking for a new house, setting up camp each night under a patchwork quilt tent. Dinner was most often a steaming bowl of forager's stew with Bea's findings of the day from forest and stream, and a pitcher of ade made with moss-filtered water and the hard-rinded, bright gold limonberries that grew plentifully in thorny bushes along the road. She whiled away her evenings whittling fantastical creatures from fallen branches of soft basswood and set out each morning well-rested and with a merry heart.

This year, her journey lasted no more than a day before she and Sir Walks-a-lot came upon a marvelous covered bridge over a brook that gurgled loudly with laughing waters. The roof was shingled in bright blue tiles glittering in the sun, and the walls were a lattice of wood and colorful glass. Built into each side of the bridge were sliding doors that led out to small balconies overlooking the creek with long wooden benches on them for resting.

It was such a pleasant spot, Beatrice lingered there for an hour, watching the nuff lazing in the sunlight on the banks and gazing down at small silvery fish that darted about in the shallows below her. If it were possible to hug a bridge, she would hug this one because it filled her with so much joy, for she delighted in all things whimsical and pleasant. She was so relaxed, she hated to get up, but instinct pulled her onward down the cobblestone road into the distance.

Impatient to find out what was over the horizon, she urged Sir Walks-a-lot on until they crested the hill. A thrill ran down her spine at the sight of a large house painted as pink as the first blush of dawn. While the color was certainly eye-catching, it was the nine rounded turrets that really excited her. Beatrice was a connoisseur of turrets and immediately started mapping out a purpose for each of them: a conservatory, a library, an astronomy tower, a cocoon for napping. The possibilities were endless.

In the land of Lichen, people changed their houses the way hermit crabs change their shells. Whenever they got restless, the size of their family grew or shrunk, or they simply got bored of their old decor or location, they would pack up their things and move on in search of a new dwelling-place, leaving the old one behind so someone else might make use of it. Nobody paid rent or fought over houses. There was always the perfect number and style to suit every person at any given moment but first you had to find an empty house. Beatrice kept all her fingers and toes crossed that this house would be empty and waiting for its next tenant.

Jumping down from her patient nuff, she strode up the wide front steps to a door made of sea glass with an inlaid mother-of-pearl frame. A large, black filigree door key rested in the lock with a note attached to it by a pink ribbon:

Welcome! This house has been loved by all who entered its doors. May it surround you and protect your hopes and dreams. Each of us who have occupied these walls have added to their splendor. Feel free to add your own touches while preserving that which is already here. Don't forget to leave the key in the door when you choose to move on!

Delighted at these friendly words, Beatrice turned the key and went in. There was a slightly dusty, musty smell such as any house will get when it is unlived in, but dancing rainbows of light bouncing along the walls enticed her on. The right front room had large windows that were hung with crystal prisms causing the kaleidoscope of cascading colors.

She started removing dust covers from the furniture, marveling over the elaborately carved scrollwork in the dark wood and the floral-patterned chairs and sofa. In one corner was a rolltop desk with a typewriter and a ream of blank paper that gave her an idea of one way she might pass her time in this delightful place once she was settled in.

Roaming from room to room, she set down a few of her belongings in each one as though to claim it for her own as she examined the things left behind by previous tenants. Her favorite discovery was a teapot shaped like a baby elephant with its trunk for a spout and its tail curled into a handle.

Beatrice's stomach rumbled at the thought of tea. Although the house was nicely-equipped with furnishings and kitchen utensils, the pantry cupboard was bare. She grabbed her foraging pouch and a wide-brimmed sun hat and went out exploring to see what she could find.

Searching the land behind the house, she was pleased to discover an abundance of root vegetables, wild herbs, grains, and fruits. She meandered through a field of wildflowers back to the covered bridge and crossed over to investigate another path winding deep into a forest. The trail looked well-used, so she followed it, hoping to find a near neighbor for company, and came upon a large clearing with a modest two-story house.

The house was unremarkable except it was painted an unusual dusky purple color. The door was bright turquoise and covered with hand-painted blooms of every variety. A screened-in porch wrapped around the building with a swing and rocking chairs to sit in and enjoy the cool breezes while watching butterflies and bees and every other kind of insect flitting among the exuberant flowers. Tickle blooms, moss berries, midnight moon lilies, and stepstone bells were just a few of the plants Beatrice recognized in the colorful garden.

A kindred spirit lives here, thought Beatrice, for she was a lover herself of insects and flowers and all inhabitants of nature.

She danced her knuckles across the front door confidently, eager to meet her new neighbor. There was no answer from within although a small wild black rabbit came up from the garden to investigate, flicking its soft ears and sniffing at her in fearless curiosity.

"Is anyone here?" Beatrice asked the rabbit.

It gave no reply but loped away around the corner of the house, looking back from time to time as though to say, *come along, follow me.*

Amused, Bea followed the animal and discovered a woman who looked to be near her own age kneeling and weeding a vegetable garden. Unlike Beatrice's own tangled up bird's nest of curls, the woman had sleek and abundant silver hair a few shades lighter than her gray skin. It was braided and looped around her head several times with still enough left for a long tail that trailed down her back to her ankles. She was all bones and angles with light lavender eyes that flashed silver in the sunlight.

"Hello!" Beatrice called out cheerfully only to be brought up short when she was met with a fierce frown.

"What do you want?" the woman asked.

"I just moved into the pink house across the bridge. I'm out exploring and wanted to introduce myself to my new neighbors."

"Did the family who lived there leave? I didn't realize."

"Yes, lucky for me. It's a fantastic place. So many turrets!"

"A little ostentatious for my taste, but I'm glad it has found a tenant. An unoccupied house has the tendency to go to rack and ruin."

"I'm Beatrice Buttons."

"Amelia Arrowheart."

"Have you lived here long?"

"All my life."

"What!?"

It was rather a rude thing to say, but Beatrice couldn't help exclaiming at this extraordinary piece of information. She'd never met any Lichen who hadn't changed houses countless times over the course of their lives. It was one of the best things about being a citizen, this freedom to roam. Afraid she'd offended her new acquaintance, Beatrice was relieved to see Amelia smile thinly.

"It's unusual, I know, but I've always been happy here and it took me a long time to get my garden the way I want it. I simply don't have the roving spirit that possesses most Lichens. What do you have there?" she asked, pointing toward Beatrice's foraging bag.

"Some odds and ends I picked up. There's no food in the house, so I've been trying to gather enough for a decent tea."

"Give it to me and I'll see what I have to add to it. You might as well come in if we're to be neighbors, although I'll warn you now, I'm not the sociable type. You'll find me moody and quiet. It's just the way I am, and I never put on a show for others."

"Sounds like what I see is what I get then," said Beatrice. "I like that."

"We'll see," replied Amelia, with a cynical expression.

They entered the house through a back door into a welcoming kitchen with red-painted cabinets and wooden counters. Amelia invited Beatrice to sit at a small round table in one corner and set a plate of pound cake and a pot of limonberry jam before her guest to tide her over while she brewed up a cup of tea and rooted through the foraging bag.

As she worked, Amelia pulled off the light sweater she had been wearing over her sundress to protect against the chill forest breeze. Beatrice was amazed to see the woman's arms were completely covered in tattoos from shoulders to the backs of her hands.

The first one she recognized was a pirate's head, complete with a tri-cornered hat and one squinty eye that winked at her. "Eat yer cake, lass. The captain and I will throw some more vittles together," proclaimed the pirate.

"Did... did..."

"Did my tattoo say something?" Amelia smiled slightly. "It did. His name is One-Eyed Jack. I've lived alone since my parents died. My tattoos are my dearest friends and somewhere along the way, they learned to talk to keep me company. I hope you're not too shocked. Most people are and think me a witch, so I usually hide them."

"Actually, I've traveled all over Lichen and seen many a stranger thing in my time. I think it's delightful. Almost makes me want to get a tattoo of my own, but I've always been too scared."

"Scared? And yet you've moved all over and traveled far by yourself?"

"I guess we each have something we're afraid of."

"Too true."

Amelia whipped up a quick soup with the ingredients Beatrice had found, adding in some vegetables from her own garden while Jack the pirate kept up a running commentary. They sat down and ate companionably enough, although Beatrice was unnerved to see Amelia staring at her with uncanny intensity.

Finally, the woman reached out a finger onto which a miniature black and white jumping spider flew from Beatrice's hat. Amelia relocated the tiny creature to a windowsill by an open window where it could hunt and go free if it wished.

"Glad you aren't afraid of spiders," said Beatrice.

"I love them and all wild creatures."

"Me too!"

A small thought crowded into a corner of Amelia's mind, casting an as yet dim light in the gloom that habitually gathered there: *Could this be a true friend, at last?*

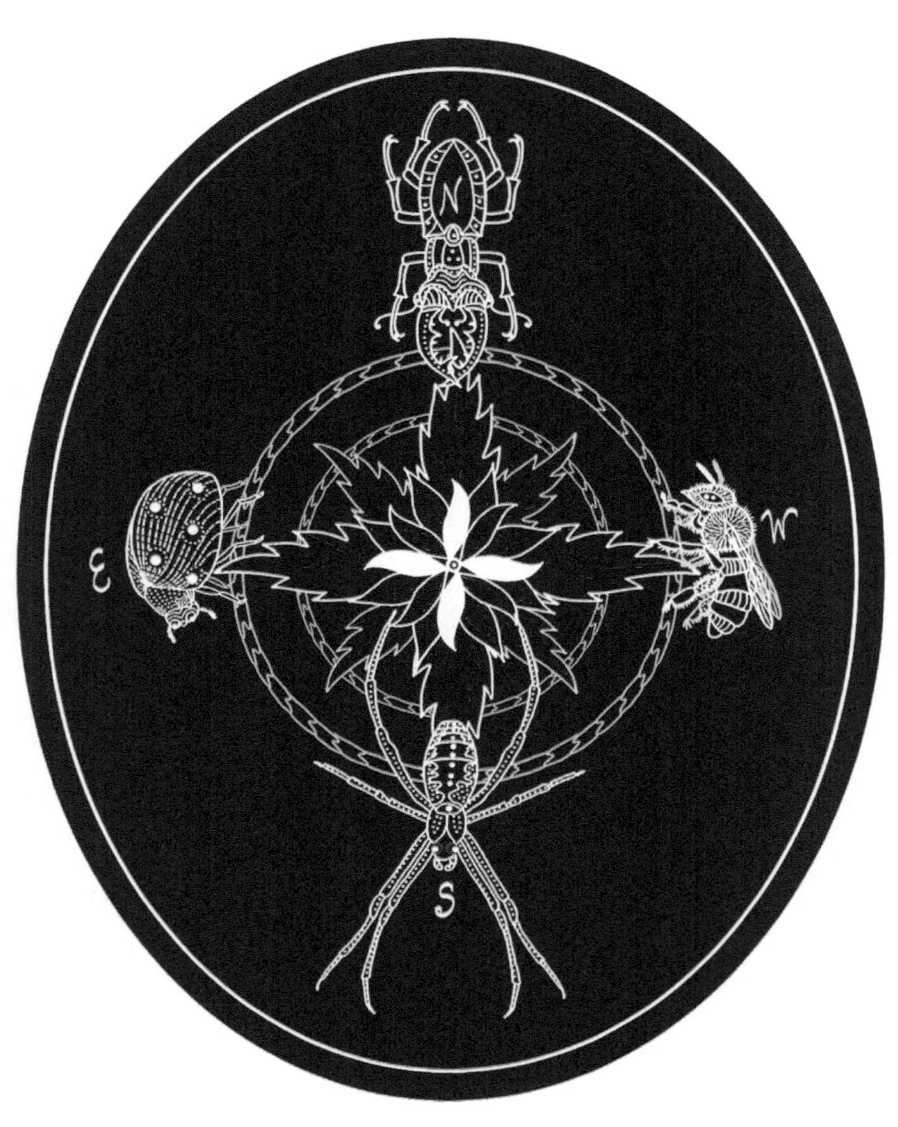
N
S
E
W

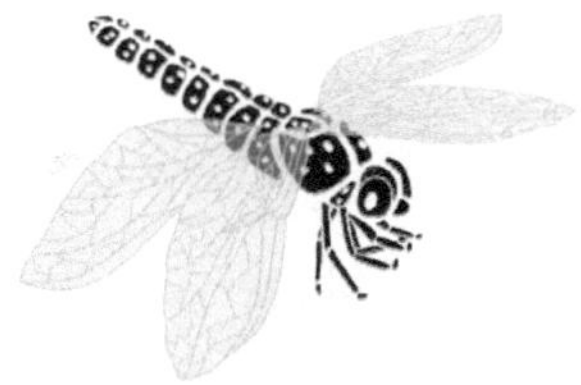

CHAPTER 2

QUIET DAYS

A CHARTREUSE TREE FROG crouched on Beatrice's shoulder, its long tongue dangling from its mouth, but Amelia decided not to mention it. She had learned in the weeks since she'd met her new friend that she couldn't domesticate her any more than Beatrice could drag a conversation out of Amelia when she wasn't in the mood to talk. Amelia wouldn't chide a nuff for not using a napkin or scold a frog for chirruping too loudly as this one was doing, so she never fussed at Beatrice's wild ways either.

In return, Beatrice was learning to accept Amelia's moods, which ranged from sunny as a bright yellow tickle bloom to as dark as a richly fuschia mamaberry. It was strange, being so unlike her own personality, but Beatrice respected the right of all beings to be exactly who they were and never asked any more of any creature that crossed her path.

They often met up at the covered bridge and sat side by side on one of the benches, Beatrice creating her whimsically whittled wood carvings while Amelia drew and wrote in her journal, chatting more and more comfortably together as they grew used to one another.

"Do you think you'll stay here long, Bea?" Amelia asked one day.

"I don't know. It's the nicest house I've lived in yet, and you're one of the nicest friends I've met, Melia, but I have a restless spirit. I love to travel and would probably be happy roaming forever. I'm afraid you'd be a bit like this piece of basswood if I tried to take you with me though. Whittling away to nothing by worry of the unknown."

"You're right. I am a homebody, but I enjoy hearing about your travels."

"Is that a map of them you're making?" Beatrice nibbled on a hard-boiled egg from the picnic basket they had brought with them and peered over Amelia's shoulder.

"Manners. This might be private."

"Private?" Beatrice asked.

"Sssssome of ussss aren't ready to ssshare every ssssssingle thought or creation," came a lisped reply from the bright red snake tattoo that slithered and curled around Amelia's right forearm. Its forked tongue tested the air, sniffing out the egg Beatrice held in her hand with interest.

"Make the varmint walk the plank, argh!" cried Jack.

Beatrice frowned and stuck her own tongue out at the pirate tattoo. "Is that how you feel, Amelia, or are your ink friends voicing their own opinions?"

"Both. I don't mind if you want to take the lead through some of our daily activities, but navigating the tangled pathways of my innermost thoughts is off limits. I don't even share them with Jack and my scarlet basilisk companion here," Amelia said, sliding a sheet of loose vellum to cover the words in her journal but allowing Beatrice to view the map she'd drawn in the margin. "I've been sketching out the places you've visited. My tattoos like to watch and imagine going there themselves someday. I don't think they're all as content as I am to stay put in one place."

"I envy you your tattoos. You always have someone to talk to."

Amelia shut her journal and pulled one of Beatrice's hands close as she reached back into her satchel for her colored pens.

"I'll give you a temporary one. A compass for your travels."

Beatrice watched the top of her friend's head as she bent over in concentration, making the drawing as precise as possible on the back of Bea's hand. She often marveled that her friend could support the burden of the mass of silver hair braided round her head and down her back. It seemed to mirror the weight of her dark thoughts. She wondered if Amelia wouldn't feel free as a bird if she cut it all off one day but would never have had the audacity to suggest it. She was learning Amelia's business was very much her own and she didn't appreciate any outside interference.

"There," said Amelia, satisfied at last with her impromptu creation. "Maybe this compass will point you in the direction of your next adventure before it washes away. In the meanwhile, it's past nap time for me."

"You and your naps," Beatrice teased her as they parted ways with smiles and waves. She ran a finger over the colorful compass on the back of her hand as she headed to her house. Though she was satisfied enough with the current state of affairs, there was always a part of her that yearned for new experiences and regretted the predictability of such placid days. She wondered what Amelia found to make note of in that journal of hers since their routine varied so little. Now, she, Beatrice, could spin quite a few tales if she so chose.

Walking back into her many-turreted abode, her eye was caught by the typewriter on the roll-top desk. She hadn't thought about writing in years, but why shouldn't she give it a try? She placed a comfy cushion in the seat of the old wooden rolling chair to sit on, plucked a piece of blank paper from the top of the stack, and carefully rolled it into the machine.

At first, it was a slow meandering hunt-and-peck as she learned where the letter keys were and stumbled over her words. There was much X'ing out of mistakes and even some cursing muttered low under the breath in frustration, but before long, she got the hang of it. As the words started flowing, the pile of blank paper diminished, and Beatrice lost track of time as her imagination took flight.

An entire day passed without Amelia seeing her new neighbor, which was unusual as Beatrice had visited every day since they first met. Although Amelia sometimes exhibited annoyance at the interruptions, in truth, she had come to enjoy having company after so many years of doing without. By the second day, Amelia decided it was time for her to pay Beatrice a visit for a change and see what was happening. As she crossed over the bridge, a small part of her worried that her compass drawing had inspired Bea to take off on more travels, but surely she would have stopped by first to say goodbye?

As she climbed the steps of the pink house, Amelia was relieved to hear a tip-tap-tapping noise. She didn't recognize the sound but was glad to find out Beatrice was still around and hadn't deserted her. She peered into a window between the olive-green gauzy curtains that floated on the cooling breeze and saw Beatrice hunched over a typewriter in deep concentration.

Reluctant to disturb her, Amelia called through the window, "It's only me! I brought you some fresh bread and a pot of honey. I'll leave them here on the porch."

The clatter stopped as Beatrice jumped up and ran to open the front door.

"Don't be a silly," Beatrice chided her. She grabbed Amelia by one arm and pulled her into the house, ushering her to a red velvet divan next to a grand piano.

"What a lovely instrument!"

"Do you play?"

Amelia set her offerings down on a low table and nodded. "A little. I took lessons as a child and have a mahogany spinet in an upstairs room I use for music and painting."

"How wonderful! I don't play a lick. Would you play something for me?"

"I never play for others, only myself. And never on such a grand instrument."

"Melia, you're so shy! You should show off more!"

"I'm not shy. I'm reserved. Something you are most definitely not." She softened it with a smile, but Bea felt chastised for her boldness all the same and blushed.

"I'll go make some tea for us," she mumbled.

"No, I will, as apology for my quick tongue. I warned you I was full of sharp edges when we met." Amelia gathered up the bread and honey. "Lead me to the kitchen and I'll make it up to you."

Beatrice guided her into a large sunny room that Amelia examined with curiosity. It was filled with white cabinets decorated with painted insects, fungi and plants. Dangling from the ceiling were dark wood herb-drying racks partially filled. The pebbled counters were covered with pots of paint and glasses with water and paintbrushes in them and a green crockery bowl filled with eggs of various sizes and colors. There was an old-fashioned cast-iron woodstove in one corner and an icebox in another. A rustic farmhouse table was surrounded by chairs carved with depictions of the moons, suns, and stars.

The kitchen opened up into a large conservatory greenhouse full of overgrown plants, but there were signs recent pruning was starting to turn chaos into order. The rooms were clean but cluttered with projects and tools. All in all, it was a warm, fragrant, and welcoming space if not as sparse and tidy as Amelia's own tastes would have dictated. She decided she might come to feel comfortable there.

Amelia filled the kettle, lit the stove, and investigated the tea tin while they waited for the water to boil. "What type of strange mixture is this? Are you trying to poison us?"

Beatrice giggled. "It's fresion, sargaroot, and dried moss berries. All good, healthy ingredients I found in the meadows out back."

"Have you been living off just what you can forage? Most people do go shopping as well, you know. You should saddle up Sir Walks-a-lot later and glide into town to pick up a few things, including some real stout Lichen tea."

"I suppose, though it's a delightful game to see how long you can go without. The forest, meadows, and creek here are full of good things. The only thing I've missed is a bar of real chocolate."

"With nuts?"

"With or without. I'm craving its smooth, rich taste."

"Well, if you don't go soon, I'll pick some up for you next time I'm in town."

The kettle gave out a piercing cry and Amelia brewed up the assortment of wild ingredients that must pass for tea, toasted some bread, and served it slathered with the wildflower honey she had harvested from her hoverbees.

"I missed you when you didn't visit yesterday, Bea," she confessed. "What have you been doing?"

"I got to thinking after we met last time about your journal and all my adventures and decided I should start writing them down. After all, I've led a very interesting life. Would you like to hear what I've written so far?"

"Yes!" came an enthusiastic chorus of voices from Amelia's collection of tattoos, including a hearty "Arrrr!" from One-Eyed Jack. The owner of the tattoos looked considerably less enthusiastic. It wasn't that she didn't want to hear of her friend's travels, but she was afraid the reminiscing would inspire Bea to take off for the road again, leaving her behind to readjust to a solitary life. But looking at Bea's hopeful and excited face, Amelia hadn't the heart to say no.

Beatrice ran to retrieve her typewritten pages and began to read her tale aloud as Amelia reached for a second piece of toast.

CHAPTER 3

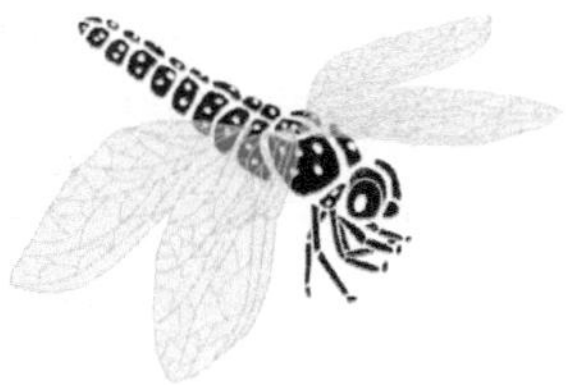

TALE OF A SEA WITCH

M Y TWENTY-FIRST SUMMER I went to visit my granny at the seaside. She lived on the edge of town so near the water, you could hear the crash of waves from an open window. Granny and I were always close, so it didn't surprise her when I showed up one day with nothing but my rucksack. It didn't even shock her I had walked a week to get there. I didn't have Sir Walks-a-lot or any other nuff yet as my parents feared my restless feet would get the better of me, but that didn't stop me from roaming.

Granny lived in a small cottage with a garden large enough to break my back with the work of it. She grew enough for her with plenty left over to pass on to the cooks at the Fisherfolk's Retirement Inn. I'd weed the garden, water it, relocate any snails and slugs foolish enough to nibble there, and of course, harvest anything ripe.

Every Monday morning, I'd load up a handcart with whatever we had excess of: jars of pepper tomato jam, mamaberry wine, and all manner of fruits and vegetables. Sometimes Granny would even throw on a few waxed wheels of cheese as she made her own from some rambunctious goats she kept too.

(Remind me, Melia, to give you Granny's recipe for that pepper jam. I made so much of it that summer, it's permanently etched into my brain.)

The Fisherfolk's Retirement Inn wasn't far, and I found myself drawn in hook, line, and sinker to a whole mess of fish tales whenever I visited to deliver food. Everyone had one except for Miss Sorcha Delaney, who instead regaled me with a story of the local sea witch. Every year, this sea witch would come into town and try to win the heart of the prettiest girl around until one returned her love and affection. One particular year, that pretty girl happened to be Miss Delaney when she was young and had wild ginger corkscrew curls that fell to her waist.

Miss Delaney was still beautiful at the unusually advanced age of 152. She told me her long life and preserved good looks were because she'd been blessed by the love of a sea witch. I was sunk when I heard that and had to stay for the whole story as I adore anything to do with enchantments and magical folk. By the time she finished telling her tale, the sun was sinking low in the sky, and I had to rush so I wouldn't be late for dinner.

I asked Granny about the sea witch when she was dipping up a bowlful of cuttleroot chowder for me. She stopped mid-scoop, staring at me.

"Beatrice, if the sea witch picks you and you fall in love with her, depending on how you look at it, you'll be either blessed or cursed to travel all of Lichen over forever. She'll come to you in your dreams throughout your life, as she'll hold your heart always, but she too is chained by her own destiny, which isn't to stay by your side."

"How dreadful!" I replied.

Granny nodded her head and gave me my soup. The warning was too late, of course. I dipped my bread in my bowl and as I sucked on the creamy goodness of each soggy bite, I daydreamed about the sea witch and what she would think of me. Was I pretty? Was I pretty enough? I had always caught the eyes of young women that longed to comb my tangled curls with their fingers, but that was silly child's play, not fit for an immortal being.

I went out that night to gaze at the moon. A soft, clear voice was singing a tale about an ill-fated albatross pair. The male flew away to seek food for his lady and their chick only to be lost in a hurricane never to return. As the melancholy melody continued, I followed the voice to see who was singing and knew without any introduction necessary it was the sea witch the moment I saw her.

Her long hair was as wavy as the incoming tide on a stormy day and of a brilliant aquamarine blue which amplified her olive-green eyes. She was long and willowy, a whole head taller than me, and radiated an aura of power. Her flowing, gauzy dress billowed in the wind like a sail and strings of seashells adorned her ankles. Banded rings of abalone shell graced each toe and pearl rings of every color bedecked her fingers.

Her throat was encircled by a necklace of teeth from creatures of the sea, and it chattered when she moved like a wind chime. I thought she had fish scales tattooed along her neck but learned later they were gills. She might live on shore, but she would always be part of the sea, able to breathe under its waters and converse with all its denizens.

She was the most dazzling being I'd ever seen, then or now, and she only had eyes for me as my own overflowed with tears from the sad song she had shared. She reached out a delicate lavender lace handkerchief to brush them away as she spoke to me.

"I am Coral, and you are the prettiest girl in town."

"Prettier than Miss Delaney?"

"Sorcha takes her last journey tonight and I cannot go with her. I am ready for another pretty thing such as yourself. Come. Take my hand and we'll walk along the edge of the waves and listen to the news the tide brings in."

"Does the tide talk to you?"

"Yes. Would you like me to teach you how to understand the languages of the waves and the sky and the ever-restless winds?"

I smiled so wide I thought my face would split in two and nodded yes. Yes to learning the languages of nature and yes to becoming her pretty, her love. With a simple whisper of a sea spell from her lips to my ear, the secrets of wild things became an open book. I could understand so much that had been unknown to me that I was overwhelmed.

By the end of our walk, the sea breeze turned cold. I shivered from the chill and the new thoughts cascading into my mind. Coral wrapped her arms around me, and I leaned my head back tucked under her chin. I could feel her hold her breath a minute before she asked me hesitantly if I would like to come back to her cottage. She promised me a warming broth to thaw my bones and a roaring fire to sit beside. I joined her willingly in the inky black of night as we walked up a rough staircase cut into the cliff to a dark structure at the top.

She ran a steaming outdoor tub for me there under the stars, and I bathed in the moonlight, encircled by tallow candles set into abandoned abalone shells. The witch washed my hair, gently untangling the curls so that they dried like round downy owl chicks, covering my head and shoulders. She prepared the broth and a plate with two slices of crusty bread while I slipped a flowing tea-length lavender nightgown over my head.

"In the morning, I'll collect your things from your grandmother's house," she said as she bade me goodnight.

When I woke the next morning, Granny and Coral were sitting at the sea witch's kitchen table and my rucksack was on a chair by the front door.

"Good morning!" I cried, delighted to see my two favorites waiting for me.

Granny frowned and gave me a sad glance. "The grown people aren't finished talking yet, child. Grab one of those mamaberries and take a little walk. Your sea witch will find you later, no doubt, after I've left."

I didn't argue the point of being called a child, for I knew in the grand scheme of things they were both much older and wiser than me, so I grabbed the fruit and obeyed without so much as a fare-thee-well to my granny. We Buttons never say goodbye even though we often take our leave. A goodbye sounds too final, like you never plan to see each other again.

When I walked outside into the daylight, I realized the sea witch lived at a famous landmark the locals called the Kaleidoscope Lighthouse. I'd seen it from a distance whenever I visited Granny but had never been up so close to it before. It quite took my breath away.

The entire thing was tiled in a vivid mosaic showcasing the wonders of nature: flora and fauna, rock and gem formations, entomology, ornithology, fungi and lichen, sea creatures and land creatures. The inside walls were painted a muted turquoise blue, and at the top of the tower, up a spiral staircase, was the renowned kaleidoscope light with its ever-changing pattern of colors and shapes that cut through the thickest fogs and steered ships away from the dangerous rocks near shore.

There were cliffs nearby with caves full of haunting tunes only heard during high tide when the caverns were unreachable by shore. The combination of the kaleidoscopic colors from the lighthouse and the eerie music gave the entire place the atmosphere of a carnival. In time, I would learn how to operate and maintain the light that kept the fisherfolk safe, but that morning, I was just in awe of being given the privilege of living in this remarkable dwelling.

I found the cut-rock staircase leading down to the ocean again and took it, looking for ways to stretch my time outside by exploring the beach. Having a playful and imaginative nature, I gathered dried starfish, seashells, fragments of coral, driftwood—anything and everything that caught my eye—and added them to my hair, tucking my curls into a seashore crown fit for a mermaid queen. I danced at the edge of the waves barely wetting my feet and sang for anyone to hear. I was young and carefree and still had a lot to learn.

The sea witch, however, was far older and wiser. Born of the ocean then cast out with the foam to fend for themselves on land or in the ocean as they chose, most sea witches were not tied to one place but were free to roam in search of adventures and new loves. When Coral was only a witchling, however, she was cursed to become caretaker of the lighthouse and live there forever.

The tower and light were very plain when she first arrived, but when you have all of eternity and cannot leave, what better way to pass the time than to add embellishments? The mosaics came first, and when every inch of the tower was covered, she turned her attention to the light, crafting the elaborate machinery and colored glass that made it unique among lighthouses and gave it its name.

When she had done everything she could think of to the lighthouse, Coral decided to build a small cottage beside it to make a cozier nest for herself and her loves. She built it out of pieces of driftwood she gathered on her walks and filled up chinks in the walls with bottles that washed up on shore.

Sometimes she found messages in the bottles and, if she was in the mood and had the power to do so, would grant the wish of whoever had sent them. The bottles also served as peepholes, but there wasn't a soul around who would have dared to peek into the abode of a sea witch without invitation. It was said if you did look in, whatever it was you saw would be firmly etched upon your eyes. No matter how hard you tried, you could never see or recognize anything else again. Nobody knew if this was true, but no one wanted to be the first one to find out either.

The furniture was from ships that had wrecked long ago, and the rugs and curtains were woven from fishing nets that had drifted to shore. Her windchimes were made from shells and sea glass tied to fishing lines, and around the cottage were curious pieces of flotsam and jetsam she collected from the beach and sea.

A petrified octopus was hugging one of the posts of her four-poster bed with its eight arms. Coral explained she'd found it that way when she salvaged the bed and thought it wrong to remove the poor creature. I eventually carved three more from driftwood to keep it company on the other posts.

Herds of dried seahorses galloped along the fireplace mantel, and a tabletop with a spore board pattern painted on it was where we spent many an hour playing with small sand dollars and cat's-eye seashells as markers. It is a unique and lovely house that will be forever etched upon my memory.

When Coral had finished her cottage and decorated it to her liking, she brought her first pretty one to live with her. In exchange for her lonely life tethered to the lighthouse, the sea witch laid claim to the fairest lass of the land, but only if she could win her love. If you give your heart to the witch, you are bound to her for life but are allowed to roam all of Lichen in her place.

When you are too tired or old to roam any longer, there is always a place at the Kaleidoscope Lighthouse waiting for you. Miss Delaney lived there in the cottage for many happy years with Coral until her advanced age made it safer for her to move to the Fisherfolk's Inn. The night she died was the night I met Coral and won a place in her heart. It might sound cruel she didn't take time to grieve first. As an immortal, she looks at death as part of life and didn't grieve for what was a long and joyous time together for her and Miss Delaney.

In exchange for my love, the sea witch gave me many gifts, chief among them the ability to communicate with and be at one with nature. I can forage and find food wherever I go and am never afraid of any living creature. She offered to change my appearance so I might look however I wished and stay forever young, but I chose to age as you see and be my natural self. She offered me immortality, but I declined it then, having no wish to outlive everyone and everything I've known. There is a special sweetness to life knowing it must come to an end, but that is not to say I might not change my mind someday.

We lived together for a blissful year in the driftwood cottage and it was during that time I began to whittle. For some, carving wood is simply a way to keep their hands busy, but for me it is a form of storytelling. Each creature I make has a soul that I discover in the wood. I send them back to Coral so she knows I haven't forgotten her.

While I was living at the cottage, I discovered the locals believed the sea witch forbade me to leave her sight, but it wasn't true. We knew from the start that our time together would be brief, and that made us cling to each other all the more and feel no need for other company.

Coral loved me deeply but told me I had one of the most restless souls she'd ever encountered and was destined to roam more than any other creature she had met. I didn't believe her at first, but then on my next birthday, I woke up with itchy feet and knew I must travel and see more of Lichen or I would never be content again. She must have known as well because she'd already packed my rucksack and walked the first part of my journey with me before leaving me at twilight to return to the lighthouse where she is condemned to spend each night.

She visits me now in my dreams so I can tell her about my travels and the places where she can never visit. It may seem an unconventional relationship, but when you love someone as much as we love each other, you don't need to be physically together to never feel apart. Leaving her on my birthday was like a present in itself, as I always look forward to a new adventure each year instead of looking back on it as the day we parted. That is why I always move on my birthday. To celebrate and take advantage of the freedom which is the greatest of the many gifts she has given me.

CHAPTER 4

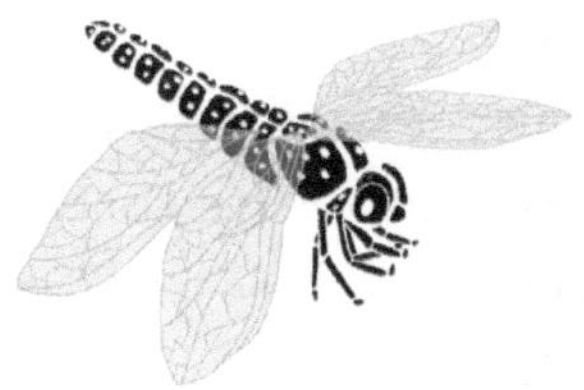

FLOATING

"THE END," READ BEATRICE.

"Well," said Amelia, "that was quite a tale. You have a vivid imagination. I could almost believe it was true."

"It is true! Every bit."

"You have a sea witch lover who lives in a kaleidoscopic lighthouse and visits you in your dreams?"

"I can see it sounds odd when you put it that way, but it doesn't make it any less true. Don't you believe me?"

"I suppose it's not for me to say, really. I've never ventured far from this place and have no idea what mysteries Lichen holds beyond it. It's always quiet and sedate around these parts. The only unusual phenomenon we have locally is a floating building."

"A what!?" Beatrice exclaimed.

Amelia snorted. "Haven't you noticed it when you've been roaming around? It's hard to miss. Looks like a storm cloud at first glance, but when you look more closely, you can see it's a building made of gray stone. No one knows how it got up there or what it means but it doesn't seem to do any harm, so we mostly ignore it."

"I have to see this. Show me!"

They walked outside and Amelia pointed over the trees to the west. "There. How could you miss it? Don't you ever look up at the sky?"

"I must admit lately I've had my head down, foraging and watching the fascinating insects around these parts. Besides, who expects to see a building floating in the sky? If I glanced at it without knowing, I would think it was just another cloud. What do you think is up there? I wish we could see." Beatrice's natural curiosity and thirst for excitement was making her practically burst from her skin.

"Like I said, nobody knows, and no one has figured out a practical way of getting to it. There was a bit of a panic when it first appeared, but it hasn't caused any harm. We're used to it now."

"Melia, I've lived in almost every kind of house and structure in Lichen, but I've never visited a cloud house. I have to find a way to get up there!"

"If anyone could do it, I'm sure it would be you. Maybe your witch can tell you the secret."

"You're joking, but I'm going to ask her in my dream tonight if she's ever heard of such a thing."

"Okay then, report back to me your findings, but for now, it's been quite an afternoon, and I've missed my nap. I'll see you tomorrow, Bea. I did enjoy your story."

"S-s-s-s-so did I," said the snake.

"And I," said the pirate. "That was a right good yarn, lass. Tell yer sea witch hello from old One-Eyed Jack."

The friends parted in good cheer, although Amelia was still dubious about Bea's story and Beatrice was miffed that Melia didn't believe her.

That night, in her dream, Bea discussed the situation with Coral.

"Some people are rather pedestrian-minded," said her lover. "It takes a creative soul such as your own to believe in magical beings."

"But I think Melia is creative. You should see the things she draws, and she writes in her journal constantly. Her problem is she's never traveled. When you've seen as many sights as I have, nothing seems impossible. She has such a skeptical and stoic nature. Why, there's even a floating building right over her town, and yet she takes it in stride as though it were nothing at all!"

"A floating building? Sounds like powerful magic. Be careful, beloved. I cannot protect you from strong sorcery at such a distance. Promise me you will leave such trickery alone. No, don't. I know you can't promise me. Your inquisitive nature will not allow you to rest without solving this mystery, but do try to be a little cautious, for me."

"For you, my love, anything," Beatrice agreed, yet when she woke up, she was already full of plans and schemes and hurried outside with a pair of binoculars to take a closer look at the cloud.

As she stepped off the last of her front steps, she was shocked to find the drop much longer than usual and almost stumbled to her knees in her surprise. She turned to examine her house closely and was amazed to find it was floating several inches off the ground. She was passing her hand under the foundation to confirm what her eyes were seeing when Amelia strode up, flustered and flushed from her walk.

"Yours is doing it too. I thought it was just mine. What can it mean?"

"Maybe we're going to float right up into the sky like that cloud building!"

"Oh, no! You don't think we brought it on by talking about it yesterday, do you? Did you say something to your witch? Maybe this is her doing."

"I thought you didn't believe in Coral? Besides, she knew nothing about it. In fact, she was worried about me. Said it sounded like strong magic that could be dangerous."

"It seems quite dangerous to me. Floating houses, indeed!"

Although sorry for her friend's distress, Beatrice, as might be expected, was delighted at this turn of events, considering that a great adventure had come to her for a change instead of having to seek one out. She hoped their houses would reach as high as the mysterious cloud building and thereby, they might discover a way to visit it.

Amelia was not so thrilled. In fact, she was dismayed that her safe and secure life was literally shifting under her feet. For a few days, it was easy enough to step off the house or use a ladder to get safely back on solid ground, but the process seemed to be accelerating from day to day, so neither woman was surprised to awake one morning to find their houses floating over two hundred feet above the ground.

Without the trees and hills in the way, Amelia was able to use a pair of opera glasses to peer over at Beatrice's house to see how she was reacting to the situation. She watched in horror as Bea dipped a toe off her front steps as though testing the temperature of the water at the beach and then jumped.

Beatrice plunged almost to the ground and then bounced back up, floating in a cross-legged position as if she was held up by the air around her. Amelia could see her friend laughing as she twisted and turned to test the properties of this new medium.

Finally, Bea lay flat on her stomach and swam through the air over to Amelia's house using a modified breaststroke. "What do you make of this?"

"Terrifying," said Amelia. "It can't be safe. What does it feel like?"

"It feels like swimming in the ocean without getting wet and without having to worry about not being able to breathe. It's strange, but not unpleasant. I could get used to it, I think. Why don't you give it a go?"

"Why in Lichen should I do such a thing?"

"For one thing, it may be the only way to get back down there."

Amelia looked down dizzily at her gardens far below. Bea had a point. She didn't want to be stuck up here forever. Screwing up more courage than she had ever needed in her life before, she jumped, screaming in fright. Beatrice caught her hand, gripping it strongly enough to give her the confidence to paddle her feet like a duck while her friend pulled her along in the sky. Slowly her nervousness gave way to a cautious excitement. The feeling of being weightless and flying above the ground was like a dream she often had, but this was real life.

As she gained confidence she wouldn't plummet suddenly to the ground, she struck out on her own, enjoying the view from on high. She was pleased to see her flower beds looked as neat and tidy from above as they did at ground level. Beatrice zoomed hither and yon, calling out to Amelia to come look at this or that. It was fun but exhausting.

Amelia was the first to call a halt to their exploration. "Come eat some lunch with me. I feel like we need a moment to sit down and think about what all of this means."

Beatrice was reluctant to stop, as she was having so much fun, but then her stomach growled loudly.

"Okay," she answered it with a laugh, "settle down in there. Lunch it is."

They swam to Amelia's house and discussed their new situation over a bowl of rich vegetable stew that Amelia warmed up over the stove. They decided the sensible first thing to do was investigate whether they were the only ones whose houses were floating. For all they knew, the same thing was happening to everyone in the land of Lichen.

Though she wasn't much of a long-distance swimmer, Beatrice volunteered to venture out after lunch to explore the neighboring houses and town to see who else was floating sky high. She was both elated and puzzled to discover it was only she and Amelia and the mysterious cloud building that were up in the air. Everyone else was going about their business as usual.

She was most surprised that while people were agreeable about answering the questions she shouted down to them from above, they felt no need to bombard her with ones of their own about her odd predicament. It was hard to believe they weren't more amazed or shocked, but Beatrice decided maybe the lack of curiosity was a regional characteristic after all instead of being confined to her unadventurous friend.

Beatrice found it very odd to discover a part of Lichen where folk ignored rather than explored the unexplained, but she had met all types in her travels. She returned to Amelia to report on the many sincere good wishes sent their way but with no offers or suggestions to help resolve their weird state of affairs.

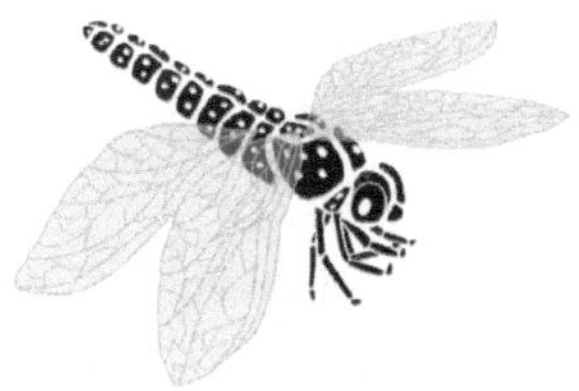

SKYBOAT

ALTHOUGH NO HELP WAS forthcoming from the local inhabitants, unbeknownst to Amelia, Beatrice had formulated a plan of her own. If they were going to float up to the heavens like birds, Bea anticipated they might need something to travel in. Sir Walks-a-lot was unaffected by whatever allowed them to float. Like all nuffs, he could glide for short distances, but not as far as her adventuring mind was imagining they might go, and neither she nor Amelia were in good enough shape to swim for hours or days at a time. What they needed was a boat to sail the open skies.

Beatrice began gathering supplies and materials as soon as their houses first started to rise from the ground. In the early days, before the floating got too bad, she pulled a long-handled wagon from the comfort of Sir Walks-a-lot's back, riding to the dry goods store in town with a shopping list in hand. She sought out boards and nails, bought anything and everything stored in wooden barrels, soft mattresses, and gallons of paint in every hue under the suns. She chose bolt after bolt of silk fabric, large eyelets, rope and many other odds and ends.

She was able to store all of her purchases away in her house before it floated too far into the sky to make it practical. She then cleared furniture and plants out of the conservatory off the kitchen as it was the only room large enough to house the boat while she built it. There was a wall of folding glass doors to the outside through which she could push the completed craft out into the sky, hoping it didn't simply crash to the ground when she did so.

Beatrice gave a lot of thought to the design of her skyboat. She knew she wanted it to mimic nature, something whimsical and fun that might entice the cautious Amelia into an adventure. She had spent hours among the flowers and plants outside watching the insects and other creatures. One day, a large emerald-green dragonfly landed on her boot and a bright blue damselfly roosted on her maroon and pink paisley trousers.

She watched the two as their iridescent colors shimmered in the sun and it gave her an idea. What if the boat could be made almost invisible when viewed from above by painting the top green to blend with the grass and trees and the bottom blue to blend in with the sky when seen from below? The form of the dragonfly suggested living quarters which could be in the fat abdomen part of the body. The elongated part would be perfect for sleek aerodynamics when flying along in the sky and sails could mimic the delicate, fluttering wings.

Beatrice told Coral about her schemes when they met in her dreams. The sea witch laughed in delight at her fantastical ideas. She kissed her lover's eyelids so her eyes would see exactly what needed to be done, wrapped her close in her arms so her body would have the strength to build it, then weaved a spell of flight, air-worthy design, and beauty, whispering it in her ear and sealing it with a soft kiss on the lips.

"This kiss will fill your boat with my love, which offers its own protection. Name her for me, sweetheart, so I will always be with you wherever you go. And don't forget to leave Sir Walks-a-lot in the care of a neighbor before you venture off. I know how impulsive you can be."

Beatrice awoke refreshed and eager to complete her project. The unnatural strength she'd been gifted helped make short work of the construction. She used the rounded wood of the barrels to build the main body of the ship, caulking the whole thing airtight for storms and painting the body in the green and blue colors she'd chosen.

The interior she painted a pale pink with buttery yellow floors to create a bright and cheerful ambience. It wasn't large, so to economize on space, Beatrice built in pea pod-shaped sofas that doubled as beds with a soft mattress on each. They were painted bright green, and she added round pillows so they mimicked the pods from the garden. She laughed, thinking Amelia would get a kick out of the veggie-inspired furniture.

She installed a potbellied cook stove next to the tiny kitchen area. It wouldn't require much fuel and could be used for cooking and heating. The boat was stocked up with the most practical supplies she could think of: grains, canned vegetables, jars of pickled eggs, big wheels of cheese, dried fruits, chocolate bars, seasonings, herbs, and tea. Water was stored in barrels, there was an icebox for cold foods, a discreet bathroom area, and drawers and shelves were added wherever there was room to provide additional storage.

One of the last things she did was paint a spore game board onto a table that folded down from the wall. She had carved a special spore set where each game piece was a mushroom recognizable from pilgrimages to Fungi Ridge with Blessed Baby knights, Pillars of the Deep as queens, and kings that looked like Beatrice and Amelia as Record Keepers because, why not? It was amusing to make a set of pieces that were completely unique and honored the most treasured traditions of Lichen.

Beatrice was fussing with finishing touches one day when she heard a voice calling her name. Before she could stop her visitor, Amelia stepped through the conservatory door from the kitchen.

"What in Lichen are you building, Bea? Looks like a bug. Is it a fancy planter? Garden sculpture?"

Although disappointed her big reveal had been ruined, Beatrice bubbled over with excitement that she could finally show off her pet project and hard work.

"It's a skyboat, of course. I built it in here so when I launch it, I can push it out the conservatory doors into the sky."

"What will keep it from falling to the ground?" Amelia asked skeptically. Just because their houses floated didn't mean a boat would. She walked closer, inspecting every surface as she waited for Beatrice's answer.

"These balloons," Beatrice said, pointing to four large rubber spheres dangling above the craft. "Coral enchanted them so we can fill them up with buoyantly pleasant thoughts and never have to worry about them deflating. And the engine runs on soap bubbles, which are lighter than air, so if they float, we float." She looked at Amelia expectantly.

Amelia blinked twice at this outlandish explanation, but instead of arguing, she sighed and said, "Guess we'll see."

It was as close as Amelia ever came to saying, "I have faith in you and hopefully it will work out," so with that, Beatrice had to be satisfied.

She gave Amelia the grand tour, which didn't take terribly long as it was not a large vessel. Reluctantly to herself, Amelia admired the design and the skill of Bea's craftswomanship, but outwardly she pursed her lips and furrowed her brow with anxiety. "We" float must mean Bea intended an adventure that included her. Amelia's stomach knotted at the idea, but her curiosity won out in the end.

"I must admit it is very nice, Bea, but will it work?"

"Only one way to find out," said Beatrice.

With Amelia's help, she began moving the skyboat along a log launch she had built to make rolling the boat outdoors easier. They pushed the boat out into the air, holding their breaths as it bobbed briefly before the buoyancy from the balloons kicked in. Luckily, Beatrice had remembered to moor the boat to the house by ropes tied to one of the turrets so it didn't float away without them.

They swam to the boat and climbed aboard. Beatrice cast off the lines, starting the engine and adjusting the rainbow cloud of balloons above her head as a steady stream of iridescent soap bubbles trailed behind the ship. She turned the captain's wheel as they made a circuit around the house for a practice run.

"I can't believe it works!" Amelia exclaimed.

"Of course it does. Told you I knew what I was doing. Let's take it for a spin."

"We did take it for a spin," Amelia objected, looking over the side as her long braid flew behind her like a kite tail in the wind. "Now you can fly me back to my house. That's as far as I'm interested in going."

"But what about the cloud building? Aren't you the least bit curious about it? We could investigate it now!"

"It might be dangerous."

"That's part of the fun! C'mon, we'll take a quick look around and if anything is too scary, we'll jump back in the boat and skedaddle."

"I suppose..."

"Adventures on the high seas!" yelled One-Eyed Jack. "That's for us, mateys!"

Amelia rolled her eyes. "Outvoted, I see. Okay, but I reserve the right to call a retreat whenever I want."

"Deal!" cried Beatrice, pointing the bow of the ship skyward with glee.

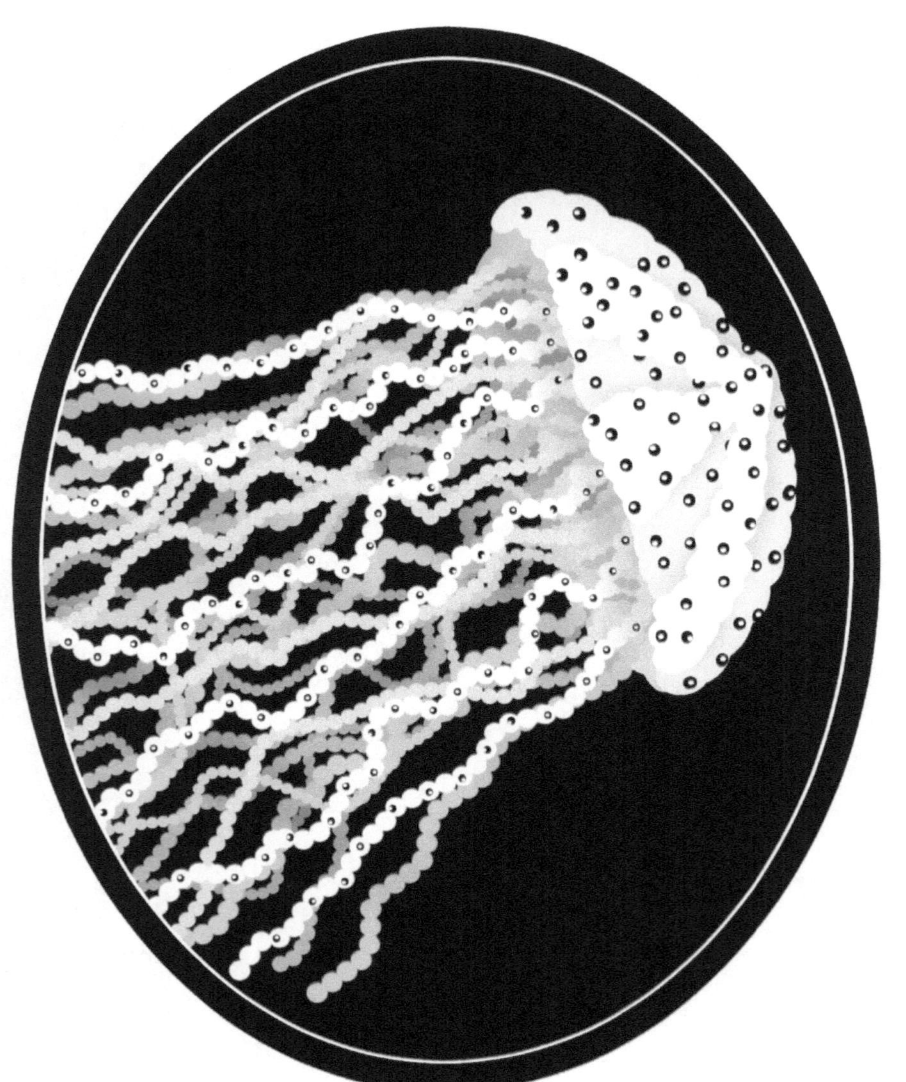

CHAPTER 6

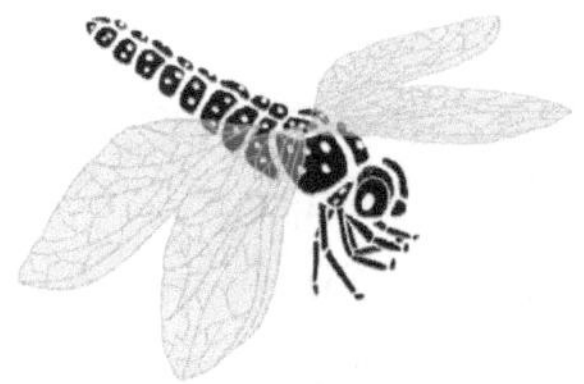

THE OBSERVATORY

T HE SHIP MADE SHORT work of the distance, and they were soon dropping anchor at the floating building. They were surprised to find the doors to the imposing stone structure unlocked. A spacious marble lobby was adorned with a swirling spiral staircase that led up to a metal platform under a domed ceiling. The lobby floor was covered in an elaborate pattern of tiles in bold yellow, blue, and white. An enormous telescope poked through a hole in the ceiling.

"It's an observatory," Amelia said. "For studying the suns and moons and stars."

"I love it! Look, Amelia!" Beatrice exclaimed, pointing toward a guest sign-in log resting on a pedestal at the foot of the stairs.

They leant over and read the last note that was recorded there in a tidy, elegant script:

Please make use of this observatory if you can. It was once on solid ground but floated up into the skies and took us with it. We continued our studies and were working on theories about our levitation until the day our two little boys ran away. They're a mischievous pair and we're worried what they might get up to, so we're going in search of them. We hope to return one day and continue our work but until then, we hope someone else may find our telescope and scientific notes of use.

"Kind of brief," said Beatrice.

"Concise," Amelia corrected.

Beatrice rolled her eyes and began to look around. There had to be more to their story, like names or a date. It was so dusty, it must have been years since anyone had been there, so perhaps it wouldn't be considered too intrusive to sort through the belongings that were left behind for more clues. She pulled a bandana from her trouser pocket and swiped at the furnishings as she investigated.

Amelia decided to climb the spiral staircase and take a closer look at the telescope. She blew a two-inch-thick cottony blanket of dust from the lens then pulled a linen handkerchief from where it was tucked into the end of her sweater sleeve, lightly batting at the layers of grime on the gears and mechanical wheels of the instrument in an ineffectual effort at tidying.

She bent down to look through the eyepiece and was startled when a gauzy tentacle drifted past her vision. Thinking a floating piece of lint was obstructing the lens, she polished it again with her cloth before taking another look. This time there was no mistake: there were long tentacles that looked very much like the pictures she had seen of ocean jellyfish.

"Bea, come look at this!" she called out, wondering what it could mean. Maybe a waterspout sent a jellyfish up from the sea into the sky. How strange that it looked as though it was floating in the air just like it would in water.

Beatrice stepped up and peered through the lens. She turned one of the knobs for better focus then leaned back looking up at the roof. "Amelia, I think there are some amazing creatures living up here in the sky. That looks like a jellyfish made of cloud!"

"But how is that possible?" Amelia asked, sinking down into a nearby chair. "I've never heard of such things as cloud creatures before."

"I keep trying to tell you Lichen is full of magic and marvels. Haven't you been listening to my tales? We've only been able to see the tip of the iceberg from the ground. Now we have this amazing opportunity to get a bird's eye view!"

Amelia stood up and looked again, this time turning the wheel to spin the telescope around for a wider look. There was an entire school of pink jellyfish, cloud-like creatures with long streaming tentacles that performed an elegant dance before her eyes as they lazily circled around the observatory.

While Amelia was preoccupied with this miraculous sight, Beatrice continued her exploration downstairs. She came across an oversized book that was cumbersome and awkward to hold. The front of the book was covered in drawings of animals and a large childish scrawl stated STAY OUT: THAT MEANS YOU TOO!!

Beatrice hesitated a moment at this forbidding warning but then shrugged and opened the book anyway. If she had wondered about the missing boys mentioned in the guest log before, she definitely had an idea of what they were like by the collection of boogers wiped on the inside of the cover.

She loudly groaned, "Ew!" Nasty, foul little scrappers. Beatrice wasn't sure she was so anxious to find out more about them after all.

Cautiously, she grasped the edges of each page to turn them, afraid of what she might discover, but found the rest of the book was safer to explore. It was full of photographs with detailed descriptions and notes. She gathered the two missing boys were named Bix and Click.

Bix was the younger, seven-years-old at the time of the latest birthday photo of him. A ginger-haired boy with a galaxy of silver freckles that looked like a sky full of stars on his dark gray skin and flashing mischievous-looking dark eyes. Click was ten with a shock of snow-white hair and electric blue eyes and a much paler, almost silver skin.

Click was a self-proclaimed Famous Photographer just waiting to be discovered, and to be fair, his photos were captivating, with detailed captions written out in his imperfect handwriting. One of the most interesting was of the observatory when it was still on solid ground. Bix was hanging upside down from a puzzle tree in the garden while a couple Beatrice presumed were the lads' parents examined a picnic table covered with maps, papers and open books with the remains of a feast laid out around them.

Beatrice's stomach grumbled loudly at this reminder of food. Amelia glanced down at her. "You should feed the beast that lives in your belly before everything within a hundred miles is alerted to our presence."

Setting the book aside, Bea walked outside to their skyboat to fetch a fuschia-colored mamaberry for each of them. Mamaberries are as big as your hand with one large round berry known as the mama and lots of smaller berries attached known as the babies. It is one of the most nutritious fruits that grow in Lichen. They are very juicy and make tongues, lips and fingers blush purple and red. She handed one to Amelia before she began to nosh on her own.

Once their hunger was satisfied, they sat down to look at the lads' journal and took turns reading aloud the entries. The earliest pages were filled with photos of their family, local wildlife, the observatory and its surroundings, celestial sightings and creatures they had observed through the telescope. Descriptions on each page were written in the same childish hand. It was evident at this point in their lives, the observatory was still tethered to the ground.

But then, about halfway through the book, they came upon a photograph of a magical-looking object. It resembled a small crystal ball that contained an entire galaxy within, painted in swirls of pink, gray, and rainbow-colored stardust.

The entry written under the photograph read:

My new ball I found when Bix and I were building sand sculptures at the sea. It was bobbing along and I retrieved it. I was making a sky leviathan and Bix was building the observatory.

Amelia made an appreciative noise as she examined a photo of the sand sculptures. Such extraordinary detail! The eyes of the leviathan captured the soul of the creature, and in the windows of the observatory sculpture you could make out their parents at work. It was hard to believe a ten- and a seven-year-old boy made them. Snotty or not, they were talented little fellows.

After a few more sea photos, Beatrice turned the page to a photograph capturing the observatory in the first phases of detaching from the ground. From page to page, they examined the evidence as it slowly rose into the sky as their own houses had.

Under the last observatory photo, Click had written:

It was the ball! I held it and wished we'd fly into the sky to see everything up close and bam! Our house is floating. It's a wishing ball and nobody's taking it from us! Bix wished we could swim like the sky creatures and now we all float. Mom and Dad are trying to figure out what happened so Bix and I are running away. We'll snag some of the leftover scones from tea and catch a ride on the cloud turtles and see if we can find the sky leviathans.

That was the last entry.

Beatrice looked at Amelia with concern. "There's strong magic at work here. I think we need to track down these two before they wish for the wrong thing and do any worse mischief."

Amelia was flabbergasted at the very idea. "This building started floating so many years ago and these journal entries are from way back then. Those two could be anywhere by now or even dead. How could you possibly hope to find them?"

The excitement drained out of Beatrice's face. "You're right. It would probably be a wild goose chase. I know what—I'll borrow the journals and scientific notes and sail to Coral's lighthouse. There's not much about magic she doesn't understand and she can advise me on how to find them. I'll drop you off at your house first. I know you aren't interested in traveling so far."

Amelia was conflicted. It was true she was a homebody through and through and had no desire for adventuring, but the idea of meeting the sea witch and finding out if Beatrice's fantastical stories were true was so intriguing, she thought she might be tempted, just this once.

"I'll come with you." Amelia said, feeling very brave and pleased with herself. "First, it was only the observatory floating. Now our houses. Who knows how far this will spread. It could disrupt the whole countryside. And if this ball is so powerful, you're right that these boys may have gotten in over their heads and caused even more harm. But I hope we find them soon and can get back to our normal schedule."

Beatrice was more than a tad impatient with Amelia's aversion to adventure because it was so foreign to her own nature. However, the opportunity to introduce her new friend to her true love and prove she had been telling the truth was far more important. This was turning into an absolutely amazing day!

The Sea
Witch

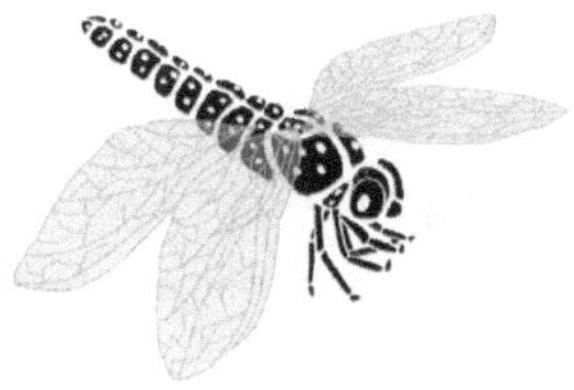

THE JOURNEY BEGINS

WHEN THEY HAD DRIFTED far enough away from the observatory, Beatrice unfurled the skyboat's sails for the first time to supplement the balloons. She heard a gasp from Amelia and turned toward her friend in time to catch her grinning in delight at the unexpected sight.

The sails were pastel shades of every color with segmented ebony stitching to mimic a real dragonfly. They beat through the air with a great *whoosh* as the boat took flight. The sun shining through the wings produced an ever-changing stained glass window pattern on the floor and sides of the boat. The design and effect of the wings exceeded even Bea's own expectations, and she was gratified to see Amelia was also impressed.

As they gathered speed, Amelia's silver braid trailed behind the boat again, attracting the attention of the school of cloud jellyfish. She pulled her braid back toward her as the jellies followed like fish caught on a line.

Beatrice took out her knife and began to carve a relief of one of the curious creatures into the wood of the boat. "Perhaps they think you're an odd-looking jellyfish with only one tentacle."

With knitted brow, Amelia turned to Beatrice, ready to disparage such a whimsical notion, but then reconsidered when she realized how flattering it was to think these beautiful creatures might see her as one of their own.

"The skyboat is lovely, Bea. Why didn't you enlighten me when I referred to it as some kind of bug? I can't believe I didn't notice the likeness it bore to a dragonfly until now."

"I knew you'd figure it out sooner or later, and I wanted to surprise you when I spread the sails."

"You're a genius. I've never seen anything more gorgeous or better designed."

Bea blushed in delight at this rare compliment from her friend. Secretly, even she was surprised at how well the skyboat worked. It sailed through the skies like a real dragonfly, zipping and soaring and dipping to catch downdrafts. In fact, the boat became rather over-exuberant, and before she knew it, Beatrice was flung overboard.

Since she could float, she was in no immediate danger, but there was no way she could swim fast enough to catch up to the racing boat. Amelia wasted no time flinging her long braid out as a lifeline for her friend. Bracing one foot against the boat's railing, Amelia pulled on the hairy rope to bring Beatrice alongside.

"Thanks," Beatrice said as she hauled herself back onboard. She eyed Amelia curiously. "Didn't that hurt?"

"The Arrowhearts are famous for the strength of our hair. My father had a braided beard so long that he would often use it as a fishing line, but perhaps we would do well to tie ourselves to the boat with actual rope to be on the safe side."

Their tethers gave them a sense of security, but an even better solution was waiting for them when they went down below to prepare a bite of supper. They discovered a fancily-wrapped parcel sitting in the center of each of their pea pod sofa beds. Delicate turquoise blue paper tied up with curlicues of silver ribbon gave way to a giant clamshell that opened to reveal a pair of clogs that looked like they were covered in seaweed.

A note written on lavender paper rolled up like a scroll contained an identical message to each of them:

Greetings, lovely ladies! The funny thing about dragonflies is they are talented acrobats and if you aren't careful, you might fall out of your skyboat. These magical shoes will keep you safely adhered to the deck no matter how rough your sky seas. They will never fail you. I look forward to your visit –Coral

"How did she know we needed them and that we're on our way to see her?" asked Amelia.

"I told you she was full of magic, and the best part of magic is surprise gifts!"

Amelia held her pair of shoes next to her long, narrow feet in disappointment. "Mine are too small. Still, it's the thought that counts."

Beatrice snorted. "A sea witch never makes a mistake. Magic is one size fits all. Try them on and you'll see." She slipped her own shoes off and slid into each clog with a soft sigh. They were incredibly plush, like walking barefoot in lush velvety cushions of moss. She thought she might never remove them again.

Amelia tried her pair on and was chastened to discover they fit perfectly despite her reservations. A splutter of laughter sounded from the tattoo on her shoulder.

"I've no doubt they're mighty comfortable, Captain, but I must say it looks like a pair of barnacled feet ye have now," One-Eyed Jack observed.

Beatrice laughed too, standing up and twirling, discovering her clogs did hug the floor as well as any barnacle. Though she could dance, it was tricky, as every time she lifted a foot it made popping, suction cup sounds.

Amelia turned her back so Beatrice couldn't see her face and began shaking uncontrollably.

"Melia? Are you ok?" Beatrice asked.

Amelia spluttered and gasped and finally let out a nonstop belly laugh. She fell to her knees unable to stop chortling at the comical noise the clogs made. "Nothing has tickled me so much in years! At this rate, I'll be doing good just to be able to crawl."

Beatrice was relieved and surprised. She'd rarely heard Amelia laugh before. She didn't mind making a fool of herself if it helped her friend lighten up.

They bustled about the galley kitchen, giggling at the funny sounds of the clogs as they wove around each other to put together a simple meal in the tiny space. Amelia had to admit the seaweed shoes made her feel more secure once she got used to them. At least she didn't have to worry so much about tumbling out of the boat.

After supper, they climbed on deck and watched as the sun set and the skies dimmed. The seven Lichen moons shone far above their heads, drowning out the distant lights of the villages they passed over. Navigation was easy as Beatrice's love for Coral was like a homing device pointed unerringly in the direction of her beloved sea witch's lighthouse.

They watched in amazement as the jellyfish clouds that trailed the boat glowed neon in the darkened sky, their bioluminescent tentacles shining every color of a rainbow. It was a glorious sight and a comfort to the two women flying through the night, but eventually the jellies grew bored of the strange wooden creature they had discovered and drifted away.

Without the distraction of the beautiful creatures, Amelia had more time to think about her predicament as they went below deck to prepare for bedtime. She was farther from her house than she'd ever been in her life, having never spent so much as a night away before. Not to mention hurtling through the air on a skyboat of all things, with a friend who sometimes appeared overly reckless in her adventurous spirit.

Amelia couldn't help but appreciate that having discovered the observatory and the lads' journal as well as having the unique ability to travel by air, they had a responsibility to see what mischief Bix and Click were up to with their wishing ball, but it didn't make her happy about it. She wondered if they wouldn't have been better off returning and explaining to someone in authority what was going on. But then she imagined trying to convince anyone of the bizarre events. They'd probably be laughed at and sent away with pitying looks. Dismissed as a couple of middle-aged kooks.

Beatrice could sense her friend's fears. "I know you're worried about being away from the comforts of your house and garden, but anywhere can be comfortable if you have a friend with you." She reached into one of her many pockets and pulled out a carved snowbear cub and a charming penguin and handed them to Amelia.

"Take these. I find running my fingers over the wood helps me relax. Tuck yourself in, close your eyes, and I'll tell you a story about the time I traveled to the Bitter Lands, which are covered with snow and ice the year round. I followed a waddle of penguins on a grand march across the ice and rescued a young snowbear."

"Is this another of your tall tales?"

"All my stories are true. You only have to believe in them. Now close your eyes or no story."

"Let's hear it, lass. Nothing better than a good yarn," said Jack.

Amelia gave the pirate tattoo a dirty look but had to admit, it might distract her from her worries. "Very well, but I can't promise to believe it."

"That doesn't matter," said Beatrice. "It doesn't change the fact it happened exactly this way."

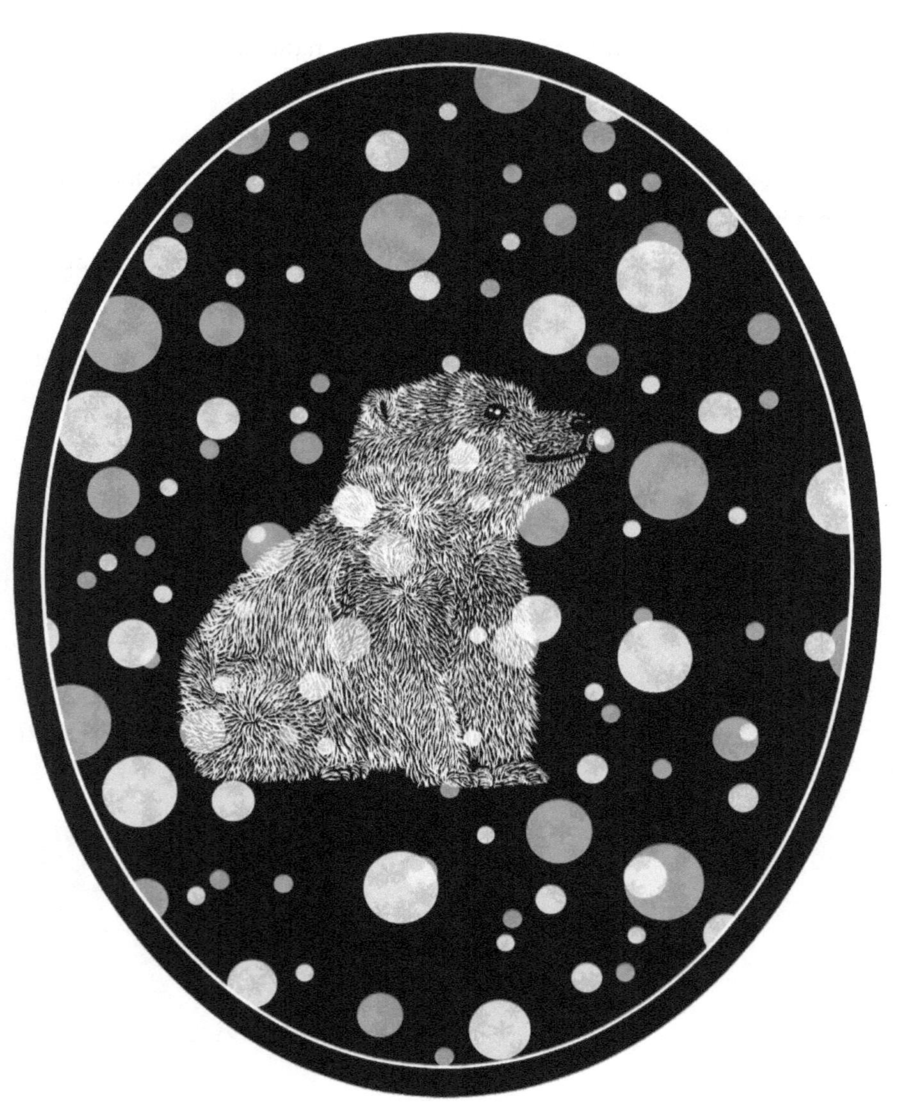

CHAPTER 8

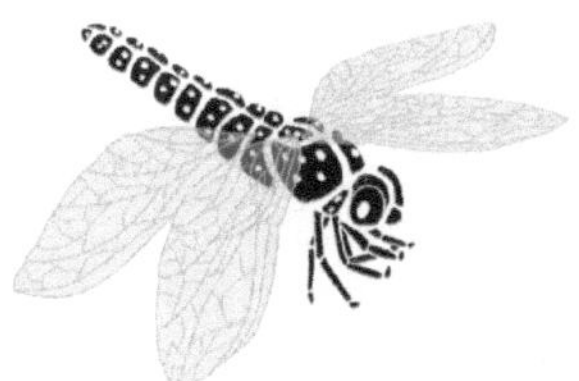

BEATRICE IN THE BITTER LANDS

WHEN CORAL AND I first parted ways, I caught a lift on a fishing boat headed to the Bitter Lands. I had never been anywhere so cold and longed to see my breath spiraling in the frosty air and experience life in a frozen environment. I helped the crew to pay my way, swabbing the decks and assisting the cook in the kitchen. After two weeks of sailing, we reached the southernmost port of that icy country and disembarked at a small coastal town.

The cold made my face sting, but I was so excited, I twirled in circles, dancing in time with a shower of snowflakes I tried to catch on my tongue. I pirouetted into a dry goods store to buy warmer clothing. A red hunter's cap with ear flaps that covered my neck, waterproofed and fleece-lined for comfort. A thick boiled wool coat so black and shiny it made me look like a fat beetle. Then I saw a pair of snowshoes, something I'd always wanted to try. I put them on and the store clerk laughed at my attempts to walk, assuring me I'd get better with practice.

I then turned my attention to food supplies. I hoped to be able to forage some things, like fish or berries but in such an inhospitable environment, it seemed wise to fill my rucksack with tea, grains, dried herbs, spices and fruit, chocolate and pemmican bars, honey, and as an afterthought, several bars of tallow, which in an emergency could serve for food. Flint for starting fires and a sturdy and versatile pocketknife completed my kit.

"Are you joining the expedition?" the shopkeeper asked me, seeing I was out-fitting myself for a trek in the wilderness.

"Possibly," I answered, intrigued at the notion. "What expedition are you talking about?"

"Tannen Troop is leading a group to search for a legendary ice castle. Most of us don't believe it exists, but he's an impractical dreamer. You look like the impractical dreamer type, too, so I thought maybe you were planning on tagging along."

Smiling tightly, I paid for my purchases. A funny little man with long tufts of hair sticking out from the sides of his head like spun sugar shouldn't cast stones, but I have a thick skin and didn't mind if he found me peculiar. Besides, I was excited about this talk of ice castles and an expedition. I wasn't afraid to strike out on my own, but having never explored a frozen land before, it didn't seem a bad idea to start out as part of a larger, more experienced group until I got the lay of the place.

I tracked down Tannen Troop on his ship, *The Ne'er-do-well*, where he was eating his lunch in the galley. The captain was a squat, powerfully-built man with tangles of red wooly hair and a droopy red mustache. He looked like someone had thrown a freckle pie in his face, the spots were so numerous. I sat down and introduced myself, asking for a berth on board and offering to work for nothing to pay my way and use my gift of wind and weather craft to aid our voyage.

"You've the look of a lassie who's missing her mama. Sure you don't want me changing your nappy and kicking your arse back to where you come from instead?" he asked through a cloud of noxious pipe smoke.

I nearly turned around then, not wanting to put up with such snark, but I was so curious to travel north, I swallowed my pride and decided to try honesty. "No, but I miss my witch. Have you ever heard of the sea witch who keeps the Kaleidoscope Lighthouse? That's my Coral."

"Aye, any who've sailed have heard of your sea witch. So, you're her latest fair one? Hm, don't know if that makes you a jinx or a good luck charm, but I think I won't give you the boot. Last thing I need is for a sea witch to be angered and sink my ship." He sliced a hunk of bread off the loaf and after he'd smeared it with butter, he stabbed the knife into the table between the fingers of my left hand.

"I might not throw you off my ship, but it don't mean I'll kowtow to the likes of you neither. Pull your weight and tell me if you sense a change in the winds or weather and you can ride along with us."

He got up, retrieving his knife and waving it once more in my face as a warning before leaving me alone in the galley. I licked the blood from my hand where he'd nicked the skin. He was right to be worried about angering Coral, but he hadn't been careful enough. She always knew when I was hurt or ill and would exact her revenge in some way or another.

I awoke to a ruckus in the morning as Troop tipped me out of my hammock to the ship's floor. The captain no longer had hair of red or any other color. In retaliation for drawing my blood, Coral had cursed him to live without a single hair on any part of his body. He was livid, shaking his fist and swearing at me, but it was like spitting in the wind. Coral had made her point and he now knew the penalty for harming me.

Despite the rough start, I settled into the crew well enough. My ability to talk to the winds and predict the weather was much admired by the other sailors, and even the captain had to admit it was a useful skill to have on board. We made good time at first, but the farther north we ventured, the more ice we saw, until one day we became stranded by floes on all sides of us. Most of the crew worked on chipping and picking at the ice to try and loosen it while the rest of us passed the time by fishing to replenish our food supplies for the next part of the journey.

The other sailors were agitated and annoyed by mischievous seals that popped their dark, sleek heads in and out of the holes we cut in the ice and stole the fish right out of their hands. I had the foresight to toss a string of pearls into my hole before I fished, however, and was left in peace.

That was a little trick I learned from Coral as she'd warned me I might encounter shapeshifters along my route. Shapeshifters are seafolk who can turn themselves into any creature of the sea to better navigate the ocean waters and are notorious for playing tricks on land dwellers. It's always wise to placate them with a gift. My present seemed to do the trick for I caught more fish than all the other sailors combined. A good lesson to be kind to everything since not every creature or situation is what it appears to be.

After two days of work, the captain decided the ship was truly stuck and we might as well begin the overland part of our expedition from where we were. The ice sleds were brought up from the holds of the ship, and we hitched up some seals to the harnesses. Bitter Land seals are notoriously swift on the snow, sliding on their bellies for miles before they have to stop and build up momentum again. We threw fish in front of the animals to entice them if they became disinterested in sliding and there were plenty of fresh seals in that part of the Lands to trade out when ours became too tired.

Most of us shared a sled with three or four others, but the ship's photographer had one sled all to himself and his equipment. He'd wrapped everything in cushioned furs to preserve them and keep them from freezing and cracking. Might seem silly to bring so much heavy equipment on an expedition, but the ice castles were legendary. Photographs of them would ensure his fame throughout Lichen if he succeeded.

The scenery didn't change much as we traveled, just flat ice and snow until one day in the distance, we noticed a long black line near the horizon. When we got close enough to find out what it was, by golly, by gumbo, it was a waddle of penguins! A spark was kindled in my heart. I longed to see what life with them would be like. Fairy ice castles that sparkled in the sunshine like crystal sounded amazing, but I was drawn to these creatures of the land and sea and thought Coral would want me to follow them.

At our next stop to rest and capture new seals for the journey, I gathered up my things and told the company I was going to join the march of the penguins. A few of the sailors were sad to see me go, but most were too focused on their quest to care. Certainly the captain wasn't sorry to see the last of me given that I was the cause of his eternal baldness. I strapped on my snowshoes and set out at a steady pace to catch up with the waddle.

They walked in a line that stretched as far as the eye could see, marching in pairs, two by two. The only sound to be heard was the crunching of snow under their feet and the howl of the blasting wind. The birds were black and white with lilac and turquoise tufts of curly feathers protruding from their ears. At first glance, it made them appear whimsical, foolish even, until I studied their faces closely and saw their looks of determination. I wondered where they were going—that is, where *we* were going since I'd decided to throw my lot in with them.

Some of them glanced at me curiously from time to time as I walked beside the line, but mostly they didn't seem to care about me. They had a destination in mind and that was what filled their thoughts. We marched through the night with a sky full of gloaming, which was as dark as it got there during that time of year. They chattered to each other occasionally, but never slowed their progress. I grew tired and wondered if they ever planned to stop and rest. Finally, I reached the limits of my strength and lay down in my tracks, curling up in a ball for sleep.

It wasn't the smartest move as I might have frozen to death and should have at least taken the time to light a fire or build a shelter, but I'd never been so exhausted in my life and couldn't bring myself to care. I was ashamed I couldn't compete with the stamina of the birds, but they'd been practicing this journey for a lifetime while it was all new to me.

Luckily, the penguins must have taken pity on me. When I woke up a few hours later, I found they'd surrounded me in a protective huddle like they were shielding one of their own chicks. They took turns bearing the brunt of the icy winds while others rested more comfortably. When they noticed I was awake, they chirruped the news, repeating it up and down the frozen tundra to the rest of the crowd. The penguins reassembled into their pairs and set off again.

I marched with them for several days and might have continued to the end—for I was interested in finding out what their final destination might be—except I caught a glint of light, something catching the rays of the sun that distracted me from their mission.

We were passing an ice cave, its gaping mouth hung with icicles taller than me. My curiosity was immediately aroused. How deep was it? Was it inhabited? What if it was another entrance to the fabled ice castle Tannen had talked of? I knew I would regret it forever if I didn't stop and find out.

Waving and blowing kisses to them, I called out to my companions: "I'm leaving you now. Thank you for letting me travel with you and thank you for protecting me while I slept."

Many of them raised a wing in response and cooed softly to me as their endless procession traveled past. I collected several lilac and turquoise feathers from the ground as souvenirs, tucking them carefully in a pouch for safekeeping, then set off in the direction of the ice cave.

Inching inside cautiously, I was enchanted by music created by the winds whistling through the icy stalactites. It sounded like a calliope, only gentle and soft. Then I heard another noise, a pitiful cry so mournful that I recklessly rushed farther into the cave to see what it was.

It wasn't long before I found a little snowbear cub, snuggled up to its mother and tugging on her trying to wake her up. I was terrified at first as full-grown snowbears are formidable creatures, but when I saw the larger snowbear never moved, not even to breathe, I knew it must be dead.

The poor cub looked up at me as I approached and loped over to drag me closer to its mother. It was very young and so alone, my heart went out to it, and I was determined to do what I could to help.

Figuring it must be hungry, I rummaged through my rucksack to find something, feeding it dried fish mixed with some of the tallow and one of my pemmican bars. It was more content after that, but I knew I couldn't keep it fed for long on my own. I watched as the poor thing raced around its mother, pawing at her and tagging her to play a game, not realizing its mum's playing days were no more.

I decided to spend the night there and ask Coral what to do in my dreams. This is what she told me: "When the little cub is asleep you must take off your coat and other outer garments and roll in the scent of the mother snowbear, then put your things back on and roll in her scent again. After that, dig a hole in the snow to give her a decent burial."

"I couldn't possibly lift her," I answered, knowing the creature must weigh hundreds of pounds more than me.

Coral smiled and sang an incantation to me. "Now you can and will, my beloved. The scent will trick the baby bear for a while into believing you are its mother, even though you don't look the same. He'll follow you until we can find him another family. Listen to your instincts, for they and I will guide you along your path."

I followed Coral's instructions to the letter, the extra strength she had given me equal to the task. Exhausted from burying the poor dead bear, I returned to the ice cave and noticed my supplies had been magically replenished. I started a small fire and made a cup of tea and a bowl of oats with dried mamaberries to share with the cub. A bucket had appeared, and I discovered it was full of milk—snowbear's milk, I assumed.

The drowsy cub woke up and sniffed the air. It stared at me, puzzled. I smelled like its mother, but I could tell it was trying to work out why I looked so different. When I brought it the milk, it drank hungrily though. No matter how much the cub drank, the amount of milk in the bucket stayed the same. I was worrying how I was supposed to drag a sloshing pail along with us when I noticed the milk disappeared once the cub was full. I could tie the bucket to my rucksack until the cub was ready for feasting again.

I ate my breakfast, sharing bites with the cub, and then indulged it in a wrestling match, sensing it was eager for playtime. I sang a song about snowbears my mother sang to me when I was little, rubbing the cub's ears and cuddling with it as it dozed by my side.

"Little one, when life closes a door, we don't try to reopen it, we look for another. Let's explore this cave and see if it has another opening."

Shouldering my rucksack and clicking my tongue at the cub who followed me closely, we ventured farther into the cave. I turned on my flashlight and the ice sparkled like gemstones along the walls as the light bounced around.

We'd hiked at least a mile when the pathway opened into a larger cave chamber with a lake of clear water lit by sunshine streaming in through gaps in the roof. I caught sight of a female snowbear and her two cubs playing on the far side. My little cub got excited and called out to them, running over as fast as he could to join in the fun. The mother bear eyed me warily, rising on her hind legs to her full height.

I spoke quietly to her, hoping she might understand the feeling behind my words if not the sounds. I told her how the cub was orphaned and alone. That I hoped she would adopt it as it didn't belong in the care of people. She seemed to understand I meant no harm as she turned away and supervised her brood, now increased by one. I backed quietly away, not wishing to draw the cub's attention to my departure. I sensed Coral's presence and knew she approved of this happy ending to my adventure.

"Why, Amelia! I do believe you relaxed so much listening to my tale that you've fallen asleep. Maybe you'll think you dreamed the whole thing. It's just as well. You'd only think I made it up like my other stories. Sweet dreams, dear friend," Beatrice whispered and lay down to sleep too.

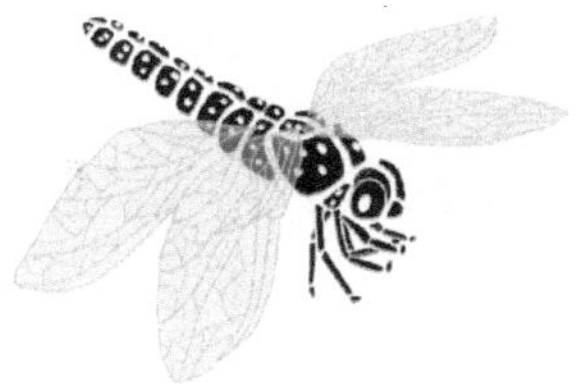

CHAPTER 9

THE LOSS OF A FRIEND

THE CRIES OF SEAGULLS and crash of waves woke Amelia. She opened her eyes to find a waterfall of aquamarine blue hair and a pair of lively olive-green eyes staring into hers.

"You're..." she started to say.

The sea witch smiled, amused at how Amelia struggled to finish her thought.

"You're real," she said with her mouth agape.

"How astute. Would you like me to pinch you to demonstrate you're not dreaming?" Coral teased.

"No, thank you," Amelia replied, unable to stop staring at the gills around Coral's neck. She pulled her covers up under her chin, greatly intimidated by this magical being.

"Wakey, wakey beloved," Coral cooed to the sleeping Beatrice.

Beatrice smiled up at her and stretched out her arms in welcome. "Hello, wife of mine."

"You never told me she was your wife!" Amelia said in surprise.

"You didn't believe she even existed, so what did it matter?" Beatrice snuggled against Coral. "You guided us here as we slept. What a delightful surprise to wake up to."

"If you're real then the Kaleidoscope Lighthouse must be too?" Amelia asked.

Coral gestured up the stairs. "Your skyboat is tethered to it. Have a look."

Amelia hopped out of her pea pod bed and slid her feet into the seaweed clogs, creeping up the stairs slowly as if afraid of what she might find. She peeked over the edge of the boat and gazed at the lighthouse. Nothing could have prepared her for its extraordinary beauty. Her friend had described it in detail, but some things have to be seen to be appreciated.

"Let usssssss sssssssee," said her snake tattoo.

Amelia complied by lifting up her arms and resting them on the railing. She could have stayed there all day soaking in the astounding scenes depicted in the intricate tilework. While she studied the curious building, clanging sounds and delicious aromas from below deck spoke of breakfast being prepared. Soon Beatrice and Coral came up top with bowls of steaming vegetable soup, soft boiled eggs, thick crusty bread slathered with butter, and mugs of stout Lichen tea.

As they enjoyed this sumptuous feast, Beatrice filled her wife in on what they had discovered at the observatory and about the magical object the boys had used to such ill effect.

Amelia asked the sea witch, "Do you think we'll always float away from the ground now, or do you have a way to give us our land legs back? I want to be able to work in my garden without worrying about drifting away."

Coral dabbed daintily at her mouth with a purple linen napkin. "I need to see the journal and get a look at a photo of the ball before I can give you a definitive answer. I think your lads may have a Wizarding Ball of Intention. If that's the case, they can make things happen, but they cannot undo them. It doesn't mean it can't be undone, just not with the Ball of Intention."

"If you stop us floating, does that mean I can't fly anymore?" asked Beatrice. "I like keeping my options open, you know."

Coral laughed at her wife. "Yes, dearest, I know it very well. I might be able to work a spell that way if you like."

"Think how handy it would be, Amelia. You could paint the second story of your house easily. Repair the roof without worrying about falling off. It has an upside if you think about it."

Coral sipped her tea and looked at them both. "It also depends on the purpose for which you were given flight. It's possible it is only a temporary gift and would wear off on its own. These complicated variables are why a Ball of Intention should never be given to children and most especially not to children who don't understand the power of their wishes."

Deep in thought, her brow furrowed by worry, Bea retrieved the photo journal from below decks and handed the tome off to her wife.

Coral caressed Beatrice's cheek. "We'll sort this out, love, don't worry."

The witch opened the big leatherbound book, and spying the dried snot inside the front cover, pulled a soft brown drawstring pouch out of the pocket of her dress. She retrieved a pair of tweezers and a small cream vellum envelope from within it and scraped up some of the messy residue, saving it in the envelope and returning the pouch and all to her pocket.

Amelia and Beatrice sat watching this surprising operation in silence and continued to hold their tongues as Coral studied the photos and inscriptions in the book one by one. Instinct warned them it was best to wait until she finished her tasks rather than interrupting with impatient questions or meddling observations as they were tempted to do.

After she shut the book, Coral looked out to sea for a while before addressing Amelia and Beatrice. "Your gift of flight may come from the wish the lads made with the Ball of Intention that caused the observatory and eventually your houses to float. I will give you a spell that will maintain your ability to fly in case the magic from their wish wears out at an inconvenient time that might lead you to plunge to your deaths. I'll put the spell on a necklace you must wear at all times."

The Sea Witch took off two of her own necklaces, mumbled a spell into them, and kissed each before beckoning to Amelia and Beatrice. Coral placed one with an albatross carved out of an abalone shell around Amelia's neck. She placed a seagull carved from dried coral around her wife's.

"To activate them, say: 'I want to fly.' That's all it takes. When you want to walk on the ground, say: 'I want to land' and you will gently touch down. To make sure you don't lose them and no one steals them from you, I've added a special binding that only allows you to take them off if I reverse the spell."

"A fantastic safety precaution! That should safeguard us on our own without you." Beatrice gazed at her wife longingly. How she wished Coral could join them. She knew they had to leave soon to track down the missing boys, and it didn't make it any easier knowing she would once again have to leave her love behind.

Amelia watched her friend closely. Though she had never been in love herself, she could imagine something of what Bea felt. She wondered if there was a way to break the curse or spell that bound Coral to the lighthouse so the couple could be together always, but it seemed impertinent to ask when she had only just met the witch.

Her tattoo of a seal from the Bitter Lands on her forearm had no such qualms, however. It was captivated with Coral and was drawn to learn more about her. It spoke up in a soft, lilting voice. "Is it a spell or a curse that keeps you here? Who bound you to the lighthouse, and is there a way we can help?"

Coral smiled down at the bright-eyed seal. "It's a long, painful story that we don't have time to go into right now. You'll have more than enough on your plates in finding and dealing with these wayward lads." She looked more closely at the seal tattoo. "But how do you come to be trapped as you are, my little shapeshifter?"

At Coral's words, the seal tattoo shed its skin. In its place, was a parade of ever-changing figures: a mermaid, a moonfish, a red crab, and finally, a beautiful young girl. Amelia stared in amazement. She'd gotten used to her tattoos talking and even moving around occasionally from place to place on her skin when they grew bored, but she had never seen such a transformation before.

"It's the Ink of Lost Souls that bound us to her skin. None of us are free," the shapeshifter confided.

Amelia gasped in shock and mortification at this news.

"You view them as your friends, don't you?" Coral asked Amelia gently. "Did you realize they were trapped?"

"No," she answered, aghast. "I'd no idea. I thought it was ordinary tattoo ink until they started talking to me, but it just seemed like a neat trick. I never dreamed they had their own souls and wanted to be free. They never said so before."

"Probably the magic that binds them forbade them from complaining until they came across another magical being such as myself. This is the work of a powerful sorcerer. When souls lose their way, they can be tempted and trapped. They must have been caught in the bottle of ink used for your tattoos. I can free them from being bound to your skin, but then it will be up to them whether to stay with you or move on, either in this life or into another realm according to their natures."

Amelia looked down at her arms stoically. "I can't pretend I won't miss them, but I would never keep any being caged that longed to be free."

The sea witch nodded in approval and held up her hands, running them along Amelia's aura with graceful, swirling motions, creating a tickling sensation that made her shiver. A hissing sound came from Coral's gills and a wild incantation conjuring all the sounds of the ocean poured from her lips.

As the last word sounded, the ink of the shapeshifter stretched like a rubber band, pulling away from Amelia's arm and bursting into its own being of flesh and blood. The beautiful young woman of the tattoo stood before them with aqua blue, lavender, and pale pink wavy tresses trailing down the dewy seaweed woven dress she wore. Her shapely bare legs stretched as she wiggled her toes in delight against the surface of the boat's decking.

"Thank you! Thank you for my freedom. My name is Noe. I can't believe I'm finally free! Thank you, lovely sea witch. And thank you, dear Amelia Arrowheart, for your years of friendship, but I must return to the ocean where my heart yearns to be. If ever a boon you need that I or any of my kind can grant, simply speak your request across the waters and the tides will carry it to us and we will come to your aid." With that promise, she climbed over the boat's railing and dove gracefully into the sea below, disappearing beneath the pounding waves.

CHAPTER 10

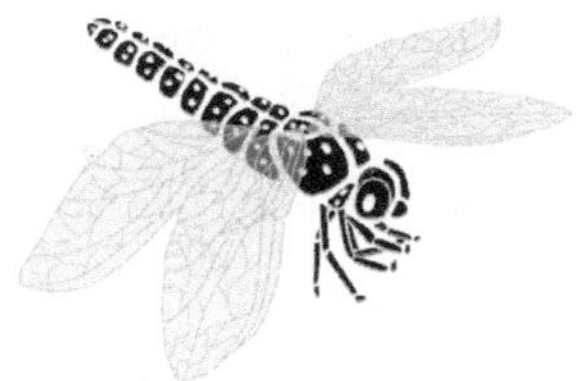

CORAL'S ADVICE

AMELIA HUGGED HERSELF FIERCELY, torn between grief at the loss of a friend and happiness at the shapeshifter's joy. For once, the rest of her inks remained silent. None of them made an immediate move to leave, but she knew it was only a matter of time before more of them decided to abandon her to live their own lives. She couldn't blame them for wanting to be free, but it was a lonely feeling to think they could leave her behind and she might never see them again.

Beatrice watched her friend with pity, but she knew Amelia hated being the center of attention and would not welcome sympathy at her loss. She decided to change the subject to a more disgusting one. "Perhaps you'd care to share what you're going to do with your new snot collection, wife of mine?"

Coral laughed deep and long. "Much can be done with the smallest part of a person left behind. Always remember that." She pulled out the vellum envelope. "This will become an ingredient in a tracking spell that can pinpoint where these boys are to the last nth of an inch."

"So you think we should go after them?"

"Definitely. The only way to end the spell on your houses is to find these brothers and discover the exact nature of their wish. Once I know the details, I might be able to reverse it."

"Must I go too?" asked Amelia, anxious at the idea of further adventures.

"I wish you would," Coral said gently. "My wife is precious to me. Since I cannot leave this lighthouse, I would feel better if she had a companion on such an uncertain journey."

Amelia was very unhappy at the idea of traveling so far with no destination or timeframe in mind, but something about the sea witch's trust inspired her to nod her head slightly in acceptance at this unfortunate fate.

"Before you both leave, I will ask you to give me something of your own. That way, if you ever get separated or lost, I can track you down. Hair, a nail clipping, a laugh, or even a sigh will do. I can work with most anything. But for now, bring me a little pot I can burn this in," she added, indicating the brothers' snot.

Beatrice jumped up and went below deck, returning in a few minutes with a small iron cauldron covered in etched runes.

The sea witch took it from her with a smile. "After all these years, you still have it. I am pleased, my dear." She reached into the multitudinous pockets of her dress, pulling out pinches of this and that. "If you haven't the gift of magic, this isn't a spell you can replicate. Sand and salt represent the sea, soil and powdered clowdis root represent the land, spun sugar and two drops of rain to represent the sky, all swirled together." She snapped her fingers and a neon green fire lit up the tiny cauldron.

"Land, sky, and flowing sea, show me where these brothers be." Coral dumped in the boys' nasal residue which turned the flame a rich mulberry color. She examined the changing patterns for some time before making a contented sound of satisfaction.

"If you follow the migration path of the cloud jellyfish, you will find Bix and Click, and perhaps even their parents too." She added two more pinches of spun sugar to the flames and three puffs of smoke rose up. "It will take you three days to reach them from here."

"Three days is a long time," Amelia fretted. "And what do we do when we find them? They might be all grown up by now. How are we to convince them to tell us what we need to know? What if they use the ball against us?"

"There are too many unknown variables for me to answer your questions. The future is often unseeable. Try not to worry about things we cannot yet predict. Spend some time here resting before your journey. I can teach you of the things you may encounter in the sky. Plants to harvest when you run low on food. Which creatures are friendly and which are not."

Beatrice held up her coral bird necklace. "Does this work now? Can we use it to walk around in the house?"

The Sea Witch laughed lightly, got up and stepped off the boat, disappearing into her cottage.

"She didn't answer you," Amelia said.

"She didn't need to. It was silly to ask and I know it. All I have to do is follow her and find out on my own. Even I am not allowed to waste her time with foolish questions," Beatrice replied, walking to the side of the boat and jumping off.

Amelia ran to the side to see what happened.

"I want to land," Bea said and floated gently to the ground.

Amelia followed suit, and they entered the witch's cottage. She was immediately overwhelmed at the multitude of different things there were to look at in every direction. She was delighted to see carved wooden figures on almost every surface, picking up a heron standing on one leg.

"Look, Bea, your carvings!"

"Yes," Coral confirmed. "They each come to me with a story to tell. The wood sings of why she made them, how she was feeling, and how they fit into her life and journey while she is away from me. Like you, I spend most of my time alone, preferring the company of my wife above any other, but these gifts keep her close to me."

Amelia continued her exploration of the many marvels to be seen. She walked up to the peek-a-boo glass bottles cemented into the walls and looked through the spyglass seeing everything outside through the unique lens of each piece of colored glass. And every direction she looked inside, there was a new wonder to behold. All she could think about was how in Lichen would she ever be able to capture this beauty in the drawings she made in her journal.

She realized Bea and Coral were watching her with more than a little amusement. "I've been unforgivably nosy, but you have such a beautiful cottage, I couldn't help myself. I want to try and memorize every detail so I can reproduce it later."

"Don't bother. I wove a spell around it," the sea witch explained. "Even if you spent the rest of your life here, you would always find you couldn't remember a thing about it when you tried to draw or describe it. Beatrice is my wife, so she is able to write about it, but even from her description, you wouldn't be able to sketch it. I protect our privacy that way."

Afraid Amelia would take umbrage at this mild admonishment from Coral, Beatrice leapt in again to turn the conversation. "Why don't you tell us about the skies now, my love?"

Amelia settled down in a comfortable chair across from where Beatrice and her wife cuddled close together on a plump sofa as Coral began her lecture.

"You've seen the cloud jellyfish for yourself. These lads wrote they were off after the sky leviathans who mate once every ten years with lunar leviathans that descend from the stars. I hope you'll have the opportunity to witness this most wondrous event that few are privileged to observe. There is also every kind of sky creature you can imagine from what you know of the seas. Cloud dolphins, starfish, cephalopods, schools of every type of fish. You might even catch sight of a cloud skydragon, though they are tiny and not easy to spy."

"Is there anything we should be wary of on our travels?" Amelia asked, ever cautious of the unfamiliar and unexplored.

"Storms are to be respected, just as they are on land, and there are some creatures that may confuse you for prey or seek to play pranks on you for their own amusement. And whatever you do, don't ever trust or tempt a kraken," she said with a stern look before changing the subject without further explanation.

"Our next topic is food. Numerous plants grow in the sky. No one knows why or how any more than we understand why there are cloud creatures, but they do exist nevertheless. There are things similar to onions, seaweed, mamaberries, and potatoes that grow whipped and sweet like toasted meringue. I'm sure you'll learn as you go. You can trust Beatrice when it comes to what is safe to eat. Her foraging talents will never lead you astray," Coral added.

"It's like we've shaken Lichen upside down and instead of falling into the sea, we fell into the sky and now everything is changing and nothing will ever be the same," Amelia observed with a tinge of melancholy.

"You're sorry for the loss of your shapeshifter friend," Coral stated. "I cannot undo what's been done nor would I choose to, but I am sorry if it makes you sad." She ran her fingers through Beatrice's curls and braided them into a crown atop her head. "Try not to worry too much about your ink. Until you've had your freedom stolen by another for almost a millennium, you cannot imagine what horror that instills in the heart, mind, and soul. I, too, have experienced loneliness and regret, but all things should be free and have a choice and say in their destiny."

Amelia agreed with the sea witch, but it was still a loss to know her tattoos could now walk away from her at any time. As the sun sunk lower on the horizon, Amelia announced she would sleep on the boat to give the married couple a chance for some time together, though in truth, she craved time by herself to think about everything that had happened during this eventful day.

Left alone with her wife, Beatrice reached up to begin unbraiding her crown. "Won't you ever tell me how you became tethered to this place?"

Coral stopped her wife's hands. "Leave your crown for tonight. You'll be gone tomorrow, so indulge me. You have an exquisite neck hidden by a wall of hair. As I said earlier, you have enough on your plate with these brothers. My story will wait, but it involves a kraken, so heed what I say and keep well clear of them. They are a deadly foe." She kissed the back of her wife's neck, wrapping her arms around her. "Come bathe in the moonlight with me. Tonight is a night for love, not woes. Come."

The next morning, as they broke their fast in the witch's cottage, Amelia was solemn and quiet. One of her favorite tattoos, an elaborately-detailed snail, had crawled away from her skin overnight and was nowhere to be seen. One-Eyed Jack, however, was in his usual place and in an even more chatty mood than usual, flirting nonstop with the sea witch. Beatrice scavenged through Coral's herb stores and other supplies collecting what she thought they might need for their trip. Then, the witch called for Beatrice to sit back down beside Amelia.

When she had their attention, she began. "I haven't told you what to do with the wizarding ball."

She laid a chartreuse-colored silk scarf upon the table. It was large enough any of them could have rolled it up and used it for a belt. "Treat the Ball of Intention with care and don't ever touch it with your bare hands. Wrap it in this scarf and put it in your pocket for safekeeping. Do not interact with it under any circumstances. If the brothers will come with you, bring them to me. If not, I'll advise you what to do in your dreams, Beatrice." She pulled out another silk scarf of a deep plum color and handed it off to Amelia, while Beatrice took the green one.

"Shall we load up? It's time," Beatrice said, getting up and walking out the door with an armful of supplies.

Amelia looked at the sea witch in confusion.

Coral smiled. "Buttons never say goodbye. Apparently, you haven't found that out yet. She spoke to you because you're going with her. She won't say another word to me, and you're mistaken if you think she will come give me a farewell kiss."

"That's incredibly rude! I, at least, will thank you for your hospitality and for freeing Noe and the others," Amelia said politely.

The witch laughed. "Really, it is the only way Buttons are rude. One day when she does move away, she won't say goodbye to you either. Don't force her to as she would consider it bad luck."

As soon as Amelia was on board, they untethered the skyboat from the Kaleidoscope Lighthouse. Beatrice climbed to the crow's nest and turned her face to the morning breeze, sensing fresh adventure on the wind.

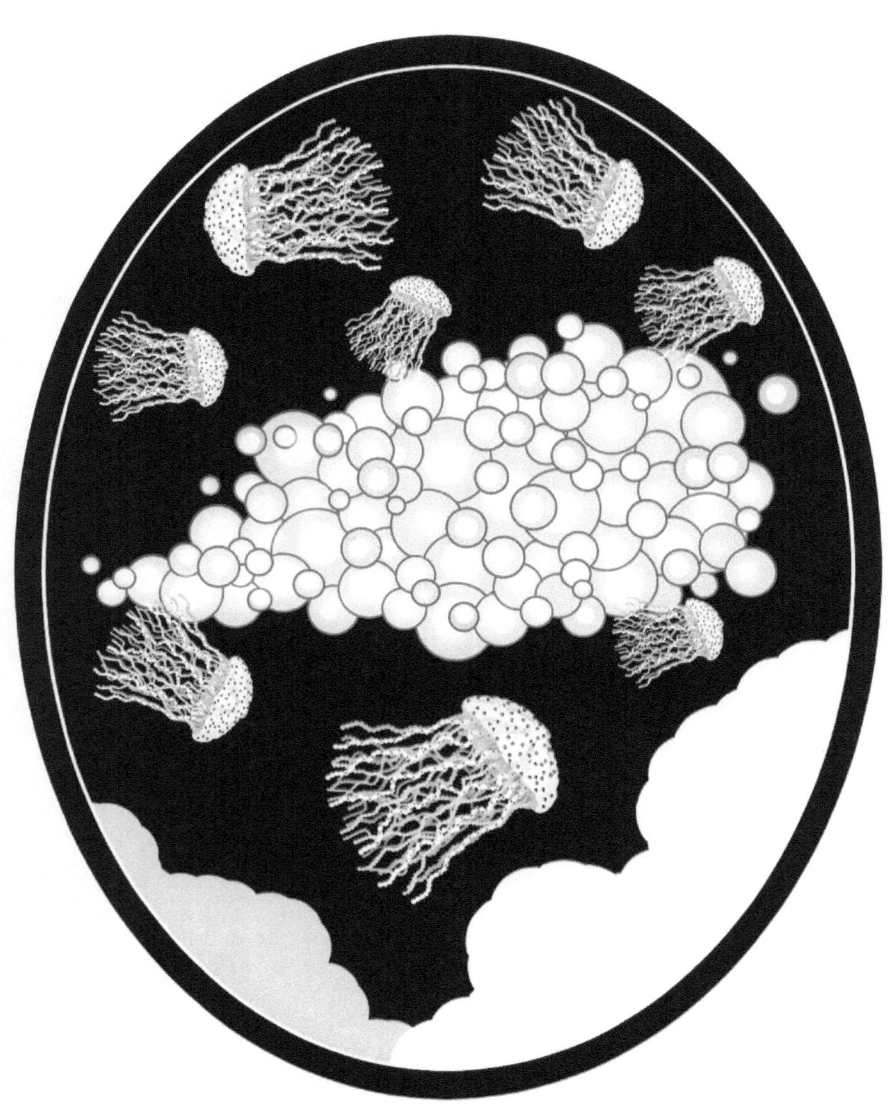

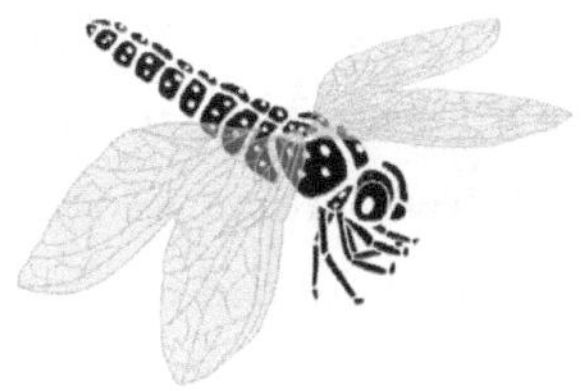

CHAPTER 11

A Meeting

"A RE YOU TRYING TO avoid me?" Amelia asked, after noticing how many times Beatrice swam to the top of the skyboat's mast and stayed high in the air above her.

Beatrice looked down and grinned. "Don't be a silly! I'm talking to the winds. The ship is guided by my thoughts tied to Coral's magic, but the winds let me know how to adjust our direction to make the best time."

"Bea! Look! The first plant in the sky!" Amelia leaned over the edge of the boat.

Pulling a telescope from her pocket, Beatrice extended it to see what Amelia was shouting about. It was weird to find mamaberries in the sky, as if someone had pitched them as high up as they could throw. "Grab one, Melia!"

Amelia reached out and inched the fruit closer with the tips of her fingers until she could pick it from the bush. She examined the berry, holding it up to her nose and inhaling deeply. The scent was reassuringly like the ones she'd eaten all her life. Amelia settled down into a cozy corner of the boat and pulled her knees up to her chest, smelling the mamaberry and watching the ever-changing patterns in the clouds.

Beatrice slid down the mast and sat next to Amelia, grabbing a handful of babies from the mamaberry and munching them. "Tastes much the same, only lighter, like they're mixed with whipped cream. You know, if we can catch up with these lads quickly, you'll be able to return to your own plants soon. You must miss them."

"Just as you miss your witch. I don't understand how you can leave her all the time."

Beatrice shrugged. "I've always had the itch to roam from the time I was a wee lass, but it's the same curse that binds Coral to the lighthouse that makes my heart yearn to travel now. I get sick if I stay in the same place too long. It's a horrible, hateful feeling to constantly be driven from my love, but it's our destiny. Granny warned me it would be even before I decided to answer Coral's siren call."

Amelia frowned. "If it was a siren call that means you didn't have any choice in the matter."

"She had the power to call me, but she couldn't make me stay or give my heart to her. She can't even force me to be immortal if I don't want to be. It wouldn't be true love if it was only a spell. She'll live forever but will never accept a lover who doesn't choose to be with her. I don't know if that's her own preference or part of her binding."

"Well, I hope one day the mystery of her curse and a way to break it will be revealed, but in the meantime, this cloud mamaberry won't fill us up. I'll make us something more substantial to eat," said Amelia, heading below deck.

"I do miss you, Coral," Beatrice whispered to her seagull necklace, giving it a kiss with berry-stained lips. She sang the song of the heartbroken albatross that the sea witch was singing when they first met and salted the wind with her tears.

They journeyed on and began to discover not only more cloud plants, but the sky creatures Coral had promised. A pod of dolphins that were no larger than your average house cat leapt along beside them, chattering and squeaking as they performed dizzying acrobatic feats. A ponderously large and slow cloud sea turtle swam above them, shadowing the deck from the suns with its enormous bulk. A school of fat fish surrounded the skyboat's balloons, kissing them with their pursed lips as though exploring the taste of these unfamiliar objects.

On the second day, they caught up to the jellyfish migration. They adjusted their course to the pace and direction of the beautiful cloud creatures while keeping their eyes peeled for any sign of the missing boys.

"We know what they look like as children from their photos," Amelia said, "but we have no idea how long ago that was, how old they are now, or what they might look like as adults."

Not in the least discouraged, Beatrice reassured her friend cheerfully. "We can simply watch for anything out of the ordinary. Coral said we would find them on the third day, so I'm sure we'll discover something tomorrow."

"I wonder if they'll be glad to see us or will they resent us tracking them down? There's no telling what they might do to us with that ball if they don't want to be found. It gives them a frightening amount of force, and they've had years to practice using it. Plus, they may be grown men by now. What if they overpower us?"

"Don't worry so much, Amelia. Coral's a formidable witch. We can call on her to defend us if these fellows try to give us trouble. But let's wait and see. All this speculation won't help us until we find out what we're dealing with."

Amelia nodded as though in agreement but privately continued to fret and imagine all sorts of dire outcomes of their mission. They had no reason to believe Click and Bix were the least bit interested in having anyone interfere with whatever schemes they were up to, and she didn't understand how they were supposed to stop the brothers if they put up a fight. She spent a restless night worrying while Beatrice slept as soundly as a hibernating snowbear.

The third day dawned. Bea ascended to the crow's nest for a better view, pulling out her telescope and scanning the sky around them. She spotted a large bubbling mound floating along, a teeming mass that looked like a million spit bubbles stuck together. She stared, not knowing what to make of it. It wasn't a cloud creature. It looked more like someone had drawn a sketch of an oobble and conjured it to life.

"Maybe that's them!" she hollered down to Amelia.

"What's them?"

"That oobble."

"What in Lichen is an oobble? Is this the beginning of another one of your stories?"

"An oobble is an amoeba-like creature that looks like it's made out of bubbles. They live in the sea. I didn't make it up and it's not a story. I couldn't swear on it, but I think the brothers must have drawn one and wished it to life, because that looks more like a drawing of one than the real thing. And it's so big! What if it's their boat?"

Amelia held up her pair of opera glasses to get a closer look as Beatrice descended the mast to join her on deck. The oobble definitely had the look of a pencil outline and the color of the bubbles looked like white vellum. How curious!

Through the windows of the bubble structure, she thought she saw movement. Two small figures suddenly popped out on top of the mass of bubbles and started waving at them. They appeared to be shouting but were too far away to be heard. Same shock of white hair on the older brother, Click, and same ginger hair on the younger Bix as in the photographs. Amazingly, it looked like they hadn't aged a single day.

Still children after all this time! Beatrice and Amelia exchanged a look of mutual shock and apprehension. Neither were overly fond of kiddies and worried if they would be able to relate to these little people. They waved back tentatively, much to the seeming delight of the brothers.

Beatrice fought back a wave of nausea as she remembered the booger-filled journal. She wondered if they'd retained the habit of picking their noses so much.

I better not find any snot wiped on our boat if they come visit us, she thought, grimacing in disgust.

As the ladies drew close to the oobble, they were finally able to hear what the boys were shouting: "Ahoy there! Are you friend or foe?"

"Friends! We come seeking you in peace. You're Click and Bix from the observatory, aren't you? Did your parents ever find you?" Beatrice yelled.

The brothers exchanged a glance, frowning before the older one answered. "Yes, but it's kind of complicated."

Beatrice grabbed a green and white rope from the dragonfly's deck and tossed it over to the lads. Click caught and anchored it to the sea of bubbles that made up their unique craft, and Beatrice and Amelia used the tether to pull the two boats alongside each other.

The older boy, Click, looked gravely disappointed when he got a closer look at Amelia and Beatrice. "It's a pair of grannies! Grannies answered our rescue call."

"Who are you calling grannies?" Beatrice asked in irritated dismay. She supposed it was true she and Amelia were of an age to be someone's granny, but the thought had never occurred to her before.

"Should we leave, so someone younger can come instead?" Amelia snapped. She was relieved in some measure to find they didn't have to deal with full-grown men but was also in no mood to be insulted by a pair of naughty lads who were the cause of her being torn away from her beloved garden and comfortable house.

"No, don't go!" the younger boy, Bix, replied quickly. "We haven't seen anyone else for ages. Since we ran away, the only people we've met are Mom and Dad. We can't even touch the ground anymore. You're probably the only ones who'll ever come." Bix looked totally dejected, whereas Click presented a more indifferent face to the ladies.

"Very well, but watch your manners if you want our company. I'm Beatrice Buttons and this is Amelia Arrowheart. My wife is the sea witch of the Kaleidoscope Lighthouse and she'd like to help you. Are you interested?"

"We are. Cross my heart and hope to spit," Bix said as he crossed his heart, spit in the palm of his hand, and offered it to Beatrice.

Beatrice's eyes widened as she looked in revulsion at Bix's proffered hand, but she fought back a wave of nausea as she spit into her own, clasped the boy's, and shook it firmly once. Bix looked at Beatrice with a new air of respect and smiled at her. Her bravery also earned a slight smirk from his brother.

Amelia watched this ritual with dismay, appreciative of Beatrice's sacrifice in order to gain the lads' trust but immensely grateful it wasn't her hand.

Click hawked like he was also going to spit in his hand only to be stopped in his tracks by Amelia. "That won't be necessary. Beatrice's handshake speaks for us both."

The boy swallowed back his gob of spit at this rejection causing Beatrice's stomach to give another twinge.

"Where are your parents?" Amelia demanded. "You said they found you but it was complicated. What did you mean?"

The brothers exchanged a glance.

"Look, we read your journal. My wife has it for safekeeping, but we know about the ball you found and the wish you made," Beatrice told them.

Click crossed his arms and confessed. "It was an accident. We were still new at working the ball and hadn't any clue what might happen. They caught up to us and were badgering us to come back with them. I wanted a moment to think and said I wished they were nothing more than one of my photographs."

"He didn't mean it," Bix insisted with teary eyes. "He spoke without thinking and then we couldn't figure out how to reverse the spell. They move around in the photo and were able to talk to us at first, but they can't anymore."

"You didn't wish for them to shut up, did you?" Amelia asked suspiciously.

"Not exactly. They were yelling at us and we thought it. We didn't know then that the ball could read our minds," Click clarified.

"It's understandable, I suppose. Nobody of any age likes to be scolded. It makes you feel bad," Beatrice said sincerely, for there was nothing that irked her more than being reprimanded. "This ball sounds like a burden that's caused you a lot of trouble. Would you consider allowing one of us to carry it for you? We'll turn it over to Coral, and she can try to fix everything that's gone wrong."

"Can she make it so we stop being children? Bix said he wished we'd never grow up before I could stop him," Click revealed.

"She was sure she could find a way to reverse most any spell you cast," Beatrice said. "Do you know how old you really are?"

"We don't have any way of knowing for certain how long we've been up here," Bix said, reaching into his pocket and pulling out the gleaming wizarding ball. "But it's been decades."

He made as though to hand over the ball, but his brother reached out and grabbed it. "Let's think about this for a minute, Bix. Some of our wishes have gone wrong, but others have turned out amazing, like our boat. Why should we turn over all this power to a couple of grannies we just met? What's in it for us?"

Amelia snorted. "You've made a pretty fine mess of things as far as we can tell. Causing things to float that have no business floating, trapping your parents, forcing them to be silent, defying nature by not growing old. If you had any decency at all, you'd feel ashamed of the trouble you've caused and be eager to set things right, for your parents' sake if nothing else. Don't you love them at all or feel sorry for their fate?"

Click hung his head but still looked defiant. It was Bix who grabbed the ball back and held it out to the two ladies. "I love them very much and want to free them if we can."

Beatrice reached into her pocket and pulled out the chartreuse silk scarf Coral had given her, placing it over her hand and holding it out to receive the ball. Bix dropped it into her covered hand, and she bound the magical object up tightly before placing it into one of her pockets.

"Did you wish for someone to help you? Is that what made us start floating?" Amelia asked, for it still seemed a curious thing that no one else in their community had been affected.

"We've been alone so long, we finally decided to ask for someone to find us who would have the power to undo our wishes," said Bix. "We should have done it sooner, but it's easy to lose track of time out here."

"Did you ever happen to find out anything about where the ball comes from?"

"It belongs to a kraken," Click replied.

Beatrice experienced a strange sensation at this mention of a kraken. Coral's warnings of how dangerous they were sounded in her ears and she suddenly found it hard to breathe.

So this is what it feels like when your life spins out of control, she thought. Her eyes rolled up into the back of her head and she fainted, falling flat on her face, quite ungracefully.

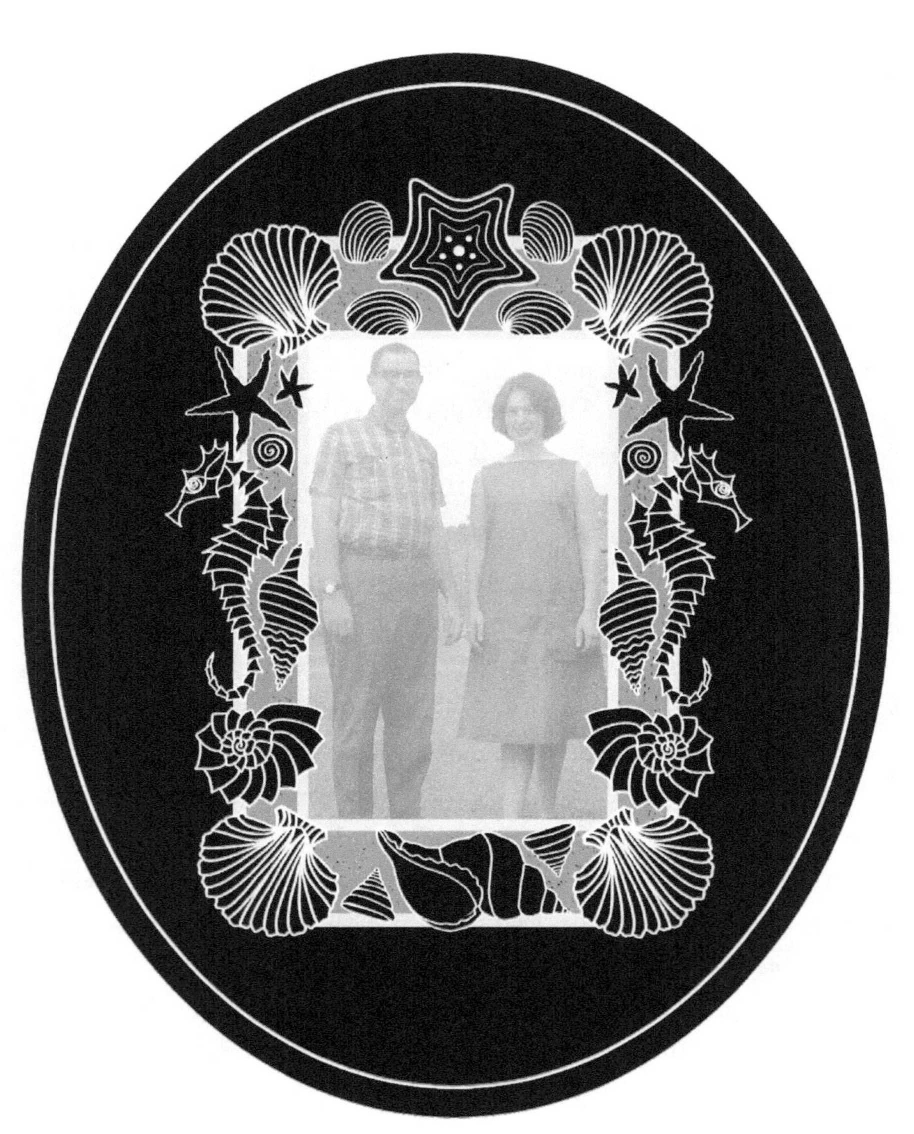

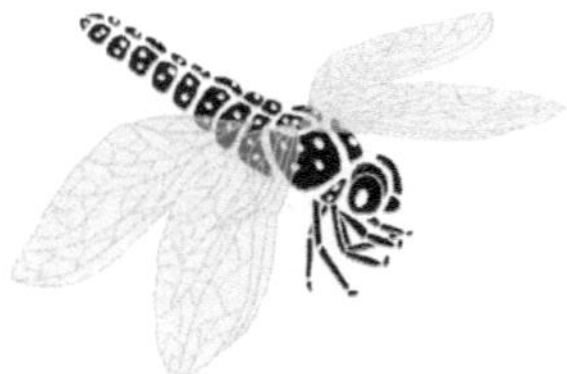

CHAPTER 12

A DANGEROUS DISCOVERY

BEATRICE AWOKE ON HER back with a soft pillow cushioning her head. Amelia was dabbing her forehead with a cool cloth that smelled pleasantly of hickleweed and limonberry.

"What happened, Bea?"

"I don't know. I think I had a kind of premonition when Click mentioned the kraken. Like I was drowning, spiraling downward to the bottom of the deepest part of the ocean. There was terrible danger and unbearable pain and loss. I feel awful, Melia. It was my idea to go on this adventure and find these lads. You were perfectly happy before I dragged you into this, and now we could be in big trouble. You should take the boys to Coral. I'll return the Ball of Intention to its rightful owner to see if that will solve our problems."

"Nonsense!" Amelia said. "Coral is your wife, not mine. You should take the lads to the lighthouse, and I'll go see about this creature," she added with a bravado she wasn't sure she truly felt.

"No, if something happens to me, Coral will be more motivated to come to my rescue than yours. If the kraken is the same one who tethered her, it's the only creature I've ever heard her speak of with fear. Coral is immortal—the life of any mortal but me wouldn't seem worth the risk of confronting her worst enemy. She'll do what it takes to rescue me, though. At least, I think she will, and if I'm wrong, at least you'll get to go back to your normal life."

"You're entirely mistaken about being responsible for dragging me off on an adventure. When the brothers wished for help, we both started floating so obviously we both were destined to undertake this mission. And besides, I wanted to come. You didn't have to work hard to talk me into it."

Amelia sighed before continuing. "When Coral gave us these necklaces, I wondered why she gave me the albatross which crosses such large distances when her own wife is the grand traveler. I kept thinking she should have given me the seagull which mostly hovers around the same area all its life. But now I think she gave me the albatross to inspire me and build confidence that yes, I can do this."

"Besides," she added. "We don't even know if returning the ball would be the right thing to do. If this kraken is so powerful, giving it a magical object that can turn its thoughts into reality hardly seems like a wise thing to do. We should consult with Coral before we make any decisive moves. All of this sorcery stuff is over our heads!"

While unconvinced her vision was not predestined to come true no matter what they did, Beatrice agreed that waiting to ask Coral's opinion in her next dream would be prudent.

In the meantime, Bix and Click offered to give them a tour of their most unusual skycraft. The ladies climbed aboard and were surprised to discover the oobble didn't just look like white vellum paper. It felt like it was made of vellum too, but the strongest that had ever existed. All the same, it was a little unnerving to feel like they were drifting along on nothing more than an elaborate paper boat.

The lads explained the oobble floated in the sky without any assistance, but they were unable to guide its course reliably. Instead, they were at the mercy of the whims of the winds and wherever it decided to blow them next. They agreed to keep the oobble tethered to the Sea Witch so the dragonfly boat could tow them where they needed to go.

"I don't see a door. How do you get inside?" Beatrice asked.

"Try saying I-N," Bix said, spelling out the word. "It works for us. I wonder if it will work for you?"

"IN," said Beatrice and disappeared.

Amelia looked at the lads warily, not trusting them, but One-Eyed Jack laughed and shouted, "IN!" Amelia felt herself passing through a series of tickling bubbles until she touched the interior floor. The lads joined them inside, explaining leaving was as easy as saying "OUT" and the whole process reversed.

The ladies barely heard them as they were completely entranced by the interior of the ship. The bubbles still looked like bubbles from inside, only now they were as clear as soap bubbles rather than opaque. They could see three hundred and sixty-five degrees in every direction. Two giant lily pads served as beds while the lotus flowers in the center unfolded to create pillows and bedding. The lighting fixtures on the wall were jellyfish-shaped.

"Are these real jellyfish?" Beatrice asked.

"No, but they sure look like it, don't they?" Bix said with pride.

"What makes them work?" asked Amelia, hypnotized by the realism of the sculptured lights.

"Wish craft."

"Do you want to meet Dad and Mom?" Click asked. He pulled his white bangs away from his forehead in a nervous upward thrust.

Bix walked over to a jar full of paper-wrapped chocolates and picked up a photograph leaning against it. Its frame was composed of an artful arrangement of small starfish and seashells. There was a kind-looking couple who glanced up at them and gave a shy wave.

"Are you capable of writing in there?" Beatrice asked them.

The woman beamed at them brightly and nodded.

Amelia looked at the lads. "Tell me you asked them that before?"

Bix and Click ducked their heads sheepishly. Amelia couldn't understand how two such brilliant and imaginative boys could be so incredibly thick-headed at the same time.

Their father pulled a pen and a rumpled notebook out of his shirt pocket. "Hello, I'm Moon. My wife is Star. Can you help us?"

Beatrice beamed at them. "How romantic—a cosmic couple. I can't release you, but my wife is a powerful sea witch who may be able to. We're so happy to meet you. We loved visiting your observatory."

"We gave it a good dusting," Amelia added.

"Been trapped thirty years," Moon wrote.

Bix exclaimed, "We're old!" in dismay.

Click looked at his brother while pointing at the ladies. "Almost as old as the grannies."

Amelia bristled in renewed offense, but then considered for a moment how she would feel if she suddenly found out she had missed thirty years of normal life and decided to forgive the insult just this once. She went back to examining the jellyfish lights to calm herself down.

"Call us 'ladies' if you must refer to us by anything other than our given names. We're not grannies and never will be," Beatrice gently admonished them. "This is a beautifully designed boat."

Click studied her for a moment as if she were a strange specimen before answering. "Thank you, Miss Beatrice."

Amelia sighed at the boy's sarcastic tone. She supposed it was progress of a kind. She also wondered if Coral could magic them some jellyfish lights for their own skyboat.

"We should get you back to the lighthouse so Coral can see what she can do for your parents," Beatrice suggested.

Bix opened the chocolate jar, unwrapped a piece, popped it in his mouth and replied thickly. "We can't go anywhere until after the leviathan mating season. Cloud leviathans and lunar leviathans meet up to mate with each other once a decade and it's starting now. The lunar winds that bring them together are too strong for even your boat to resist."

Seeing there was nothing more to be done at the moment, Beatrice glanced over at Amelia, who only had eyes for the jellyfish light, before saying "OUT" and exiting without further ado.

After she was gone, the brothers stared at Amelia in curiosity. "Are you going to stay here the rest of the night looking at our lamps?" Click asked.

Embarrassed at being reprimanded for lingering, Amelia also said "OUT" and vanished. She crossed over to the dragonfly boat and climbed below deck. The light was dim and Beatrice faced the wall already in bed waiting for sleep. She wished she could join her friend in her dreams to talk with the sea witch too.

After dozing off, Beatrice recounted to her wife the discovery of Bix and Click and the fact they were still youngsters, at least in looks if not in years.

"I spit and shook hands with the younger one," she added.

Coral produced a cauldron and into it she added an eccentric list of ingredients: the first chin hair sprouted by an adolescent boy along with one from a ninety-year-old woman who was both quiet and wise, a tincture of stinky zilfer, five-month-old compost sifted eight times with three cups of trueworm castings, and a very fizzy tea. Then she whispered an incantation before drinking the entire concoction down without stopping to breathe.

She put her hand in Beatrice's from which there arose a translucent miniature of Bix. The sea witch scooped up the image and placed it in her pocket. "I'll study him. There may be information he is keeping from you."

"That can't have been pleasant to drink," Beatrice exclaimed, amazed Coral was able to transform spit residue into such a thing.

"It's not very nice, but the compost will ground him in my mind and the worm castings will grant fertility to my study of the boy's nature, so it will be worth it. Life isn't always sweet, and ingredients in a spell are there from necessity, not to satisfy a craving or sweet tooth." The sea witch licked her muddy lips and kissed Beatrice on the nose.

Beatrice reached into her pocket and pulled out the Ball of Intention wrapped in its green silk scarf. She handed it to her wife who examined it before giving it back.

"The Ball of Intention isn't for you or me, but you already know that, don't you?" Coral asked.

"It belongs to a kraken, but must we return it? It's a powerful object for such a creature to have."

"There is only one kraken I know of. Its name is Myriad, the very same monster who cursed me. It is formidable and has immense power with or without the ball, but the ball will only continue to cause trouble for anyone else who tries to use it. Returning it is the only way to be rid of it, for it cannot be destroyed by any means I am aware of, and it's far too dangerous an object to remain at large."

Beatrice bit her lip. "I had a horrible vision I'm going to drown in the deepest part of the ocean. Is it too late to become immortal?"

"I would need you here in person to perform that trick. Are you sure you've changed your mind about immortality? It's impossible to undo once it takes effect."

"Perhaps. I hate to think of you taking another lover when I'm gone."

Coral looked deep into Beatrice's eyes. "I promise you this—and you know a witch promises nothing she can't deliver—I will never take another pretty again after you. You will be my only wife. I either have you or I have no one."

"But you have to take another pretty! Isn't that part of the curse?"

"No, that was my own requirement. Myriad cares nothing for my happiness. Sea witches are passionate by nature which is why we long to travel widely and love pretty things, but there will be no more passion for me without you in my life."

"If I make it out of this alive, I promise to you I will find a way to cut your tether and end your curse."

They locked ring fingers and kissed each other's wedding bands. Their next in-person reunion couldn't happen soon enough.

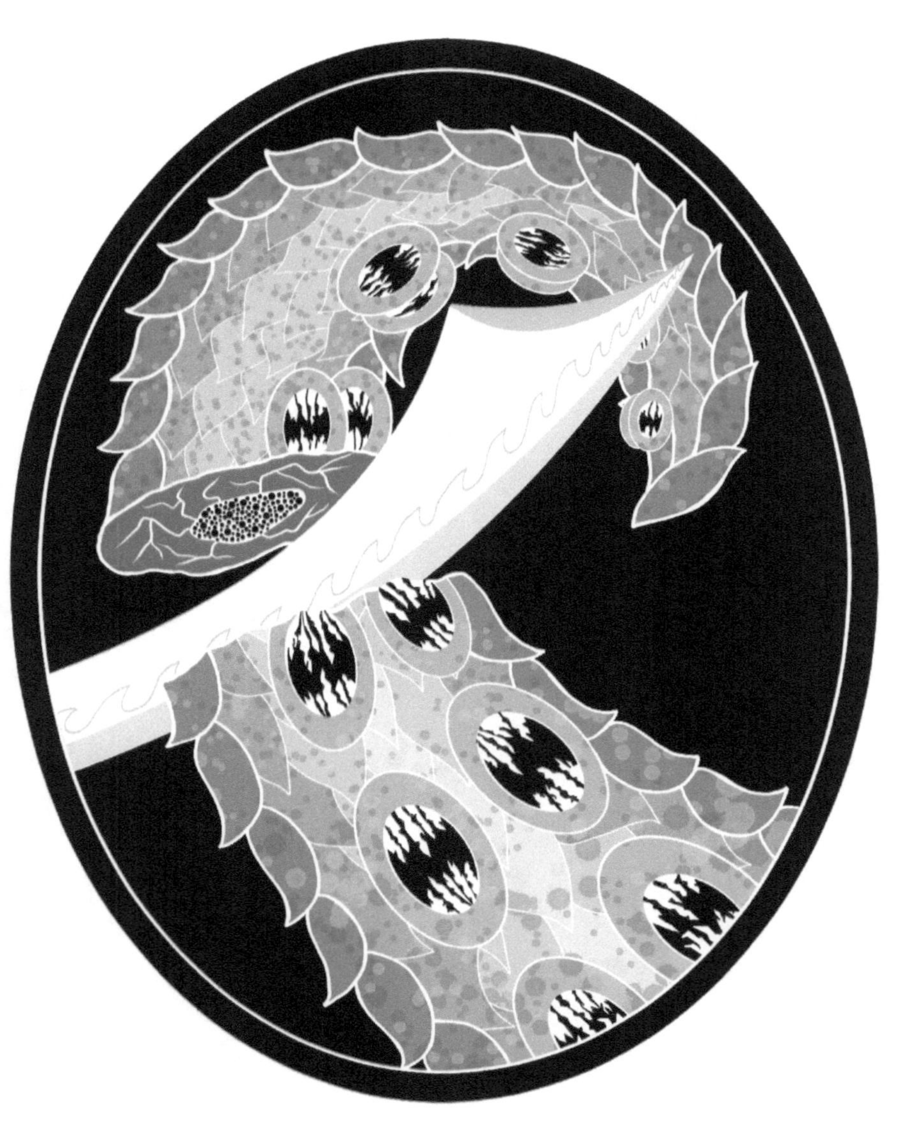

CHAPTER 13

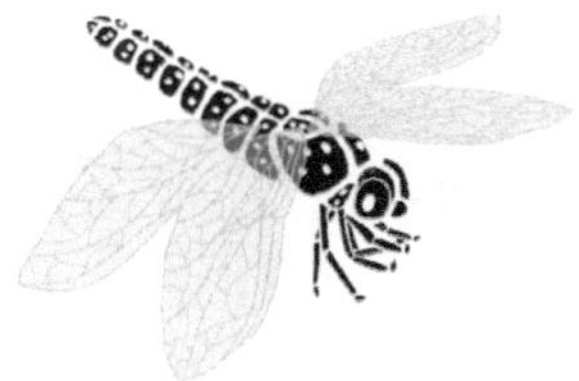

BEATRICE DEPARTS

During the night, the lunar windstream that forms during the leviathan mating season guided the travelers to the gathering spot. Once a decade, this unusual wind pattern twirled and swirled, carrying breathable air up into space. The skyboat and oobble were pulled along with the winds toward one of the most spectacular sights imaginable. That is unless you happened to be Bix and Click, who had already experienced the trip several times over and were no longer as thrilled as when they first set out from the observatory to see it.

At the foot of Beatrice's bed when she awoke were two small pairs of clogs Coral had left for the brothers.

"You figured out how to use the ball to wish for things," Click accused her as he and Bix tried them on.

Beatrice shook her head. "No, my wife visits me in my dreams and gives us things to make our journey easier. If I could wish on the ball, I'd make it disappear forever so it couldn't cause any more trouble."

The brothers marched around in their clogs, doubling over with merriment at the sucking noises they made. Click was crying, and Bix got a stomachache from laughing so hard.

Amelia tried to imagine what it must be like to stay a child for so long. To age thirty years in the blink of an eye would be hard on the boys. And what of their parents? How old would they be? Imagine the horrors of life behind a pane of glass, only to be too old to enjoy yourself when you were freed.

A haunting sound like a sawblade being played with a string bow interrupted her thoughts. The melody filled the air as white flashing shapes swam across the sky, glowing from the inside out. Amelia and Beatrice gasped at their first glimpse of a lunar leviathan. The creatures' intricately detailed skin and weird beauty were overwhelming.

And it wasn't just one—the sky was alight with an entire pod of the lunar visitors. Soon, ethereal puffs of cloud leviathans joined them, silent denizens of the sky searching for their mates. All in all, it was a ballet of light and sound that couldn't have been reproduced by even the most skillful artists, athletes, or musicians of Lichen.

"I wonder what their offspring look like and which species carries them?" Amelia asked, not expecting an answer.

"They each give birth to their own calf," Bix said, "but not until five years after they mate. The calves will be old enough to participate in the cycle themselves during the next season a decade from now."

"Isn't that marvelous, Bea?" Amelia said, unable to peel her eyes away from the magical pageantry in the sky.

But her question went unanswered as their reverie was most rudely and terrifyingly interrupted.

"Krakennnnn!" Click cried as a barrage of pea green tentacles appeared, grasping the dragonfly boat and dragging it and the oobble out of the lunar stream toward the ocean below at an astonishing speed.

Amelia and Beatrice grabbed on to the brothers and each other as the kraken known as Myriad pulled the skyboat sideways, attempting to dump its passengers out into the sea. An inky butterfly popped off Amelia's wrist in fright, fluttering its way out of the maelstrom, but it wasn't the only tattoo to peel away from her skin.

"This calls for a pirate, mateys!" One-Eyed Jack shouted as he stretched and shot off her shoulder like an arrow from a tightly strung bow.

He landed boots first on the deck of the boat in all his magnificent splendor. Bejewelled fingers and a long blond braid that peeked out from under his tri-corner hat. Royal blue, gold, and black-striped trousers and a white gauzy shirt completed his swashbuckling look. He wasted no time charging into battle, spitting over the edge of the skyboat into the depths of Myriad's eye.

The creature roared with anger at the audacity of such an insect daring to insult it. The water eddied and foamed as it thrashed its tentacles, and a booming, eldritch voice sang from the deep. "We will crush you to dust and slurp you down unless you give us the witch's slag."

"You can't have the granny!" Click shouted, shaking a fist at the monster.

Beatrice hissed at him. "It's not much better being called a granny than someone's slag."

"Evidently you've never seen the beautiful slag rocks near windler-mining camps," Amelia said, unable to resist being slightly pedantic even in a crisis. "Remember, Bea, how we choose to view a word gives it meaning."

"Haven't ye any harpoons or the like on this here vessel?" cried Jack, casting about in frustration for some kind of weapon to stave off the kraken.

"No," Beatrice replied, "I never imagined we'd need such a thing."

"Never mind!" The pirate reached behind his head as if to scratch his back and produced a long broadsword seemingly from thin air. He swung it with a flourish at Myriad, successfully chopping off the tip of one of its greedily grasping tentacles.

Eager to join the action, Click slipped out from the protection of the ladies' arms and grabbed a rope tied to the mast, swinging himself round to the other side of the boat so he could kick and stomp at the writhing beast.

Amelia's own ire rose at the mess the creature was making of their beautiful boat. If there was anything she despised, it was disorder and chaos. Although her legs were wobbling like jelly, she unwound her long braid and sprinted toward the kraken with determination. Her hair was strong and heavy and she wielded it like a whip, striking the tentacles and leaving long welts that enraged Myriad still further.

Now only Beatrice and Bix were left clinging to each other on the opposite side of the boat.

"Maybe if we return the Ball of Intention that would satisfy it and it would leave us alone," Bix suggested.

"I suppose it couldn't hurt at this point," Beatrice responded, "though I'm not sure it will do any good."

She reached for the handkerchief in one of her numerous pockets and pulled it out, swinging it like a shepherd's sling. The ball whistled through the air so fast and accurately that it disappeared down the kraken's maw in a trice, provoking a fit of coughing that momentarily reduced the creature's fighting spirit.

"Lichen righted!" shouted Bix, much impressed with Bea's throwing precision.

Unfortunately, Myriad recovered all too soon and the battle raged on. Amelia and Jack had fallen into a rhythm of taking turns slicing at the monster with hair and sword respectively while Click darted in and out stomping with all his weight on any part of the monster he could reach.

It was a life and death struggle as Myriad both delighted in fighting and was a formidable opponent. The combatants noticed that no matter how often they injured it, the hurt soon healed up as though it had never been. It even regrew the tentacle end Jack had chopped off.

"Grab all the rope ye can muster, mateys," the pirate cried. "We'll see if we can't wrap this brute up like a birthday parcel!"

Amelia, Click and Jack maneuvered ropes around as many tentacles as they could reach and wound them as quickly and tightly as possible. Their determined effort succeeded in causing the kraken to loosen its grip on the boat and drop back into the sea.

Filled with a burst of sudden hope and elation from its delighted passengers, the dragonfly's balloons grew more buoyant and pulled them high up into the sky, away from the ocean surface and danger.

"Lichen definitely righted now," Click said with a whoop as he and Bix exchanged brotherly handshakes in relief.

Amelia smiled shyly at the ruggedly handsome pirate who had once adorned her skin. "Thank you so much, Jack. You helped save the day!"

"No problem at all, Captain. It was good to be back in action again, just like the old days with me own crew."

Beatrice simply grinned at them all, delighted she had escaped Myriad's grasp and thinking how relieved Coral would be when she found out. She was still grinning when a slimy tentacle reached over the side of the boat, grasping her round the waist and pulling her over the side in a flash.

At the same moment, Amelia's braid was grabbed by another tentacle. Amelia held onto her hair with both hands as she was yanked off her feet. She would have gone sliding overboard if it hadn't been for Jack's quick reflexes. He sliced the braid clean off, so it disappeared into the ocean along with the kraken and Beatrice.

Those left on the skyboat stood frozen in shock and horror except for Jack, who dived gracefully over the side of the boat and disappeared beneath the waves. The others watched anxiously for an unbearably long time before Jack resurfaced.

He was alone.

Hot tears flowed down Amelia's face as she lowered a rope to the pirate, who made quick work of clambering back aboard.

"I'm sorry, Captain. I tried to follow, but the fiend was too fast and dove too deep for me. I'm afraid Beatrice Buttons is gone."

CHAPTER 14

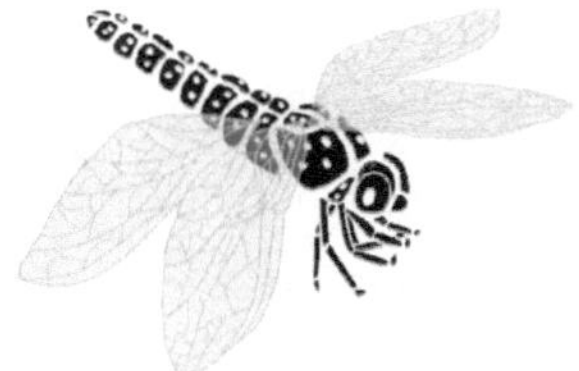

RETURN TO THE LIGHTHOUSE

"L ICHEN WRONGED!" CRIED BIX, choking on his words.

"What in the name of every beast in the sky does that mean—Lichen righted or wronged?" the pirate asked.

Amelia swept her fingers through her roughly shorn hair as she answered mournfully. "It means every little ripple in Lichen is felt by all and affects all for the good or for the bad because everything is connected. Beatrice's loss is not only a loss for us but for all of Lichen."

She wept silently, mostly for her friend but at least a few of her tears were for her lost braid. Her head was so light, like it might fly away without the comforting heaviness of her hair to weigh it down. She felt exposed without her crowning glory, but there was no time to dwell on it. "We'd better try and get back to the lighthouse quick as we can. Maybe Coral will know what to do, though how I'll bear to break the news that we've lost her wife, I can't imagine."

Amelia didn't have to wait long to find out, for that very night the sea witch visited her in a dream. "I've come to you because I can't reach Beatrice. Your beautiful braid is gone! What's happened?"

Relaying as many details of the battle with the kraken as she could remember, Amelia hoped it would allow Coral to glean some insight that might help them discover Beatrice's fate.

At the end of Amelia's recitation, Coral nodded sadly. "I feared as much. Myriad will play with her like a new toy before tossing her aside in death or worse, but I'll feel if she is out of this life forever. So far, I do not sense that. I'm sorry for the loss of your hair. I know it was important to you."

"It would have been a small sacrifice to make if only we could have saved Beatrice."

"You all made a valiant effort. I'll cast a spell to retrieve the boats more quickly to the lighthouse. When you arrive, we'll make a plan of how to rescue Beatrice. Until then, get some sleep, friend of my wife."

Coral touched Amelia lightly on the forehead with one finger, sending her off into a deeper and more restful repose.

When Amelia awoke, she found a gift waiting for her by her bed. Strong magic emanated from the present as she carefully untied its silver ribbon and fanned open the lavender tissue paper wrapping to see what the sea witch had left.

It was a large journal with the seven moons of Lichen etched onto the cover, their shapes subtly waxing and waning as the skyboat sailed through the sky. The pages within were the color and scent of the weak tea Beatrice preferred, brewing it from the herbs she foraged. The back cover was hollowed out to accommodate a voluminous pocket filled with drawing utensils of every kind and color, fastened with a coral button shaped like a fish. The sea witch had anticipated everything Amelia might wish for in a new journal, and the thoughtful present brought some small measure of peace to her troubled mind.

Distracted from her examination of the lovely book by a rich baritone voice on deck, Amelia wrapped herself up in a snug gray wool cardigan and climbed up to take a peek. She spotted Jack swinging himself nimbly and cheerfully round the ship's riggings as though he hadn't a single worry in his head.

He looked down and spied her lurking. "Good morning, Captain! Might scalawags like me and those brats on yon strange vessel expect a bite from ye, fair lady, or do we whip up our own mess around here?"

Made shy by this once familiar companion brought startlingly to life and still embarrassed by her rough-shorn locks, Amelia bent down too quickly in her haste to retreat into the cabin. She hit her head on the deck with a resounding "OW!" followed by an indignant "IN!" With mortification, she remembered she wasn't on the oobble and that trick wouldn't work.

"Yes," she called in answer to the pirate's questions, disappearing below deck with what dignity she could muster before realizing she had not been terribly clear. Popping her head up once more, she added, "That is, I will make us a meal."

Jack's robust laughter followed her as she ducked down again. She blushed to think what a fool she'd made of herself. Would she ever get used to the shock of her familiar ink friends springing to life? It was very disconcerting to interact with them as full-bodied beings in their own right rather than the flat images crawling across her skin.

She recovered herself enough to focus on the task at hand, and soon the four travelers were sitting down to a meal of pickled eggs, wedges of mellow orange cheese, hot crusty bread slathered with creamy butter and mamaberry jam, and piping hot Lichen tea to wash it down with.

Bix and Click were fascinated by the pirate and stole many furtive glances at Jack's black velvet eye patch. It had a unique design of a lunar leviathan formed out of sparkling gems.

"I thought no one from the ground except us had seen lunar leviathans before. How can you have one on your eye patch?" asked Bix.

"I guess I'm not from the ground, am I?" Jack replied with a wink of his good eye.

"What in Lichen does that mean?" asked Amelia.

"I'm not from Lichen at all is what it means, Captain."

His audience goggled at this outrageous statement. How could someone not be from Lichen? Where else was there? The seven moons? The suns or the stars? It was too much to fathom. No Lichen had ever speculated about life existing elsewhere before.

"It might be more than ye can easily ken," he continued, "but all that black space ye see out there at night is full of life. Lichen is only one tiny dot of a planet among countless others."

"Planet," Click said slowly, trying to work his lips around the foreign word. "What's a planet?"

"I guess ye could think of it as a type of ball up in space, like a moon but larger. Smaller than suns though. Most have creatures or folks of one kind or another living on 'em, and each planet has things that make it special. Lichen, for instance, is terrible small yet ye have seven moons and three suns. That makes it unique among the planets I've journeyed to so far."

"We're a planet? One among many?" Amelia repeated, trying to get used to the concept. No one she knew had ever called Lichen anything but home. Everyone had houses they lived in, but they all had one home: Lichen. To learn there were other beings living on other worlds was startling.

"How did you come to Lichen if you aren't from here?" asked Click, enraptured by the space pirate's tales.

"The Ink of Lost Souls traps ye from wherever it finds ye, whether land, sea, sky, moons, other planets, the hereafter." He hesitated, unsure exactly what Lichens believed happened after they died.

"Will you go back now you're free?" Amelia asked, half afraid of the pirate's response. She'd gotten used to Jack's company in the many long years he'd lived as ink on her shoulder and even though the reality of him in the flesh was a bit overwhelming, she knew she would feel the loss if he left entirely.

He poured another cup of tea and gazed off at the clouds and the rising suns. "I'll do me part to help ye find Beatrice Buttons first, but when I've done what I can, I'll ask that sea witch if she has enough magic to send me home. I yearn to be among me own kind once more."

Bix scrunched up his freckled face in disgust at the admiring looks his brother was giving the pirate. "A load of bosh," he said under his breath. "There might be unintelligent animals elsewhere, but there aren't people living anywhere but in Lichen and you're silly to believe it."

He picked his nose, rolled the snot up into a ball and made ready to wipe it under the table, but Amelia saw what he was up to and shot him a meaningful glare. He grimaced at her and flicked the nasal nugget off the side of the boat instead, thinking that grannies were stupidly fussy about boogers.

In contrast to his outwardly good-natured demeanor, Jack was feeling lost and discouraged as he climbed up to the crow's nest after breakfast. He missed conversing easily with Amelia, who was timid around him now that he was no longer simply a drawing. And he'd never be able to convey to her and the boys what his old life was like in his solar system with technology and scientific knowledge that was so much more complex than their own.

When he was still a tattoo, he'd felt like he was stuck in a dream or a nightmare, though he'd grown more or less resigned to his fate. Now that he was supposedly free, it was more like being trapped between the pages of a fairy tale. Witches, shapeshifters, a kraken, the Ball of Intention and the rest of it. Nothing like it happened where he came from.

He'd enjoyed his previously freewheeling rogue lifestyle and longed to get back to it. The only familiar thing here was the lunar leviathans which were well-known on his planet too. Nothing good could come of further entangling himself in the lives of folks who were so wrapped up in their provincial affairs and understood little of his concerns or of the variety of worlds and societies beyond their own.

Jack decided he would be friendly and help in the search for Beatrice, but that would be it. He didn't want to live in Lichen forever and never see his home again. The very idea was infinitely depressing.

As he thought about his woes, Jack noticed the dragonfly's balloons were beginning to deflate, allowing the skyboat to drift dangerously near to the ocean's surface.

"We're sinking. How do we inflate the balloons, Captain?" Jack shouted down to Amelia.

"Positive thoughts. Beatrice said we can fill them with hope and joy."

Jack was aghast. "What a diabolical choice! How are we supposed to conjure up hope and joy in our current plight?"

Then he remembered Noe, the shapeshifter tattoo. She'd been able to return to her watery home, maybe that meant he'd be able to return too. He thought of the things he'd missed and imagined being back on his own ship, traveling in familiar skies with his old crew around him. How happy he would be!

Did the boat lift a fraction? He looked up at the balloons and saw they weren't quite so limp. He looked down and saw Click and Bix dancing wildly in their clogs, the sucking noises they made against the deck causing them to laugh hysterically as always. The balloons seemed to catch the boys' exuberance and expanded again to their proper size, much to the pirate's relief.

"What's that out there?" Click suddenly cried, leaning far over the railing and pointing into the distance.

An elaborately-carved door mounted upon a stone throne of sorts was floating toward them. The throne was covered with a fascinating array of whirling, twirling gadgets and gizmos that dazzled the eye with a tempting invitation to explore.

Jack slid down the mast to the deck and grabbed Click's shirt to jerk him back. "For the love of all things, lad, don't get close to it!"

"Why not? It looks like fun. We should lasso it in!"

"It's a dangerous trap! The stuff nightmares is made of. It appears and disappears all over the universe, moving on after it captures some unsuspecting fool." Jack broke out in a cold sweat but still held fast to the boy, pulling his wriggling charge back into the boat.

"Tell him the ressssst," insisted Amelia's snake tattoo.

"It was created by an evil sorcerer to snare lost souls. It's how I was trapped me own self," the pirate admitted. "One of the crew unwittingly called it to us by thinking gloomy thoughts. Banish all ideas of being lost, fight off despair, or ye too may end up in a bottle of ink, yer existence squandered as ye become nothing but a drawing on another's skin," he said in a rattling rasp of a voice.

He glanced over at Amelia. "Is it ye that's despairing, Captain? You're worried about Beatrice Buttons. Afraid she's lost forever and ye failed yer friend, but it's not one bit true. None of us was strong enough to defeat that fell beast."

Amelia bowed her head to acknowledge she'd heard him, but it was one thing to know you'd done nothing to be sorry for and another to feel it in your bones.

Part of her wished she could go through the floating door and escape their current troubles.

"If you move one toe in the direction of that door, Miss," Bix shouted, "I'll cover every inch of this dragonfly in balls of snot until the rustling noises heard aren't the sails but dried boogers clacking against the wood in the wind."

Amelia shot him a look of pure disgust, but he just smiled a wickedly wide grin. She couldn't help but giggle, then laugh out loud at the image conjured by Bix's outlandish threat. The joyous sound reached the door and it shot back out into space, repelled by the moment of levity.

Jack loosened his hold on Click, who slid out of his grip and stared up at the pirate in admiration. "I was wondering if you could use a first mate after we rescue Miss Beatrice. You could show me the ropes and let me travel through space with you as an apprentice," Click suggested.

Tugging on his chin and winking his good eye at Click, Jack climbed back up the mast to adjust the rigging and hollered down. "What're ye waiting for—an engraved invitation? If ye want to learn, get yerself up here."

Click grinned in reply and climbed up to join him.

Crisis passed, Bix returned to the oobble. He decided he much preferred to be alone. People were so odd and too much of a worry. Maybe it would be better to remain a child aboard his ship and let the winds take him wherever they wished. The more he thought about it, the more he liked the idea, but he decided not to tell the others yet. They might try to talk him out of it, and he was tired of talking.

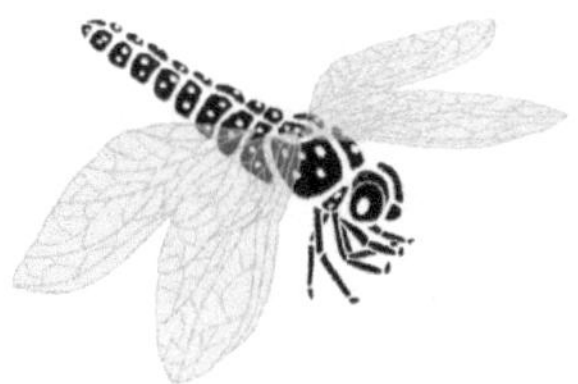

CHAPTER 15

BEATRICE'S PLIGHT

WHILE HER FRIENDS JOURNEYED back to the lighthouse in hopes of organizing a rescue party, poor Beatrice was undergoing a terrifying ordeal. Stolen overboard by Myriad, she plunged deep into the ocean, far out of reach of either hope or friends.

The powerful kraken murmured a spell while slicing a clawed tentacle along both sides of Bea's neck giving her gills. It was a relief to be able to breathe comfortably underwater, but the monster was not through with her.

Smiling cruelly, it showed off its horrible teeth, shaped like long shards of broken glass. While some were practically invisible as they were thin as a sewing needle, others cut and flashed like the rough metal of a saw blade. Trapping her with a suction-cupped tongue that held her in place, Myriad tore at Beatrice's skin.

She thrashed in the water, screaming as the kraken crunched and cracked right through her thigh bone, dropping the rest of her back into the depths as it chewed and made a snack of her right leg. Picking its teeth with a claw, it casually spoke another spell to seal her bleeding stump as Beatrice mercifully passed out.

"You may play with her, children, but remember she belongs to us," Myriad told the cephalopods pulling Beatrice down through the seaweed jungle that lined the ocean floor.

The sea creatures felt pity for the kraken's victim. Their long arms gently cradled her as they guided her to a temporary haven. Her remaining leg dragged along the sand, leaving a trail that was quickly erased as waves swayed across the sea bottom.

News of Beatrice's captivity spread quickly through the efficient undersea communication networks. From the cryptic artwork of gwibble fish to sea spiders flashing messages in their webs, to bubble-spitting oobbles and the rock tapping of crabs, word went out far and wide of Myriad's new toy. An emergency session of the Council of Seafolk convened, concerned shapeshifters and merfolk gathering to discuss the situation.

"The kraken has given her gills, but she's landfolk who bears the ring of the Sea Witch of the Kaleidoscope Lighthouse," reported a mermaid who had seen Beatrice up close.

The shapeshifters murmured in dismay and exchanged nervous glances. Amelia's old friend and former tattoo, Noe, was among them, and she experienced a thrill of fear at hearing who the victim was. She'd promised to grant a boon as thanks for being freed. Would that favor be called in now? Would the other shapeshifters risk an all-out war to rescue Coral's wife? And if they did, would seafolk such as the merpeople help them or would they swim away from the fight?

Noe sought guidance from her Aunt Lorali, a leader among the shapeshifters who was renowned for her extraordinary beauty and wisdom. Her wavy hair streaked black, white, and gray helped her blend in among the pebbles and shells when she visited the shoreline. Around her neck was a perfect strand of pearls gifted to her once through a fishing hole in the ice of the Bitter Lands by an intrepid adventurer.

Lorali advised her niece. "Coral shouldn't have to ask in order for you to fulfill your promise, Noe. You couldn't voice your own cries for help when you were trapped in the ink, yet the sea witch saw you and freed you. But it is your debt, and you alone must make the decision. I will support you either way and convince the others to help if needed."

Noe knew her aunt was right, but she was haunted by the years she'd lost during her entrapment in the ink. She couldn't imagine going toe to tentacle with the kraken and risking her newly-found freedom or even death. Little did she realize that she had attracted Myriad's attention once before.

She was still young when she lost her mother and it had grieved her mightily. Her high-pitched keening had reached the kraken's ears across the galaxy and grated on its easily disturbed nerves. It created the door to the Realm of Lost Souls to be rid of her and any other despairing creatures that might disturb its peace. The door called to the inconsolable Noe in her mother's voice and enticed her in. She spent her childhood and adolescence in the dark of the ink before reappearing as an adult tattooed on Amelia's body.

Lorali watched her niece with compassion. It hadn't been long since they'd reunited, and she was as afraid of losing Noe as Noe was afraid of losing herself again. "I know you're frightened, and you've every right to be. If you feel you can't do this, I will take on the responsibility and do what I can myself."

"Myriad has taken one of her legs," Noe whispered in horror, overhearing the news being reported to the Council.

"Poor thing. I don't believe landfolk are capable of regenerating their limbs the way we can."

"No, but it gave her gills, so at least she can breathe."

"It must mean to keep her alive for its own purposes then or it wouldn't have bothered. You'll have to make up your mind soon whether you'll help her or whether I should, for we must try to hide her away from Myriad's reach before it decides to torture her again."

"It is my debt," said Noe. "I must be the one to go."

They informed the Council of Noe's determination to spirit Beatrice away until a plan could be made for returning her in secret to Coral or defeating the kraken once and for all. The seafolk were relieved at this reprieve from an all-out declaration of war. They had treaties with the sea witches that necessitated them taking some kind of action or risk drawing the magical wrath of the witches down upon their heads, but they hoped this rescue attempt would satisfy Coral and her sisters that they were doing what they could against a formidable foe.

Noe went alone to search for Beatrice, thinking it more likely she would escape Myriad's attention than a large party of shapeshifters. Her eyes glowed like a cat's in the night as she scanned the dark forest along the seafloor. She found Beatrice where the cephalopods had secured her, wrapped in a tangle of seaweed, still unconscious from shock.

Noe gently kissed her forehead to mask Beatrice's scent with her own. The scent of a shapeshifter was a constantly evolving thing, changing as the shapeshifter changed species. You never knew when dealing with a sorcerer as powerful as the kraken whether it would see through such simple tricks, but she hoped it would buy them more time to escape.

She wrapped Beatrice's arms around her neck, carrying her on her back as she swam into a school of fish. Mirror fish swim in tight pods, their shining scales reflecting whatever is around them back at the viewer. The optical illusion the schools create provided an excellent hiding place. Noe whispered to the fish and explained her mission. They gladly shielded the shapeshifter and her passenger for, like all creatures of the sea, they both feared Myriad and delighted in thwarting any of its evil whims when they could.

At first, Noe had to hold tightly to Beatrice's arms in order not to lose her, but she gradually felt her passenger gripping tighter not only with her arms but her remaining leg which wrapped itself around Noe's waist.

"We're heading to safety. Hold on, petal," Noe murmured.

And hold on Beatrice did. The closer to the surface they swam, the rockier the waves that shook and slapped at them. Finally, Noe pushed up and out of the water and the school of fish into the open air. Beatrice gasped, forcing the water out of her lungs and gills, then slid farther down, resting her head on Noe's shoulder before passing out again.

Knowing sleep was a blessing for her wounded passenger, Noe shifted into a sea turtle, providing Beatrice with a large shell bed as she swam along the surface. For a strong swimmer like a shapeshifter, the burden was no more than bearing the weight of a small child. She cleaved the water with mighty strokes, anxious to be relieved of her responsibility and return to the safety of her home as soon as her task was complete, her debt to Coral repaid.

Noe and her aunt had thought of a sanctuary where they were sure Beatrice would be well-hidden but also welcomed and cared for. It was time for Coral's wife to meet the oldest and most powerful sea witch of all.

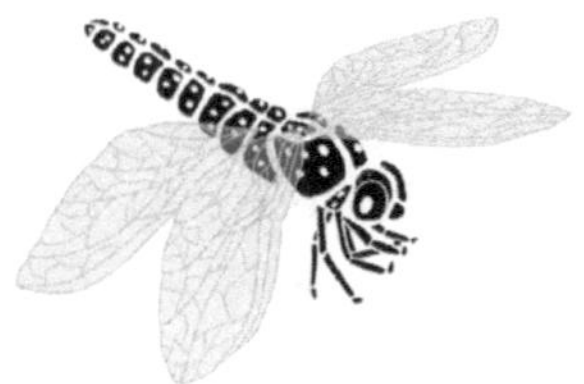

CHAPTER 16

STORMY

BEATRICE AWOKE IN A comfortable bed and beheld a woman with deep violet blue hair and chocolate brown eyes. The thought of chocolate made Bea's stomach growl, and she reached up to feel the lovely, silky hair and found her touch was tolerated with amusement.

"Where am I? Who are you?"

"I am one of your wife's sisters. My name is Stormy, and this is my house. Did Coral never tell you how sea witches are as connected as the sea foam is frothy when it tosses us up on land as babes? I knew at once when Noe brought you to me that you belonged to my sister and she would want me to care for you. Best to stay abed and rest. Myriad has dealt you a fearful injury."

Bea looked down tearfully at the empty place under the covers where her leg had been.

"No need for tears. You're lucky to be alive. Few survive an encounter with the kraken. I've made a pair of crutches to help you walk when you feel stronger. I could have conjured you an artificial leg, but it will be better if Coral does it. She understands your heart and soul and will make you something that perfectly suits you."

"You mean the two of you can't magic me a real one like I had before?"

"Some things are beyond the reach of even our powers. Myriad ate your leg, my pretty, and I'm afraid it's gone forever. Have Coral fashion a new one for you. Blood and feeling won't flow through it like you're used to, but if your wife creates it, she can imbue it with protection that no other can. She chose well with you, little warrior bride, so brave. I will hide you until Coral can come for you or we can deliver you to her."

Beatrice's lower lip quivered as she swallowed back her tears. "Then I guess I'll have to stay with you forever. The kraken has her tethered to the Kaleidoscope Lighthouse so she can't come for me. She might not want me back anyhow."

"Don't be foolish. Of course she wants you back, and besides, I hope she won't always be tethered. There's a storm brewing out at sea and Myriad may soon be fighting one last great battle against all who dwell underwater. After that's over, who knows what might not come to pass?"

"Are there other krakens?" Beatrice asked. "If not, it must be lonely to be the only one of its kind."

"Are you actually feeling pity for something that ate one of your legs?"

"It probably feels so alone. Maybe that's why it acts the way it does."

"I should dump you back in the ocean! Ever since it arrived, the kraken has left a path of destruction, misery, and death. No matter what horrors a being encounters in life, it has a choice whether to become sour and cruel or turn to love and kindness. Myriad has turned to hate. It saved you from bleeding to death not as a mercy, but because it has further plans for you."

"I suppose."

"You suppose!" In a fit of pique, impatient with Beatrice's line of reasoning, Stormy lifted her up like a doll and carried her out of the shelter that served as the sea witch's abode to the far end of the beach, leaving her there alone on the warm sands until the tide started to roll in.

When she fetched Beatrice back again, the sea witch found her patient to be chastened and subdued. Stormy bathed and dressed her and made sure she ate some nourishing seaweed soup. Conversation was avoided by both, but when Beatrice retreated to the bed and refused to get up again, Stormy finally spoke.

"Did you know that even immortals can die?" Stormy asked, pulling Beatrice into a seated position. She started combing the snarls, knots, and tangles gently from Beatrice's hair, deftly braiding it into a crown atop her head just as her sister liked to do. "Not in common ordinary ways, but they can be killed by a creature as powerful as Myriad. It is a hateful, murderous thing. No one knows exactly where it came from, but it's rumored to have fallen into our ocean from a distant sky.

There has never been a kraken before, and hopefully there will never be another one, but that is not reason enough to pity it."

She cupped Beatrice's face in her hands. "It's one thing to decide to stop talking, but quite another if you think I will allow you to succumb to the depths of depression by staying abed all day. You need to get up and practice with your crutches. Regain your independence."

Beatrice couldn't meet Stormy's eyes. A tear slid down her cheek but otherwise she showed no sign of acknowledgement or agreement.

"You are my sister's wife. Coral is one of the strongest of us, so I can't imagine she would have been attracted to a weakling. That means somewhere deep inside of you is a strength you haven't shown me yet. You must fight against this feeling lest it eat you alive like a corruption from within. Look at me! Look at me!"

Beatrice raised her eyes finally at that plea.

"You've lived a playful, safe, protected life until now and this injury has been a terrible shock, but you mustn't lose hope. You're a fool if you think there won't be a day when Coral will either come for you herself or send someone to fetch you. Be worth saving," Stormy admonished her.

"I'll try," Beatrice replied, and with that, the sea witch had to be content.

After grudgingly practicing with the crutches, Beatrice sat down to eat lunch with Stormy. "Does Coral know I'm here?"

"No, we decided it was best if we didn't tell her yet. The kraken keeps watch on her and would pick up on her thoughts. You must stay here where you'll be safe until either Myriad is defeated or we can figure out a way to get you back to the lighthouse without risking your recapture."

"So, I'm your prisoner?"

"You are my guest and my sister-in-law. Coral is the youngest of the sea witches, which makes her most precious to us, so in turn you are too."

Beatrice sobbed as she confessed her secret fear. "Coral gave me a necklace, and now it's gone. She said she was the only one with the power to remove it. I'm afraid its absence means she wants nothing more to do with me."

Stormy shook her head at such sentimental nonsense. "Myriad still has ultimate power over my sister. If a necklace she gave you that only she could remove is missing, it was likely taken by the kraken itself. You still have your wedding ring. If Coral was through with you, she'd have taken that too. You are suffering greatly, but don't ever doubt that the love you and Coral share is true."

Stormy contemplated her next words carefully.

"I could weave a spell of protection for you, but your wife might think it undermines her right to defend you. Or worse, she might think I am trying to claim what is hers and would want to either fight me to the death or give you to me and be done with you."

"That's too big a risk to take for being safe," Beatrice agreed. "Guess I'll wing it the best I can. Why doesn't she come to me in my dreams anymore?"

"I'm not sure. Perhaps Myriad noticed the connection and severed it with a spell of its own. If it was safe, I would transport you back to Coral immediately. I love my sister and her mopey little wife," she said with a wink, hoping to lighten Beatrice's spirits, "and want them to be together."

Beatrice gave her a tiny smile which Stormy took as a positive sign.

Even though Beatrice soon mastered the use of her crutches, as a matter of precaution, Stormy carried Bea on her back over the rockier terrain as they traveled down the beach and away from the witch's shelter. Beatrice didn't appreciate being carried around like a toddling infant, but she could see the common sense in it.

"Where are we headed?" Beatrice asked.

"A small journey to see a few of my other sisters. That's all you need to know for now," Stormy replied.

"Do all magical beings in Lichen come from the sea?"

"The sea and the sky, although some Lichens mistakenly believe we witches are from the land and just prefer to dwell by the sea."

"Have you no parents?"

"How is it in all the years you've been married to my sister these aren't questions you asked her?"

"With all the traveling I do, I tend not to wax philosophical when I'm with her. Our time together is too precious. She can also be cagey about not answering questions if she doesn't want to, you know. I knew that she had sea witch sisters, but she never spoke much about any of you."

"That sounds like Coral. Her tethering to the lighthouse has left her feeling isolated and separate from her own kind. My breath is short from hiking and carrying you upon my back. Spend this time gathering questions in your mind. When we stop for the night, you may ask anything you want and I will answer to the best of my ability. Until then, either shush, sing pretty songs to me, or regale me with tales of your travels to help pass the time."

Beatrice was silent for a few moments considering which to do. Finally, she sang *The Ballad of the Weary Traveler*, a song Coral would sing to her in her dreams when she was on the move, sleeping in her patchwork quilt tent. The words spoke of hope and the importance of keeping your spirits light, releasing the stress of the road back into the ground where it re-energized Lichen and made the land burst forth with fresh flowers and new saplings and all good growing things.

Stormy was astounded to realize Beatrice's voice was weaving an incantation on her that left the witch feeling rested and energized. She felt as if she could walk forever without stopping. Landfolk didn't possess magic. How was it Beatrice was able to build such a spell?

The sea witch decided not to mention anything to Beatrice about it yet. Best to think on it and consult with her witchy sisters first, but there was no denying it was strange and needed further investigation.

When they stopped for the night, Stormy finally allowed Beatrice to ask the questions she'd thought of while they traveled. Beatrice obliged by unleashing such a barrage of queries that it made the sea witch's head spin.

"Enough! Not another word, Beatrice Buttons. You've asked, I've listened, and now you will show me patience and be quiet as I tell you the tale of my kind."

CHAPTER 17

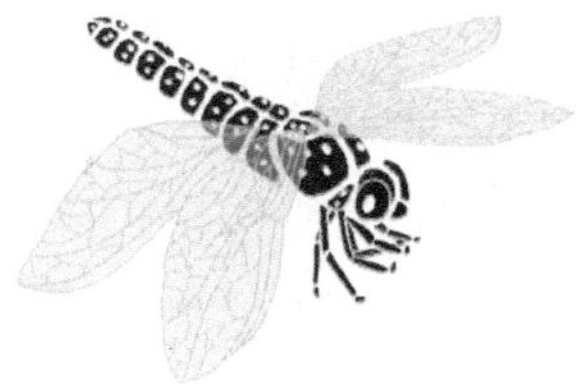

A WAVE OF WITCHES

I N THE BEGINNING, THERE was rock and there was water and there was a sprinkling of spores: cinnamon-colored dust that fell from the stars bringing new life. Swirls of neon colors and curlicues of outrageous pattern tantalized and wooed the rock and water, and from this courtship came a planet dancing with lichen, moss, and fungi. Soon, vegetation evolved and became bountiful. The land and the sea frothed with new plants and animals. The sky, having no wish to be left out of the fun, developed cloud creatures and plants of its own.

And far beneath the surface of the ocean, the Pillars of the Deep were formed—the oldest and wisest of the fungi in Lichen. Great mushroom towers that reach up from the darkest bottom lands beneath the sea and more immense than you can possibly imagine, yet well-hidden within the fathomless depths.

The Pillars of the Deep thought it would be interesting if there were two-legged creatures in Lichen. Sentient beings with power and wisdom, although not so powerful and wise as fungi because, of course, that is not possible. Since the Pillars are of the sea, they decided these two-legged beings should also come from the sea.

Much consideration went into what the creatures would be like. Webbed toes and fingers so they might swim as easily as a fish. Gills so they could breathe underwater. A connection to the Pillars so the new beings could understand the fungi's thoughts and wouldn't be lonely. And perhaps even the gift of magic so they could become guardians over the more vulnerable species of the sea.

The intense concentration of the Pillars as they contemplated these questions brought a mighty storm to life. The sky darkened and a ferocious wind blew against the sea, stirring it into waves, foam, and twirling white caps as the Pillars pondered.

With every spark of an idea, a speck came into being. Just a tiny hiccup of a thing. These specks curled up like the spiral of a snail shell as they were tossed about by the tempest. With each bump, the spirals curled and uncurled becoming something a smattering larger. Soon, they were the size of conch shells—small infants in floating bubbles of embryonic sacs bouncing along the unsettled waters.

The bubbles expanded and contracted, coming alive with these new creatures itching to burst out. They punched, kicked, twisted, and even bit. Struggled with arms as yet untried in strength. Ripped the edges of their prisons as they wormed out first one finger then another and another until whole fists curled and pulled their way to freedom. And thus, the first sea witches were born.

Each witchling gave out a roar the moment they were free, a sound that was unique to them. No witch ever forgot her own birth cry and could identify any of the other witches by theirs. This first sound of life was registered by the Pillars as the witch's true name, the essence of who they were. They took their common name from nature, but their cry was a secret signal that could be mimicked at any age and acted as a fingerprint for them.

One hundred sea witches were born that day, each of them with a shock of beautiful hair and brilliant eyes in every shade of the ocean with all its complexity and endless variation. The infants giggled and flailed their limbs as they stretched and grew, tossed about on the waves far from shore. They could communicate with the wind, the weather, the creatures of sea, sky and land, and each other. The language spoken by all Lichens evolved from witch speak, although only witches have the power to understand and cast spells.

Slowly but surely, the tempest-tossed waves pushed the witchlings closer and closer to land. The first sea witch to crawl out of the sea foam and stand upon the shore was known forevermore as the Eldest Witch, and that was me. My name, Stormy, is an homage to the circumstances of our birth as well as a hint at my own power, as storms are one of the most formidable forces in Lichen.

Next to tumble out of the waves were two witches who are often to be found in my company, Turtle and Tern. Ninety-seven other witches crawled ashore after us one by one. We must have been quite a sight, toddling about unsteadily on our wobbly legs. We sustained ourselves at first with nothing more than seaweed and other bits and bobs foraged from the beach.

The Pillars had not abandoned us, however, and were as adroit at teaching as we proved to be adept and astute young pupils, soaking up their lessons in magic and the ways of nature. Sea witches mature quickly, and we passed through childhood and adolescence into our full power as adults in what seems like no time at all in my memory.

After their success with us, the Pillars decided to bring other beings to life, further denizens of the seas—the shapeshifters and the merpeople. For a time, they were content with this, but eventually, they decided to see if they could produce people of the land as well, and thus landfolk, what you call Lichens, were born.

Like the shapeshifters, merfolk, and sea witches, the landfolk were also given gray skin. The fungi hoped this commonality would link us together and be an inducement to treat each other with love and mutual respect. Landfolk being mortal and not attuned to magic often fall short of this goal, I'm afraid, although they do tend to respect the power we witches wield.

Sea witches have been born in this same fashion ever since my sisters and I first appeared. Formed in the waters and washed up onto shore when we are mature enough to fend for ourselves, a cycle that repeats once every thousand years.

But when the tenth generation of witchlings appeared, a terrible tragedy occurred. A gigantic monster rose from the water: the kraken known as Myriad.

It flailed its tentacles about, instantly destroying ninety-nine of the witchling babies and annihilating the entire previous generation of sea witches, who had gathered on the beach to greet them as is traditional for us. One hundred and ninety-nine of my sisters were killed that day, those full-grown on shore and the new crop of babes who never got a chance to draw a single breath of air.

Only one survived—Coral.

Myriad noticed her embryonic sac shining and bobbing along the waves. Angry it had missed one of its prey, it snatched her up and flung her so hard she sailed through the air all the way into the ocean wall of the Kaleidoscope Lighthouse—only at that time, of course, it was still an ordinary lighthouse. It was a miracle Coral didn't die on impact for she was a tiny thing, hardly more than an egg, and no witchling had ever left the sea before in such an underdeveloped state.

Turtle, Tern, and myself arrived on the scene, having been drawn to the area by the death cries of our poor sisters. We found Coral in her sac. It broke our hearts to see this premature witchling thrust away from the sea before her time. I was unsure if she could be saved, but we carried her back out into the water near shore and kept careful watch over her for days.

Other sea witches gathered to assist in paying tribute to the dead and to add their blessings to the unborn as we surrounded her with love and magic. When she took her first bite through her sac and began to make her way out, there was a collective sigh of relief. She had survived.

Her tiny hands clasped the side of the hole she made and tugged. I was instantly captivated and bowed down and kissed each delicate, wiggling finger. She rewarded me with a cooing giggle from inside her sac. Unlike the rest of us, she didn't cry her way into life, she laughed. As she pulled herself out, she was caught up in an embrace of adoration as Turtle held her up for everyone to see and applaud our new sister.

Unfortunately, our celebration attracted the attention of the kraken. The Pillars tried to warn us of the danger, but we were too caught up in our joy to hear them. Myriad's curse struck our newborn witchling, tearing her from Turtle's hands and sending her back to the lighthouse on shore where she was doomed to remain tethered for all time.

We watched her float through the air to the top of the lighthouse stairs, hovering by the window, her unfocused eyes staring out to sea. I followed her there and swaddled the poor, wee thing, sharing tales of our sisterhood with her as she fell asleep.

Her growth spurt had been weakened by the ordeal, so she matured more slowly than other witches. Turtle, Tern, and I stayed with her to guard her and teach her spells, healings, and how to find the magic which belonged to her alone. When she was old enough to fend for herself, we left her there at the lighthouse as was her fate, but I helped her create a spell to call the prettiest woman nearby to her. If their love was mutual, they would become Coral's companion so she would not be too lonely.

And that, Beatrice, is how you came to know my sister and become her wife. I do believe Coral loves you most of all her pretties, and I promise you will be reunited one day, never fear.

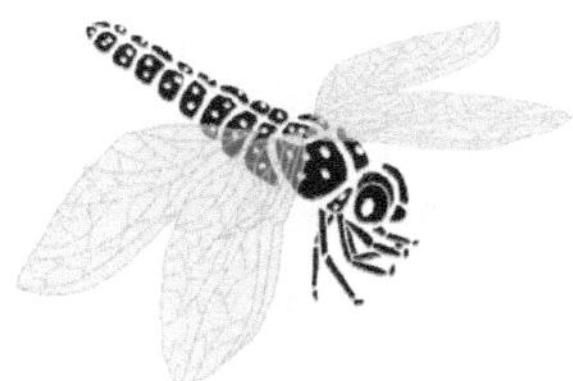

CHAPTER 18

A RESCUE PARTY GATHERS

BACK ABOARD THE DRAGONFLY boat, Amelia watched as a dot in the distance slowly grew into the Kaleidoscope Lighthouse, and her heart filled with hope. Surely, a witch as powerful as Coral must have some idea of how to find Bea, reunite the boys with their parents, and allow Amelia to return to her peaceful house and gardens.

"Ahoy, fair sea witch, we meet again!" hollered One-Eyed Jack from the dragonfly's deck.

"And greetings to you, my piratical friend!" Coral called. "I am pleased to see you have regained your former self and your freedom. Bring the brothers and the photograph containing their parents to me and we'll see what can be done."

Amelia made haste to obey the witch's orders, arriving at the base of the lighthouse with the lads in tow. Bix clutched his parents' photo, and Amelia kept a firm grip on one of each of the boys' arms as they didn't have a necklace to ground them like she did.

"Are you really a witch?" Click asked Coral.

"Yes, so be respectful and mind your manners if you want my help," she replied, placing a bespelled necklace over each of the brothers' heads to stop them floating away—a moonstone shaped like an owl for Click and a coral leviathan for Bix.

"I don't need anything from you," Bix said.

"Shall I take my gift back then?"

"Don't be dense, Bix," Click scolded. "These charms will come in handy. Besides, we need her help to change us back to the age we should be."

"Who says I want to change? I like being a kid just fine. I'm not impressed with what I've seen of being an adult. Who needs that kind of headache?" Bix answered.

Click scowled, not in any way understanding or sympathizing with his brother's stubborn position.

Coral interrupted, thinking it wiser to change the subject before a protracted family squabble set in. "Is this the photograph of your parents?"

Bix held up the framed picture for her to see, and the sea witch motioned for both brothers to come stand closer to her. Coral took the photograph in her hands and spoke a few, low words under her breath. Moon and Star were free to speak again.

"Thank you so much," said Moon. "And don't worry, boys, we don't blame you for what's happened."

Bix sniffed at his father's gentle words. "Can you release them?"

"I can try to reverse the spell and free them from the photograph," said Coral. "However, I cannot predict the outcome of them being trapped for so long under the influence of such strong magic or what exactly will happen if I free them. It's possible they might age rapidly and die when freed from the spell."

The parents whispered to one another within the photograph, then reported their decision.

"We'd prefer to wait for now," Star said, "and make sure our boys get through this challenge with the kraken okay. When we're sure they're safe, we'll make a decision."

"Very well," Coral agreed, handing the photograph back to Bix.

"Why won't you free them now?" Bix demanded.

"It's their decision to make," Coral said, giving the boy a gentle embrace with one arm. She held her other arm out to Click. "I'm sorry your parents won't be freed yet."

Click ignored her invitation for a hug. "It's up to them, I guess, but what'll happen to Bix and me when you make us our proper age?"

"Your physical appearance will change, but your emotions and knowledge, the experience you've picked up along the way should remain. It's possible one or both of you may have already passed your destined lifespan and you'll crumble to dust. I can't say for certain, although the spell to make you age would be different from the one to free your parents from the photograph, so the outcome may be different as well. You'll have to decide if it's a risk worth taking."

But Bix was adamant. "I won't grow up! I won't! We lost the chance to be a proper family once we started wishing for things on that stupid ball, and I want to spend more time with Mom and Dad, especially if they might be able to come out of the photograph one day, and do all the things we never got to do together."

"You needn't age if you really don't want to," Coral reassured him. "But I think your brother would prefer to grow up and go off adventuring on his own. Seven is too young for you to be alone. Until we resolve your parents' situation, you'll need a proper guardian."

"I want Click to stay as he is. It hasn't been so bad."

Click shook his head. "I've had it with being a kid. No one takes me seriously. I want to have my own experiences, but not as some creaking oldie."

"There's nothing wrong with the maturity of age, but I've an idea of a spell that would advance you only a little. I could make you, say, eighteen or nineteen? And then you would age naturally from there. That's old enough to take care of yourself, but not so many years ahead that you should find it too great a shock."

"Sounds good to me, but I still think you should change Bix too. He can't be a kid forever."

"We'll leave it up to your mother and father," Coral said.

"It will just be Click for now then," Moon answered. "We won't force Bix to do anything he doesn't want to. Perhaps it's time for our sons to travel their own separate paths."

Bix's eyes widened. He'd never seriously considered there would come a time when he and his brother would go their own ways. The idea frightened him, but he hid his hurt behind a scowl. "Who said I wanted to hang out with Click forever anyway? He's not so great."

Click laughed, unbothered by the insult. "Fine, then we're agreed. Let's do it!"

Coral prepared a potion filled with things she'd gathered from the ocean in an iron kettle full of seawater boiling over a roaring fire. Ground dried starfish and urchin spikes, anemone tentacles and coral flakes, seaweed strips and fish bones. She snipped a lock of Click's white hair and threw it in, instructing him to spit into the kettle. The mixture turned bright blue in a flash. Coral dipped one finger into the steaming hot brew, then drew a smear across Click's forehead while she sang a low spell.

Within minutes, his body elongated and thinned out, muscles appearing in new places and his voice sank into a lower range. Click stared down in amazement at his body, flexing his large hands in wonder, and fingering the new clothes the sea witch had magicked up for him. It felt weird beyond reason and yet familiar. He was still himself after all.

"My handsome son," Star gushed from the photograph, and Moon added, "You look like I did at your age, Click."

Bix was not so impressed and wandered off unhappily. The person he'd been closest to his whole life was turning into a stranger and wanted to abandon him. He'd still have his mom and dad in the photograph, but it wasn't the same as having a living, breathing person by his side.

Coral came over to comfort him. "I think Click will be more content now. He wants to lead what he considers a normal life but will always be your brother."

Bix looked up at her with a tear-stained face. "But if I'm too young to be left alone, and Click doesn't want me now that he's grown up, what'll I do? Do I have to go live with Miss Amelia or One-Eyed Jack?"

"Amelia Arrowheart values her privacy too much to take on such a responsibility, and Jack wishes to leave Lichen and return to his own home as soon as he can, but you're welcome to stay with me while we see how things work out with your parents. Don't forget, we still have Myriad to contend with. Don't borrow more trouble from the future is my advice."

That evening at supper, Click ate more than everyone else at the table combined. The sea witch said it was growing pains and he needed the extra nutrients. She magicked another full spread which Click tucked away mostly by himself.

After the meal was finished, Coral proposed their next course of action. "I've been meditating on the subject and have decided you should travel to Fungi Ridge."

Amelia was taken aback. Every Lichen knew about Fungi Ridge, and many made a point of visiting there at least once in their lives to observe the sacred

Luna tree and the multitudinous fungi pilgrims who climbed it in search of enlightenment.

"How will that help Beatrice?" she asked Coral.

"There you will find wise and formidable sages who can advise you on your best course of action better than I can. Trust to their guidance. When you arrive, seek out the one they call Iggy to help you."

"And how will we recognize this fellow when we see him?" asked Jack.

"Iggy is neither a him nor a her. Iggy is simply Iggy. Ask anyone you see. Everyone knows Iggy, and Iggy knows everyone."

Jack was annoyed, but as witches often spoke in riddles and refused to state things plainly, he knew it was useless to argue. With no other plan in mind, they decided it was best to follow Coral's advice.

"Before you leave," Coral said to Bix, "I will give you a present fit for the fosterling of a sea witch that may be of use to you on your travels."

She filled a shimmering aquamarine glass bowl with seawater and set it on the table. Dipping her fingers in, she next placed her splayed hands on either side of Bix's throat, tickling him. She sang a spell in the language of the sea, meant to confuse other ears from memorizing it. Everyone watched in amazement as she sliced cleanly through his skin, though it never bled a drop or caused him a moment of pain, until Bix had fully functioning gills.

"Can I breathe underwater?" he asked in delight.

"As with me, so with you." She wiggled her webbed fingers. "Look at your hands and feet."

Bix crowed in excitement as he kicked off his clogs to discover he also had webbed feet and hands along with his gills. He was now perfectly adapted to life on land or in water. Coral wished with all her heart she had given these same gifts to Beatrice before her disappearance. What a help they might have been to her! But what was done was done and what was not done was not done. No use dwelling on either.

Amelia also had a gift for Bix and Click. For each, one of her father's handkerchiefs, finely-woven of olive-green linen with stripes of gold, sky blue, and cream. "It's what you use for your nose instead of digging around with your fingers. Do you understand me?" she asked, with a weather eye on Bix, who was the worst offender.

"Yes, Miss Amelia," Bix answered, while secretly thinking his new handkerchief was a thing of beauty too magnificent to ruin with snot. *I should try to be good though*, he thought to himself, and in that moment, even meant it.

Coral had one last surprise before they embarked on their journey. She enlarged Moon and Star's photograph to life-size, hanging it on a wall inside the skyboat's cabin. The seashell frame hinged open like a door, allowing anyone from the outside to enter. Coral crooked a finger at Bix, who took a running leap into the photograph and into the arms of his astonished and grateful parents.

"We would never have dreamt of such magic!" Star cried, tears of joy streaming down her face.

"That is what we witches are for. While it might be risky to remove you from the photograph until we can predict the effects, I see no reason why you shouldn't have visitors there in the meantime. They may come and go as they please, but you and Moon must be careful not to step outside of the frame, for I can't predict what the consequences might be if you do."

While not as outwardly excited as his brother, Click condescended to enter the photo and endure a hearty clap on the back from his father and a kiss on the cheek from his mother.

Spirits much buoyed by this unexpected reunion of sorts, the travelers tethered the oobble to the lighthouse to await their return and set sail together in the dragonfly boat to Fungi Ridge.

CHAPTER 19

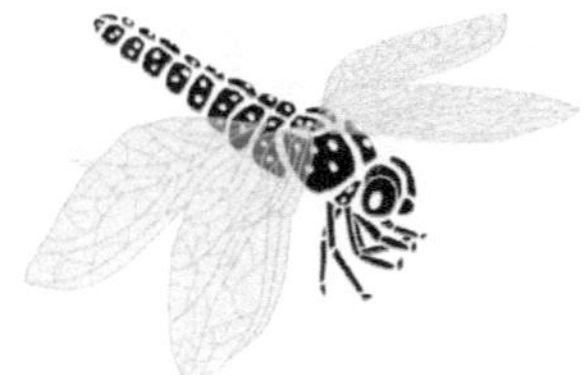

FUNGI RIDGE

B Y HARNESSING THE WESTERLY winds, the skyboat made excellent time and soon approached Fungi Ridge. Amelia, Jack, Click and Bix left Moon and Star below in their photograph and stood on deck to observe the scene before them.

In the center of the holy grove of Fungi Ridge, trails of mushrooms of every shape, color, and size could be observed climbing the deeply grooved bark of the everblooming Luna tree in orderly lines, one after another, along the hundreds of thousands of branches. Their caps and gills swayed, searching upwards, ever upwards until they could receive a solar kiss from the suns far above.

"What is this place, Captain?" asked Jack, bewildered by a part of Lichen culture that was unfamiliar to him.

"It is hallowed ground," Amelia explained. "Fungi travel from all over to pay homage to the sacred tree and seek enlightenment. The rest of us come to bear witness to these majestic and revered pilgrims."

"But to what purpose? Ye can't have much of a conversation with a wee mushroom, can ye?"

"Most of us can't, but every day, one fortunate citizen is chosen to be Record Keeper. They alone can hear the thoughts of the fungi. They make careful observation of the activities and words of the pilgrims, recording them so all of Lichen might benefit from their wisdom and insight. In this way, we remain grounded and connected to all life throughout Lichen."

"Sounds a bit daft to me," Jack mumbled under his breath, but Amelia was too distracted by trying to soak in the exciting sights and sounds to notice.

"It's always been a dream of mine to visit, only I've never been fond of traveling. It's even more beautiful than I imagined. I've studied the Record Keepers' words since I was a girl:

> *Life is brief on Fungi Ridge, where brave pilgrims attempt the trek to the top, often only to perish along the route. Though it is the highest of honors, it is also a heavy burden to be a Record Keeper and bear witness.*

The images printed along with that entry in the official records are etched forever in my mind."

"That's a sad one," Bix agreed, "but they're not all sad. The one I like says:

> *They floated up and up into the sky and found a whole new world. Full of green and good things, the soft summer breeze and the morning dew. We will settle here, they said. They spend their days watching the clouds from under their sunbonnets and life is good."*

"How lovely!" Amelia exclaimed. "Did your parents ever bring you boys to Fungi Ridge?"

"Sort of. I mean they brought Click and I was born here," Bix shared.

"Yep, born in a holy place, and he's been a holy terror ever since," Click scoffed.

"I didn't know you were a Blessed Baby," Amelia said to Bix in amazement, for she had never met one before to her knowledge.

"I may regret asking," said Jack, "but what is a Blessed Baby?"

"Blessed Babies are what we call Lichens who are born within the hallowed grounds of Fungi Ridge. They go on to lead extraordinary lives. Performing miraculous feats when dire circumstances or a crisis calls upon them or just contributing their uncommon wisdom to the improvement of life in Lichen."

Jack looked skeptical but this time kept his thoughts to himself, while Amelia wondered what Bix's contribution to Lichen would be. She knew Beatrice would laugh at the irony of the booger boy turning out to be a Blessed Baby, but she was still impressed and not a little in awe to have met one in person. There seemed to be no end to the surprises she was to experience since leaving her sedate and quiet life behind.

They anchored the skyboat to the top of a tree on the outskirts of the grove. Amelia and the boys floated down and grounded themselves with their magical necklaces while Jack climbed down a rope ladder. He noticed how quiet and meditative the other three became as they approached the place that was holy to their kind. Not being a Lichen, he didn't feel the same reverent awe but could appreciate the uniqueness of the experience. Never before had he seen as many different sizes, colors and varieties of fungi or so many Lichens gathered together.

Amelia continued her explanations to Jack in the pedantic way that was natural to her when particularly enthused about a subject. "You'll notice pathways are clearly established to protect the mushroom pilgrims, many of whom move so slowly, their movement can hardly be observed. Barely a foot a day for some of the larger species while the fastest fungi are among the tiniest, like those over there. You see the ones that are no bigger than your fingernail? They tilt their caps up toward the top of the Luna tree, except when it rains and they cover themselves like an umbrella. Isn't it fascinating?"

Her lecture was interrupted by a clear call for attention. It was not spoken aloud, however. Instead, they heard it in their minds, a telepathic message received by all except Jack since he was from a far distant planet and not attuned to Lichen.

"A NEW RECORD KEEPER HAS ARRIVED. WE CALL FORTH AMELIA ARROWHEART."

"Me?" Amelia exclaimed in disbelief.

"Ye what?" asked Jack in confusion.

"They've... they've said I'm the next Record Keeper. There must be a mistake. Maybe there's another Amelia Arrowheart here," she ventured, looking around desperately, terrified of being the center of attention in such a huge crowd.

Bix had no such inhibitions. "Here she is!" he crowed, dragging Amelia forward by the hand while other visitors buzzed and whispered in excitement at witnessing the anointing of a new Recorder.

Amelia shivered and blushed with embarrassment at being the object of so much scrutiny. She was aware it was one of the highest honors in Lichen to be chosen but couldn't help wishing with every ounce of her shy spirit that the honor had fallen to anyone else instead.

A cheery young man with pink hair and goatee bounded up to her. "Congratulations, Amelia Arrowheart! I'm Ian. My recording duties are ending. This past day has been the most amazing of my entire life! Don't you feel lucky?"

"I suppose so," she replied doubtfully. "But surely I'm not qualified for such an important position?"

"That's what I thought when I was called, but there's really nothing to it. All you need is something to write on. Do you have any paper?"

"I have this," she said, pulling the beautiful moon journal from Coral out of her bag.

"Perfect! All you have to do is listen to the thoughts of the fungi and record whichever of their movements and words seem meaningful to you."

"But I don't hear them! You see, there must be some mistake after all."

"You will. Just put your pen to paper and you'll see what I mean. Have fun!"

Ian bounded away as Amelia opened her journal to the first blank page. Her pen hovered over the pristine paper, reluctant to mar it, but as soon as the nib made contact, her mind was filled with hushed whispers, soft voices of such exquisite beauty and erudition that she was moved to tears. The knowledge that these higher beings had chosen her out of all the people on Fungi Ridge to hear their thoughts renewed her spirits and her courage.

While somewhat reassured about her new duty, she couldn't forget her old ones. She'd promised Coral and the boys' parents to look after Bix, but now would be too busy. She doubted whether Jack or Click would appreciate being burdened with the task instead.

As though he could read her mind, Bix said, "Don't worry about me. I can join the other Blessed Babies who've gathered here. I'll be safe with them while you're Record Keeper."

Amelia nodded and smiled her thanks, watching as Bix entered the embrace of the other Blessed Babies who had returned to pay homage to the place of their birth. A joyous rainbow aura encircled them all, and she felt reassured he would be in fine company.

She couldn't help also fretting about any delays in starting out on their quest to rescue Beatrice. She decided she must have faith it was part of a larger plan and would be a useful stop to them as Coral had advised. After all, the fungi were the wisest beings on the planet. There was much she could learn from them if she listened carefully.

Amelia began her day as Record Keeper by observing the slow march closest to her, recording which groups traveled together. She noted some fungi traveled above the ground, oozing along in much the same way snails and slugs move, while others traveled under the loam. If she watched carefully, she could see tiny particles of soil moving. Some of the aboveground mushrooms slowly turned their caps her way and gave a nod that anyone not patiently observant would miss. Amelia bowed back gravely and continued her work.

After an hour or two, she noticed an unusual figure perched upon a whatwhat mushroom. After her recent sky travels, Amelia was able to quickly recognize a cloud creature when she saw it. This one was shaped like a frilly seadragon and had taken on characteristics of the whatwhat mushroom it rode on in order to blend in. Anyone not watching extraordinarily closely would never have seen it.

Fascinated with the tiny dragon, she set about making a drawing of it in case it decided to suddenly fly away. As she finished her sketch, the dragon winked at her and floated up, perching upon her journal close to her hand, its leafy cloud tendrils tickling her skin and making her giggle.

"Greetings. Not many landfolk notice us," the ethereal creature said. "You must have visited the sky."

"Yes," Amelia replied, "my friends and I traveled here in a skyboat. I've seen the migration of the cloud jellyfish and the mating of the leviathans."

"And now you're a Record Keeper. Quite an adventurous life you lead."

"Oh, no! Not at all! At least, not usually. I made a friend named Beatrice Buttons recently and ever since then, I seem to be caught up in one escapade after another."

"And is this button here?"

Amelia wasn't sure Bea would appreciate being referred to as a button, but also didn't want to offend her new acquaintance by offering a correction. "No, she was taken by the kraken. Her wife, the sea witch Coral, sent us here to consult with the fungi and a friend of hers called Iggy about rescuing Beatrice. Do you know anyone named Iggy?"

"Very well. You might even say we are one and the same," came the reply.

"Friend to the sea witch of Kaleidoscope Lighthouse?" she asked, not believing someone so tiny could be who they were looking for.

"You will find if you ask the pilgrims that there is only one Iggy here and we are them. You've captured our likeness beautifully in your drawing."

"Thank you. But isn't this a little low for a cloud creature to be?"

"Have you never heard of fog? What is it but clouds come down to visit the ground? Many who never give us a second glance assume some mushrooms carry their own weather with them when they see us. We are not here to destroy the illusions of others so we never correct them, but you saw us as we are."

"I'm so happy to have found you! Coral thought you might have an idea about rescuing Beatrice."

"We understand. You focus on your duties, and we will meditate on the problem of the lost button." Saying that, Iggy floated to the top of Amelia's head and made a comfy nest for themself in her shorn, tousled locks. The skydragon was so light, she couldn't even feel the weight but decided to take it on faith the creature would not abandon her without some further insight into their problems.

Amelia returned to her observations, taking great care with her writing and sketches. When her term was finished, her notes would become part of the permanent record of Fungi Ridge so that any citizen might ponder what she had experienced and shared. She checked in with Iggy from time to time to see if the cloud creature had hit upon a plan. They liked to hum small songs in her ear or float up and down to visit with one mushroom or another, but mostly rode contentedly on her head.

"We are still meditating," the skydragon would tell her gently anytime she was brave enough to ask, so she resigned herself to being patient.

"Hang on, Bea," she whispered. "We have not forgotten you."

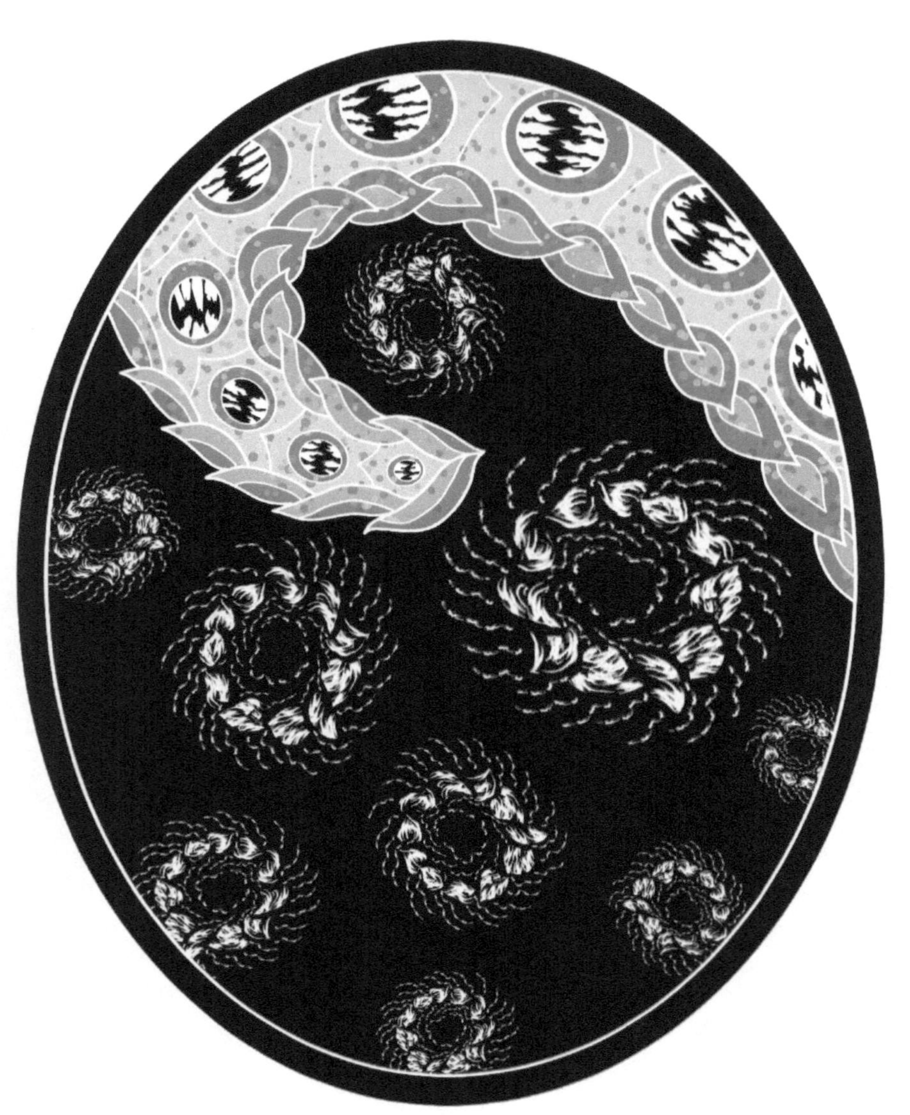

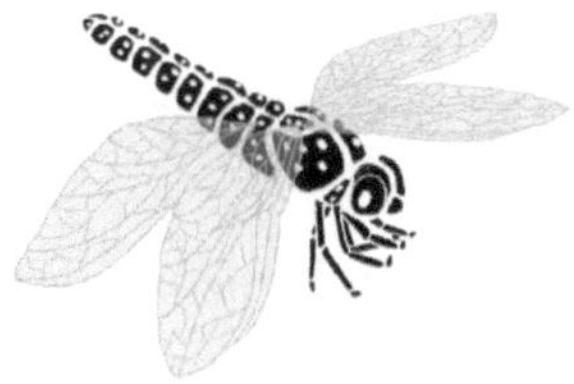

CHAPTER 20

WRATH OF THE KRAKEN

OUT AT SEA, THE waves boiled, bubbling up from deep beneath the surface with the fury of the kraken after it discovered Beatrice's escape. It had torn her leg off, crippled her, made her weak. How was it possible for her to flee? Why couldn't it perceive her scent and her thoughts in order to track her down? And what sea creatures had dared to defy it by helping her disappear?

Myriad's agitation turned the ocean an ugly shade of yellowish-gray never before seen. Schools of fish zipped off to the farthest reaches of the sea upon encountering the kraken's angry vibrations, and young cephalopods inked in fear and shot across the sea bottom seeking out crevasses to hide.

The kraken was also seeking and would not rest until it found all who aided the sea witch's wench or found the wench herself. Woe betide any creature who crossed its path while it was in this state of rage. Frenzy upon frenzy of alarms echoed as word spread of the monster's uncontainable wrath until the news reached the Council of Seafolk.

They were much divided. Some blamed Noe and Stormy for helping rescue and protect Beatrice, thereby provoking Myriad, while others sympathized and approved of their noble and brave actions. Noe's auntie, Lorali, was the wisest and most respected of the shapeshifters. When she backed her niece's decision, it became the cause of all shapeshifters far and wide, for they are loyal to each other beyond any bounds that land dwellers would recognize.

In a way, the shapeshifters had a bigger responsibility to confront the kraken than they even knew. For it was Noe who had first lured it to Lichen when she walked through the Door of Lost Souls seeking her mother. Myriad had studied her, stretching out a tentacle and absorbing her thoughts and emotions.

Puzzled but intrigued by her memories of her planet, it sent the door back to Lichen and stepped through it into the vast ocean. This would be home, it decided. This is where it would spend eternity, floating enraged and wreaking havoc on any that crossed it.

Where had it come from? Not even Myriad knew the answer to that. Its mind was full of fog. Perhaps its home world had been a land of mist, it thought. It knew its sense of hearing was more acute than any other being it had encountered. It could easily hear sounds from halfway across the galaxy, yet it had no idea what it looked like. Had it always been this way or was there a time when its thoughts were less clouded? It didn't remember its beginning and had no idea if it was capable of an ending.

While the kraken was unsure of its own form, other beings who encountered it would never forget the sight.

Its size was second only to the mighty Pillars of the Deep, and it was a putrid green color with carnation pink underside and orange suction cups on its limbs. It had twenty arms that were large and strong enough for grasping and crushing, and a multitude of tangled legs that trailed after it for miles like jellyfish tentacles. Its most fearsome feature was a puce beak that opened vertically like the wings of a beetle, revealing a horrific set of teeth sporting intricate engravings of such unusual design that they mesmerized anything unlucky enough to see them up close.

Noe had been in the ocean when she walked through the door and inadvertently led the kraken to Lichen, so the ocean is where Myriad remained, unaware of or uncaring about the land dwellers. If the monster had emerged on dry land, it would have terrorized the slow-moving Lichens much easier than the swift and canny water creatures who were adept at fleeing and hiding. A small thing to be grateful for, even though most landfolk were completely unaware of the threat lurking in the darkest depths of the ocean.

Seafolk were not so lucky. Many had suffered the kraken's wrath both before and after Coral had angered it by surviving its murderous rampages against her sea witch sisters. It had gotten revenge by tethering her to the lighthouse, but never satisfied, it had watched and plotted.

From its contact with her when it flung her ashore, it could feel Coral's emotions and capture many of her thoughts, particularly in dreams. It witnessed her courtship of Beatrice and crafted a plan. It would leave breadcrumbs of a sort in Beatrice's dream meetings with her wife that would lead her to the pink house with nine turrets near a floating observatory.

Myriad had tossed away a Ball of Intention it created and grew tired of many years before. A pair of inquisitive boys found it and made chaotic use of it. The object still retained the kraken's imprint, so it was no trouble to suggest the boys call for help and arrange for the pink house to start floating. Amelia's house had been an accident, a touch of collateral damage for an inexact spell, but it had worked out all the same. A series of orchestrated events that inevitably left Beatrice in an exposed spot far from her wife's protection and ripe for the plucking.

The kraken captured Beatrice with plans not just to eat one of her legs as a snack, but to slowly destroy her whole being as another way to torture the sea witch and remind her and her kind not to interfere within its domain. But then it tasted Coral's wife and drew from that a knowledge of her essential being. Now it understood why the witch loved Beatrice, and it wanted to love her too. In all its years of existence, Myriad had never loved anything, only hated. This new feeling was why it had imbued Beatrice with—no, it wouldn't allow itself to think of its generous gift.

Howling mad at Beatrice's disappearance, the kraken lashed out, set on destroying anything within its reach to distract itself from these disturbing new thoughts and emotions. Shells, rocks, bones, shipwreck debris became missiles whipped through the ocean like an underwater hurricane. The shrapnel shredded anything it came in contact with. An arc of emptiness widened out away from Myriad as creatures fled from its fury.

Not all were quick enough. Its grasping tentacles dredged up a school of omes, a rare circular fish that looked like rings of fire beneath the sea. They were the most harmless of creatures, but Myriad's thirst for violence and destruction knew no bounds or reason. Striking out, it slaughtered the omes to the very last one, wiping them from existence in less than a second, like a candle snuffed out forever.

This sudden extinction shook Lichen to its core. Leaves shivered on every tree, and flowers dropped their petals in grief. Four-legged creatures howled and barked and hissed. Lichens felt their stomachs roil with dread without understanding the cause. Even the cloud creatures hovered in place motionless, the loss profoundly felt by all. Was there to be no end to the destruction of the wrathful kraken?

At Fungi Ridge, the mushrooms experienced the extinction of the omes and wept and mourned in their quiet way. Some shriveled and withered in grief while others died of the shock.

Amelia understood what had happened through her connection with the fungi. Her face glistened with tears at the thought that an entire species had been wiped out, though she didn't make a peep. Iggy floated down from her head and produced a pillowy cotton handkerchief from out of the air as an offering which she accepted gratefully.

Moved by her anguish, more of her tattoos slid from her skin to comfort their former canvas. A seedling Luna tree with willowy branches stroked her back while a shimmer of hummingbirds fluttered their wings softly around her head. A stick-like insect clicked its mandibles soothingly and tickled her chin with its feathery antennae. A black rabbit wove in and out between her legs, rubbing its soft fur along her ankles.

Visitors to the Ridge gawked in surprise at this remarkable sight as many of the fungi pilgrims also moved closer to Amelia to provide their support to the Record Keeper. Their tiny spirits provided zaps of warming energy that kept her from sinking beneath the weight of her distress.

Uplifted by this outpouring of affection, Amelia resolved not to let her despair distract her from her responsibilities. It was more important now than ever to listen to the thoughts of the fungi and record their reaction to the extinction of the omes so their slaughter by the kraken would never be forgotten.

"Thank you, friends," she said gratefully to the fungi. To her former tattoos, she added, "And thank you for being my companions and a consolation to me. You are all free now. Go and live your own lives with my blessing."

The sapling bowed low to her as it sunk its roots deep into the rich soil beneath it and spread its leaves to catch the suns' rays. The hummingbirds zoomed away to feast on the nectar of the sacred Luna tree's white flowers, and the stick insect spread its translucent wings and flew up and out of sight. Only the black rabbit remained near Amelia, following in her steps and munching on the pink clover that grew in abundance on the Ridge.

As she worked, Amelia couldn't help pondering what Myriad's horrific act might mean. Had open warfare broken out in the ocean depths? If so, did any creature of the sea, land, or air stand a chance against such ruthless power? And she wondered for the thousandth time where Beatrice was and if she was safe. Would she ever see her friend again?

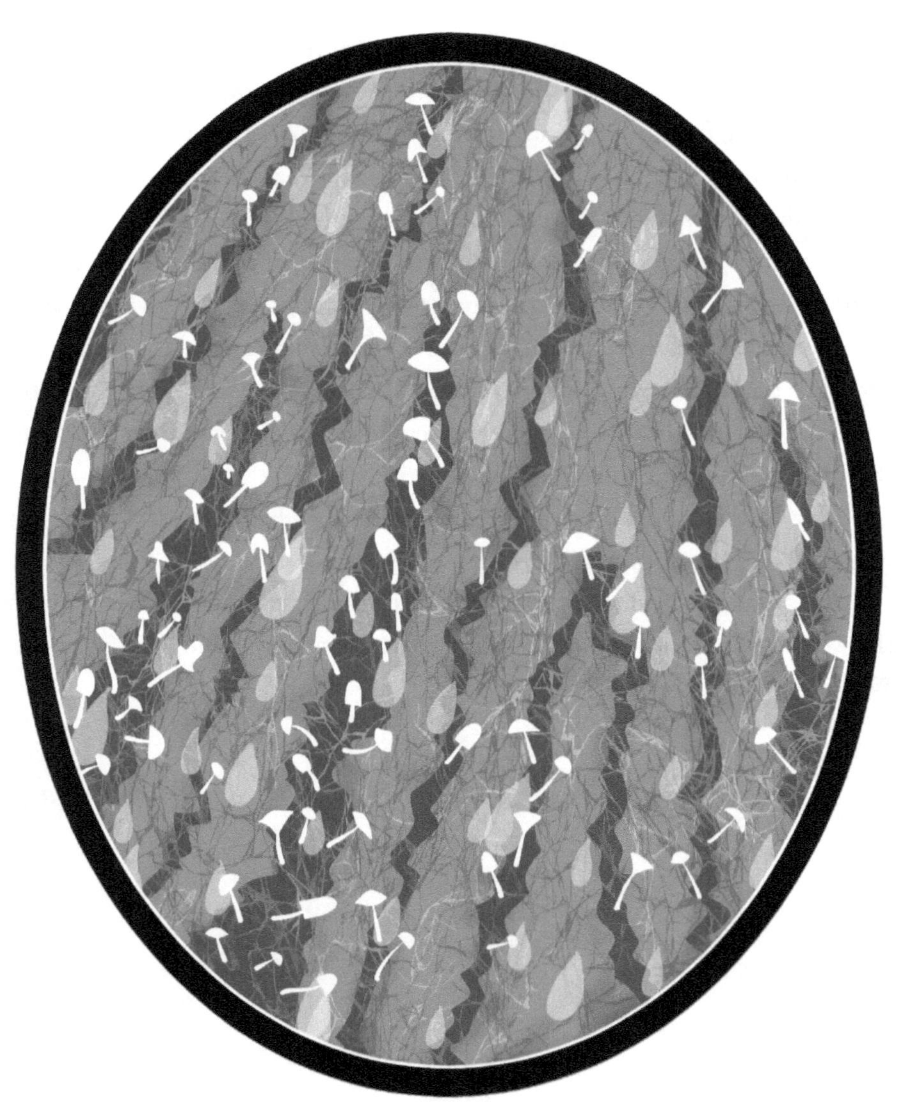

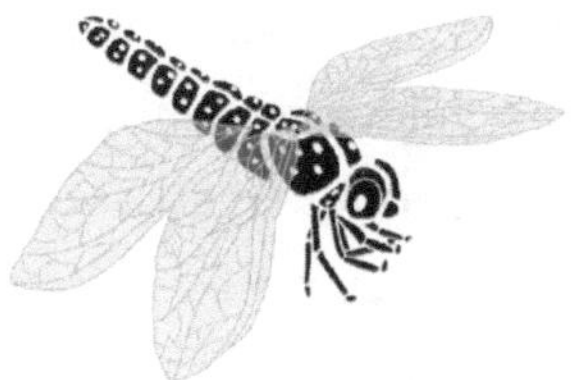

CHAPTER 21

BLESSED BABIES AND A PIRATE'S TALE

MEANWHILE, BIX WAS MAKING the most of his time among his peers. While known as Blessed Babies because of their place of origin, their ages ranged widely. Some were elderly, making perhaps their final pilgrimage to this hallowed ground while others were still children, though wise beyond their years in many cases, returning to the Ridge for the first time since their birth.

They also sensed the murder of the omes, and Bix was quick to explain the circumstances of their quest, how it was related to Myriad, and his wish to rescue Beatrice, unbind Coral from her curse, and free Lichen's ocean from the tyranny of the wrathful kraken. Typical of Blessed Babies, they listened silently, without judgment in an atmosphere of unconditional acceptance and support.

When Bix finished his tale, the Blessed Babies wordlessly split off into three groups as though by an unspoken yet common agreement. One group thrust their fingers deep into the soil, the second placed their hands on the trees of the sacred grove, and the third stretched their arms high above their heads as if to touch the sky itself. In this way, they connected with the spirit of Fungi Ridge and opened their minds to any wisdom it might offer them. For a time, there was no visible result from their actions, but then the rains began.

There are two common types of rain showers in Lichen. One is so chill and dark and gloomy that it is impossible not to feel oppressed by it, but this was the other kind: warm and loving and full of gentle raindrops backlit by the three suns and giving the appearance of liquid amber falling from the clouds.

The Blessed Babies sprang up and leapt around like an army of wild frogs, hopping and dancing and squealing in delight. "Rain! Rain! Rain!" they chanted, grinning ear to ear and collecting the amber water on their tongues.

Blessed Babies aren't exactly spoiled when they're young, but as a rule, they aren't reined in the way many children are either. They were known to be free spirits who behaved without regard for what anyone thought of them, so their antics were looked upon most indulgently by other visitors to the grove.

The mushroom pilgrims also took note of the Blessed Babies' celebration and meditated upon it, for fungi see connections and meaning in everything they observe and this event was no exception. The rains spoke a language only the fungi could understand, and they wasted no time communicating their findings to the person most anxious to hear it.

Far away from the dance of the Blessed Babies, the cloud skydragon Iggy floated down from their nest in Amelia's hair to whisper in her ear. "The pilgrims have spoken. There has been a revelation in the song of the rains. The kraken is not what it seems, and it is foretold that the lost button is the key to defeating it. She is in a safe place now but must return to Myriad and convince it she craves the power and love it offers. Only by gaining its trust and getting close enough to touch it will it be overcome."

Shocked and angered at this unexpected and unwelcome news, Amelia's first thought was that she had never heard anything more nonsensical in her life. The battle on the skyboat had shown how unimaginably dangerous the kraken could be. The fungi were mistaken if they believed she would encourage anyone, let alone her best friend, to cuddle up to such a creature.

"We know what you are thinking," Iggy said, "but we speak true. If the button does not undertake this task, then all hope will be lost for Lichen. The kraken will continue to destroy the creatures of the sea in its fury and when it is done there, it will come ashore to see what other havoc it can commit."

"But I don't even know how to find Beatrice. Besides, Coral would kill me if I sent her wife off to fight Myriad alone."

"The sea witch advised you to find Iggy because we are her friend and want to help. She will trust our advice and that of the fungi. They know where the button is. You can travel there as soon as your duties as Record Keeper come to an end. But that is not all."

"There's more?" Amelia cried in dismay, not certain she wanted to hear anything else.

"Yes. The Blessed Baby Bix has a vital part to play in events yet to come and must travel with you."

Amelia tried to censor her thoughts so as not to offend the fungi with her serious doubts that Bix could ever be of much assistance to anyone, but they heard her just the same. Fortunately, they were tolerantly amused at her misgivings, being used to the frailties and foolishness of Lichens when compared to themselves.

Sensing the gentle forbearance of these infinitely wise beings, Amelia suddenly felt very small and extremely humble. She had never missed her house and garden and uneventful life more. These grand adventures and dangerous battles were all well and good for some, but then again, the fungi had proven their wisdom over and over throughout the history of Lichen. If they said Beatrice could beat the monster, she had to have faith and do her part. But it didn't mean she had to like it!

Another of Amelia's ex-tattoos, One-Eyed Jack, had observed the Blessed Babies' joyful celebration in the rain, but the strangeness of their behavior to his eye only increased his sense of being out of place not only on Fungi Ridge but in Lichen itself. He belonged in space, sailing the solar waves, and longed more than ever for the chance to stand at the helm of his old ship once again.

Feeling low, he returned to the skyboat and went down to the cabin to see if there were any spirits or ale to drown his sorrows. Lichens not being very fond of alcoholic beverages, he found nothing but a weak beetroot wine that tasted too bitter to his palate to drink enough of for his purpose.

He noticed Click watching him and grinning at the face the pirate made as he sampled the wine. The lad was visiting his parents, having pulled up a chair to the photograph in order to chat with them.

Perhaps sensing the pirate was feeling isolated and lonely, Star invited Jack to join them. "Our ways must be unfamiliar to you, but we know just as little about your own way of life. What did you do before you came here?"

Moon nodded encouragingly and Click's eyes lit up with excitement at the prospect of hearing about life beyond Lichen. Jack pulled another chair up to the photograph, flicking his blond braid back off his shoulder, crossing his boot-shod feet in front of him, and lighting an elegant, long-stemmed pipe as he settled in to tell his tale.

"Me home is called Limbo and its people are called Loamies. Our skin color as ye see is a swirl of the colors of the soil we tend: orange, cranberry, and purple. It's dark there half the year which makes it a mighty struggle to provide enough light and heat for those that are in need. Space pirates like me harvest electrified filaments from the nests of the shrieking kiki birds on the planet Blim. It's more perilous than ye can imagine. There are terrible bad solar storms around Blim and their Navy ships will grant no quarter if they catch ye at it."

"It sounds like important work," said Moon. "Your parents must be very proud of you."

"Aye, ye would think so, wouldn't ye, but piracy is not rated so highly as a trade where I come from. 'We're people of the soil' is what Ma said to me, seeking to shame me when I abandoned the land and took to the sky. 'Loamies are ground people. We do not flit about above like birds!' she would say."

"Couldn't she see the good you were doing?" asked Click.

"Well, to be fair, it is nothing but thievery plain and simple when ye come right down to it, even though Blim has more than enough electricity to spare and it's a blessing and a boon to the Loamies to have the extra. No, I'd not seen me folks in many a long year, even before I was trapped in that cursed ink."

"How sad," Star murmured sympathetically. "But how did you come to be trapped?"

"It was during our last mission. The storms that day were the worst we'd ever encountered and me ship, *The Ghost,* was as near to breaking into pieces as I'd ever seen. I did me best to keep the crew's spirits up, but they were despondent as the ship foundered. The Door of Lost Souls can sense such despair no matter how far away, and it appeared alongside us at the height of our struggles. Several of the crew looked ready to dive overboard and into the open door, but I pulled 'em right back again. Sorry to say I lost me footing and fell in me own self."

"You're a real hero," Click said with stars in his eyes.

"Not so," Jack replied. "I only did what any captain would do to look after his crew, for they become like a family with everything ye go through together and how ye must depend one upon the other. The worst part is not knowing what happened to *The Ghost* after I left. For all I know, the ship's no more and the crew are all goners. It torments me to think I might have condemned those I saved from the door to an even worse fate. I mean to go back and find out one day if possible."

"Can I go with him?" Click asked his parents. "I've spent so long up in the skies, I feel like I've seen everything there is to be seen here. I want to travel to other planets and see what's out there."

"You don't need our permission," Moon replied. "You're grown up now, and it's past time you lived your own life now you have the opportunity."

"But Jack may have different plans," Star observed.

The pirate laid a hand on Click's shoulder. "This lad reminds me of me own self when I was his age. Restless and wild and eager to see all there is to see in the great beyond. If I get a chance to return home, ye'll be mighty welcome to come along and apprentice with me and see if the space sailing life is the one for ye."

"That's terrific! When can we leave?"

"Patience now, matey. Don't ye want to wait and find out if Beatrice Buttons can be rescued? Ye and yer brother owe her and Amelia Arrowheart a debt or two."

"But it's taking forever! When do you think we'll hear something?"

"We'll hear when we hear. If ye're gonna be part of my crew, it's time to learn to take orders. Stow yer oars and bide awhile in peace. If me pocket watch is right, the captain's time as Record Keeper will be coming to a close any time now. She'll tell us what she's found out when she's good and ready."

Click was wise enough to follow his new captain's advice, but his thoughts were written across his face plainly enough: *She'd better hurry up!*

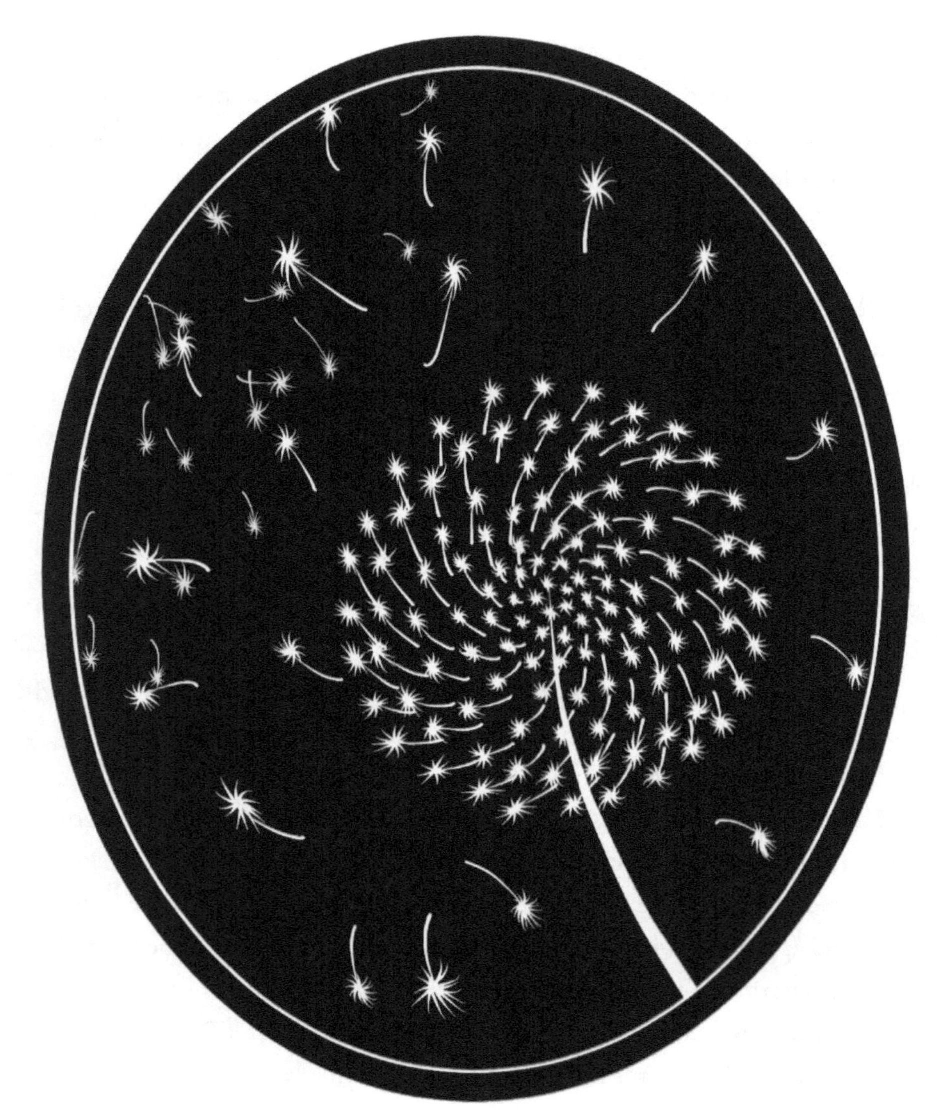

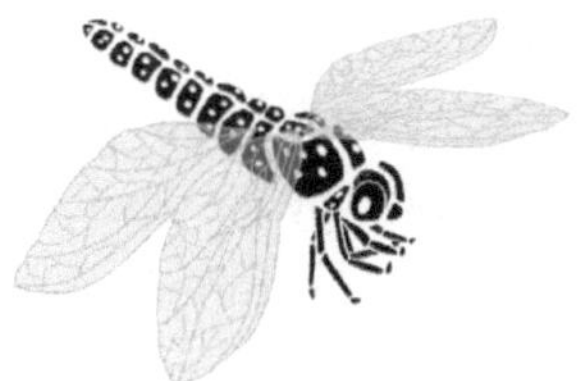

CHAPTER 22

TRAVELS WITH STORMY

BLISTERS CHAFED UNDER BEATRICE'S arms as her crutches slipped and slid along the soft, giving beach sand. She didn't complain, but Stormy noticed her exhaustion and pain, lifting Beatrice easily onto her back once more to give her a respite from her struggles.

"It's not far now. We're almost to the Great Crater. There's a tunnel system under the sea which connects many islands, but only sea witches use them. I think Myriad is unaware of or uninterested in these highways as it feels the ocean waters are the only place worth caring about. It will be the safest way for us to travel without attracting its attention."

"How cool! I can't wait to see them!"

"I love how excited you get about things, sister-in-law. It is one of your most endearing qualities."

"You weren't so impressed with me when we first met," Beatrice reminded her.

"True. I don't have the patience most of my sisters do," Stormy admitted, "but you've grown on me upon further acquaintance."

They came to the rim of a huge cavity that looked vast and bottomless.

"And down we go," said Stormy.

"How?"

"Look close. Can you see the stairway? It is constructed in such a way as to create an optical illusion, so it isn't easy for those not in the know to stumble across it. Hang on to me tightly. About halfway down, you'll see the obsidian tunnel we're looking for."

After winding down the sides of the crater for what seemed a very long time, Stormy confidently stepped off the stairs at the exact right spot for the tunnel entrance, even though it was hidden behind a curtain of hanging moss. She carried her passenger into a low-ceilinged cave. The top and sides of the cave were rough and chipped, but the ground where Stormy set Beatrice down was smoother, like it had been worn down by the passing of many feet over millennia.

Beatrice felt lost in the darkness of the tunnel until Stormy placed a hand over her eyes and cast a spell to give her the ability to see through the gloom. "For you, nothing may hide in the shadows unseen. Adaptable eyes you now possess. May they serve you well wherever your life's journey takes you."

Along with her gills and her ability to communicate with nature, this latest gift made Beatrice feel less and less like your average land-dwelling Lichen and more akin to seafolk. She was neither alarmed nor pleased by this particularly. For such a curious mind, it all added up to another adventure, albeit one more potentially life-changing than most she had experienced so far.

Not so life-changing as the loss of her leg, of course. For such an independent-minded soul, she couldn't help but be aware of how much assistance she now required. The crutches kept her reasonably mobile, but they were awkward. She hoped when she was reunited with Coral, her wife could magic her up an artificial limb that would make things a little easier.

After resting in the cave, the sea witch lifted Beatrice onto her back again. Mile after mile passed with the muffled sound of Stormy's bare feet stepping nimbly along the smooth rock and the never-ending obsidian darkness.

To pass the time during their trek, Beatrice sang every song she knew and recounted stories from her travels. Her voice was giving out by the time she spotted a tiny pinprick of light in the distance with relief. It widened out into bright sunshine as they reached the end of the tunnel and emerged onto another island shore. The sea breeze and open air were a refreshing change after the dank and clammy atmosphere of the tunnel.

"Where are we now?" Bea asked.

"One of a string of islands that cross the sea. They're called the Pearls, our own necklace of ocean treasure where we witches often spend time when we're on land, for many of us are by nature solitary creatures."

The sea witch had just set Beatrice down in the sand and was deciding on their next move when she sensed the destruction of the omes by Myriad in her soul. She began to keen in grief along with all of her far-flung sisters, for seafolk are so attuned to life in Lichen that they instantly felt and understood the loss. The note they sang was the unique energy signature given off by the omes as they perished, a final tribute by the witches to creatures that were no more.

Stormy was startled from her mourning to realize Beatrice was also singing the same high-pitched note. The sea witch lay her palms on either side of her sister-in-law's head and placed a vision of the omes into her mind. Bea's face lit up with pleasure at the sight of the unique creatures, then fell again as she remembered such lovely things were no more.

"I've never seen a live ome and now I never will!" she cried, before asking Stormy, "Did you send me the message about their death?"

"No, sea witches instinctively sense when such profound loss occurs but you shouldn't have been able to feel it or hear our keening. It is in a register much too high for any landfolk to hear."

"Then why can I?"

"Truly, sister-by-marriage, I don't know, except I've noticed a strangeness in you since we've been together. The only witches in Lichen are sea witches, and yet you can weave spells with healing magic in them. Your song renewed my energy when I was weary. I can only think Myriad has brought about this transformation but for what purpose I cannot imagine."

Beatrice shimmered with shame. "Am I an abomination? Will the sea witches strike me down?"

"Little sister, magic is a gift, never an abomination." She wiped away Beatrice's tears and peered closely at her. "Your aura is a rainbow, like the Blessed Babies. Are you a Blessed Baby?"

"No," Beatrice replied with a chuckle. "I was born at our house. My mother didn't have any birthing pains though. I slid right out of her womb while she slept in the night. She and my father woke to find me nestled at her breast feeding, with no idea how I came to be way up there on my own. Guess I've been a traveler from my very first breath."

Stormy considered this information. "You are a mystery, Beatrice Buttons. No longer just one of the landfolk but a hybrid of sea and soil and the powers they hold. One my sisterhood will embrace into our fold not only as Coral's wife but as a new breed of witch, equal in magic to us all. I think you have the potential to be of immeasurable value. Have patience and believe in me, if not yourself, for I am the oldest and wisest of us and am seldom proved wrong."

Beatrice could only smile at this advice and wipe away her tears, but it was an uneasy feeling to think she might be something new and unique in all of Lichen. The idea would take some getting used to.

"Company will be arriving soon," Stormy said. "We'll create a feast to restore our strength and raise the potency of our magic so that we may be as prepared as possible for whatever comes next."

In the growing darkness, two shapes emerged from the shadows. They were tall and thin and identical except one smiled with the corners of her mouth turned up and the other had a smile that turned down like a frown before turning up at the corners. Both had midnight blue eyes and lavender hair with vibrant yellow-green highlights.

Stormy introduced them to Bea. "These are my most beloved sisters, Turtle and Tern. Normally, we eat a vegetarian diet as we respect all sentient living things, but in times of extreme crisis, sea creatures offer up their energy to us as a precious sacrifice so we might have the best chance of defending those who reside below the waves. Weep for them if you must, honor them absolutely, but respect them by swallowing every bite while offering prayers of thanksgiving for each life."

Beatrice did weep to see the variety and number of beings offering themselves up. They crawled out of the sea or flung themselves onto the beach willingly, and she did her part to make sure their sacrifice was not in vain by eating whatever was put in front of her without protest.

Some creatures were roasted over the fire, some simmered in a makeshift clay pot of boiling water, and some were served raw. It was not always the most appetizing feast. They ate fish eyes to bring vision to their magic and raw mollusks while chanting "to the East, to the West, to the North, to the South" as they slurped them down to bring strength.

Many other unfamiliar dishes followed, and Beatrice's jaws grew wearied and sore from chewing. She didn't complain, but Stormy must have sensed her suffering. She kissed Beatrice on the forehead above the bridge of her nose with the feather-warm whisper of a spell and the aching went away. A tremendous sense of power surged through her body.

Working herself up into a frenzy, Beatrice frothed at the mouth as sea foam poured out. The witches watched in amazement and joy at this outward sign of power. She held a whole ocean of life within her body, and they marveled that Coral had swept this unusual creature off her feet and married her, almost as though their sister had sensed the greatness latent within her bride.

Stormy, Turtle, and Tern embraced Beatrice in celebration. They gathered armfuls of pink wishmaker flowers from the sand dunes and waved them, whirling in the wind like tops. The seeds broke away, twirling like ballerina dancers, spinning in pastel rainbow circles, and lofting their way off to sea. Each seed represented a hope, a dream, and even a promise for a better future.

Exhilarated from the feasting and excitement, the four witches rested on the beach, listening to the gentle lullaby of the sea as dawn rose upon a new day. What challenges it would hold they could not predict, but they were as ready for them as it was possible to be.

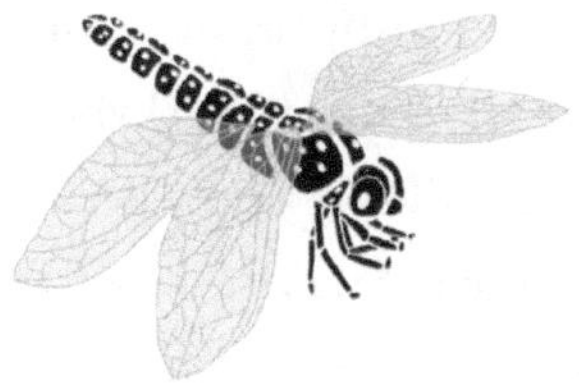

CHAPTER 23

A REUNION

As NIGHT DESCENDED UPON Fungi Ridge, Amelia struggled with a bitter-sweet mix of emotions as her recordkeeping duties came to an end. Regret at leaving behind a task she had greatly enjoyed and suited her observational talents so well fought with impatience to gather her crew together so they could set out at last to find Beatrice.

Loath to mar Coral's beautiful gift, she tore her notes from the moon journal most reluctantly but was delighted to find the book magically mended itself, reforming blank pages from the roughly torn edges. A thrill ran through her at the realization her words and sketches would become part of the permanent record of Lichen, an honor beyond any she had ever imagined in her formerly sedate existence. With the announcement of the next Record Keeper, Amelia was at last free to seek out her companions.

She found Bix among the other Blessed Babies looking happier than she'd ever seen him. She couldn't help but feel guilty at separating him from a place where he was completely accepted and free to blossom as himself, but when she waved at him tentatively, Bix ran toward her eagerly as though overjoyed to be reunited.

Perhaps this is what it is like to be loved by a child, she thought, returning Bix's grin with a dignified nod.

They had turned toward the skyboat when Amelia noticed the black rabbit was still following her. She knelt and whispered gently to it. "You'd better stay here, my friend. We are off into unknown dangers."

The rabbit only blinked its dark eyes at her.

"I think it wants to come with us," said Bix, gathering the creature in his arms. "It's so soft. I've never had a pet. Can't we keep it?"

"It's a free being now," Amelia replied, "not to be held captive anymore, but I suppose if it really wants to accompany us, we must respect its wishes."

They used their necklaces to float up to the skyboat where they found Jack and Click still chatting with Moon and Star below deck.

"What do you have there, dear?" Star asked Bix.

"A new friend," Bix said, setting the rabbit down and fetching some weavergrass from the pantry for it to nibble. "I'm going to call it Ome, in honor of those that are no more."

"Whatever are you on about?!" Click cried. "We've been waiting forever and you've been playing about with a stupid pet."

"What did I say about learning patience, me lad?" Jack admonished him before turning to Amelia. "What've ye found out, Captain?"

"The fungi have spoken. They say Beatrice is in a safe place for now, but according to them, she must return to the kraken to perform some kind of ritual in order to vanquish it."

"Return to the kraken!" Star exclaimed. "That sounds horribly dangerous. Is there no other way?"

Amelia shook her head sadly. "They say not, and they are among the wisest beings in Lichen. But that's not all. They say Bix also has an important role to play."

Click scoffed. "What could he possibly do?"

"He is a Blessed Baby," Amelia scolded, "and all Blessed Babies do at least one important thing in their lives as you must know."

"I'll have to see it to believe it." Click strode off in a huff, scuffing his feet and hunching his shoulders as he vaulted up the cabin steps and out of sight.

Bix sniffed and blinked back tears, still unused to the idea that he and his brother were no longer as close as they had always been.

"Do you have that handkerchief I gave you?" Amelia asked.

Bix nodded.

"Good. This is exactly the kind of occasion it's perfect for." She had an alarming thought. "Oh, and Bix, when your handkerchief is full, walk to the edge of the boat and shake it out. If that doesn't work, give it to me to wash for you."

Bix nodded again. It didn't seem the best time to admit he hadn't used the handkerchief even once, too impressed by the soft, clean linen to want to sully it. When Amelia looked away, he wiped his nose along his sleeve.

Jack caught his eye and gave him a wink. "Don't worry, lad. Yer brother will come around. If the captain has faith in ye, then so do I. Come up on deck and ye can help us with the rigging. It's high time we set sail!"

And so once again, the dragonfly boat took wing, following the path the fungi had indicated, but its crew soon discovered they had one additional passenger. When Amelia went below decks to prepare a late supper, she was surprised to find a delicate cloud skydragon comfortably curled up on her pea pod bed next to a snoozing black rabbit.

"We thought to come with you," Iggy said. "We may be of help with the missing button. We may not. We cannot say for certain, but we find your company restful."

"You are most welcome, of course," Amelia replied with deepest sincerity. She was both highly flattered at the compliment and delighted to learn she need not part ways with her new friend just yet. She'd become accustomed to their constant companionship and had secretly been dreading their absence, even though their propensity for referring to Beatrice as a button was disconcerting.

After journeying through the night, the travelers were relieved to see Lichen's suns peeking over the horizon as dawn broke. Below them, the waters churned. Shapeshifters, merpeople, and sea witches were gathering, prepared to go into battle should they be called upon, and the ocean teemed with every kind of sea creature swimming in all directions to escape Myriad's anger.

As for the kraken, deserted and furious, it grew ever lonelier and more obsessed with the idea of Beatrice. Its wrath at her escape and continued concealment knew no bounds, and it was obvious to all that a crisis of some sort was both fast approaching and unavoidable.

As the suns rose higher in the sky, Jack hollered welcome news from his perch in the crow's nest. "Land, ho, off the starboard bow!"

Everyone on deck rushed to the side of the boat to see. Four distant figures waved at them from a sandy island, but they were too far away to be easily recognized.

"Wonder who they are," said Click.

"Three are sea witches," replied Iggy. "Turtle, Tern, and Stormy by name. We have crossed paths before. And we imagine the fourth will be our missing button, for this is the exact spot the fungi predicted we should find her."

The skydragon was proven right and a most happy reunion ensued once the skyboat was tethered to some rocks along the shoreline.

Although not fond of hugging, Amelia was so overcome to see her friend safe and sound, she couldn't help running over and tearfully embracing her, nearly knocking Beatrice off her crutches in her enthusiasm.

"Oh, Bea! I thought we'd never see you again, but your leg!" Amelia cried out in dismay, noticing the grievous injury Bea had suffered.

"Don't worry, Melia. I won't lie. It was a dreadful shock, but I'm getting used to it. Coral will no doubt magic me up a replacement made out of driftwood or some such if I ever make it back to the lighthouse." She looked more closely at Amelia and cried, "I knew there was something different about you! Your braid! What's happened to it?"

"The kraken grabbed it when we were attacked and would have pulled me overboard if Jack hadn't cut it off with his sword. Certainly is easier to take care of now, but that's neither here nor there. I'm sorry it took us so long to find you! We've been worried sick, but Coral sent us to Fungi Ridge to get advice on rescuing you and defeating Myriad and I was made Record Keeper and had to serve out my term and we met a cloud skydragon! And the fungi said you and Bix together will vanquish the kraken. Did you know he was a Blessed Baby? And look, Click has grown up!"

Beatrice stared at her friend in open-mouthed amazement at this barrage of startling information. She was still standing like that when Stormy approached Amelia, using a long, thin razor shell to dig a ball of earwax out of her ear. The sea witch popped the wax onto her tongue where she savored it slowly, absorbing all that the fungi had told the Record Keeper from the taste alone.

"Nasty!" Bix cried with a mix of disgust and admiration.

Tern scowled at him while Turtle winked and grinned. Beatrice decided to ignore this strange procedure in favor of focusing on the last thing Amelia had said first.

"How did Click grow up? And why didn't Bix? Are their parents still trapped?"

"Click decided he wanted to grow up and go off on his own adventures," Amelia explained. "Coral wove a spell to make him a little older but not as old as his natural age. Bix, however, insists on remaining as he is, at least for now. His parents are still in the photo, but Coral magicked it to be life-sized. The frame is a door, so the boys can step into their photograph and hug them whenever they want. Coral can try to bring them out of it, but she can't guarantee the results, so they decided to wait until this business with the kraken is over since Bix is to have his own part to play and they want to make sure he's alright."

Beatrice gazed at the unpromising-looking Bix with skepticism. It seemed highly unlikely to her that the freckle-faced imp was to be a hero.

Bix solemnly pulled his handkerchief from his pocket, holding it up for inspection. "Miss Amelia gave me one of her papa's handkerchiefs so I could become more civilized in my grooming habits."

Examining the suspiciously clean linen, Beatrice would have quizzed him further if she hadn't been distracted by Iggy floating in front of her face to speak to her.

"Greetings, lost button."

"And who or what are you?"

"Bea, this is Iggy, the cloud skydragon I mentioned. They've joined our cause," said Amelia.

Beatrice's head spun. It was becoming obvious Amelia had been up to all kinds of adventures without her. Fungi Ridge, record keeping, skydragons that talked. She thought bitterly that she had not fared half as well since they'd parted, but then remembered her new powers which even now she did not understand the full extent of, so perhaps it evened out.

Stormy came out of her reverie with the earwax to confirm all that the fungi had told Amelia. Beatrice was to use her new-found magic to tame the kraken and Bix would assist in some way that was as yet unclear.

"What kind of magic do you think I'm meant to perform? How will I even get close to Myriad? The last time we met, it tried to kill me," she reminded Stormy.

"If it had meant to kill you, it could have easily. Instead, it bestowed both gills and magic upon you and seems to be lamenting your loss. I wonder if it doesn't feel some affection toward you, either through its everlasting jealousy of Coral or because of some new emotion of its own. It is possible I am deadly wrong and you will be struck down on sight, but I am rarely mistaken."

"I don't like the sound of that thing being in love with me if that's what you're suggesting, and I don't think my wife would appreciate it either."

"Coral is first and foremost a sea witch. She will understand and appreciate the need for you to be close to Myriad and perhaps even collect some part of it. After all, much of our own magic works exactly that way. Either skin cells or saliva should do. Maybe kissing would be the best option. You could close your eyes as if overcome with passion which might make the experience more palatable, allowing you to focus on the taste. Repeat the word *reveal* to yourself and I believe the answer as to what you must do next will come to you."

"Are you serious?" Amelia cried. "How can you ask Beatrice to do such a perilous and disgusting thing?"

"Magic is often neither pretty nor easy," Stormy replied, "but our powers confer unique responsibilities upon us. The kraken is a terrible danger to every creature under the sea and for the landfolk of Lichen should it ever grow tired of its watery existence and come ashore. It is Beatrice the creature is attracted to, so it is she who is in the unique position of getting closer to it than even I could manage."

Amelia would have protested further on behalf of her friend, but Beatrice placed a hand on her arm to stop her.

"I trust the wisdom of the fungi, and I trust Stormy. If they say I have to be the one to do this, then I have no choice. I'd rather die trying than allow Myriad to continue to rampage. The pain I felt at the extinction of the omes is one I'll never forget. I'd do anything to save another species from such a fate."

With that, she limped away into the sea before any could stop her. In true Buttons fashion, she didn't look back even once to wave or shout farewell. Before Amelia had recovered from the shock, her friend disappeared beneath the waves and was gone. Only a pair of crutches left floating on the surface served as testament she had ever been there at all.

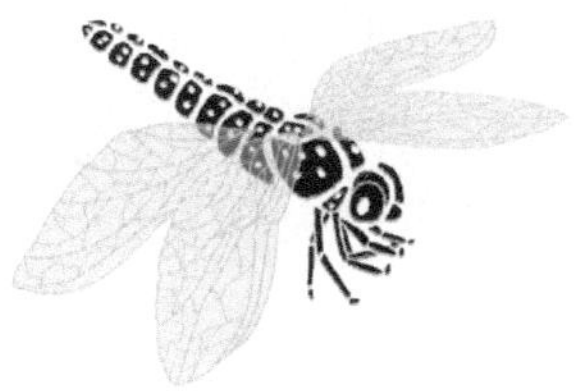

CHAPTER 24

LYING TO CORAL

"I WILL NEVER GET used to Beatrice simply disappearing without even saying goodbye," Amelia cried in dismay.

"You should understand that is the way of all Buttons by now," Stormy admonished. "She has understood her duty and means to carry it out without delay. I feel sure we will see her again. In the meantime, I suggest you return to the lighthouse until we receive further word. Leave Bix here with me since he has a role to play. We may be able to assist him," she added, indicating herself and Turtle and Tern who stood nearby.

"Can't I do anything?"

"Your time may come or it may not, the same as for the others who travel with you. It may be you have fulfilled your purpose simply by bringing word from the fungi and delivering Bix to us. I cannot say for certain. While we wait for events to reveal themselves, you can be a comfort to our sister at the lighthouse. But first, I will lay a spell on you that will prevent Coral from seeing in your thoughts what Beatrice is up to. The kraken has a psychic connection with our sister, and we do not want her to accidentally alert it to our plan."

Amelia bowed her head to the eldest witch, who lay a hand upon her, chanting a few words that sent a chill through her mind. Then Amelia, Jack, Click and Iggy reboarded the dragonfly boat, hauled up anchor, and were soon floating away into the unsettled gray clouds above.

Bix felt very small and alone as the skyboat disappeared until Turtle walked over to him and tickled him along the ribs before settling him high on her shoulders.

"What will we do now?" Bix asked the three witches.

"We'll join the other seafolk on the fringe of the battle," replied Stormy. "I bet you've never traveled to the bottom of the ocean before."

"No," he admitted, both excited and apprehensive at the idea.

"You will now, but don't fret. Every sea witch and other creature under the sea will want to be your protector. You have the power to do a great good for all of us by banishing Myriad from these waters. Do you have any idea of how you might accomplish this?"

"I've a few. I am a Blessed Baby, you know," he said self-importantly. "And we always do remarkable things."

Back aboard the skyboat, Amelia sat up in her pea pod bed, arms crossed, and prepared to square off against Coral, who had come to visit in her dream. She didn't like the idea of deceiving Beatrice's wife but knew it was in her friend's best interest to prevent the sea witch from discovering the plan and inadvertently warning the kraken.

Coral studied Amelia carefully. "You have gathered secrets since last we met. Things you either don't want to tell me or aren't allowed to."

"Stormy laid a spell on me to prevent it, so it's just as well that you don't ask."

"Stormy? My eldest sister?"

Amelia gasped, mortified she had let slip even that much.

Coral smiled sadly. "Don't worry. If the spell is one of Stormy's, I cannot break it, but it comforts me to learn she is involved. She will help Beatrice for my sake if it is within her power to do so. But who is atop your head? Is that an old friend I spy?"

The skydragon floated over to Coral. "Yes, it is us. Iggy."

"And how are you, my dear?"

"As well as can be expected, though we haven't seen our little wisplings as often as we would like. At last count, we had 26,000 offspring, give or take. Family reunions are crowded."

"I can imagine. Shall I speed your return to the lighthouse? Traveling can be tedious."

"Best not. Schemes are in motion to which we will have nothing much to offer except our patience. Let time unravel as it will."

Coral knitted her brow, frustrated at the lack of control she was allowed to exert, but if her eldest sister had forbidden Coral's curiosity, she knew she must have had a good reason.

"I suppose there's no need for me to haunt your dreams then if I'm not allowed to be a part of the plan. I will see you when you arrive. Until then, sweet slumbers," Coral said with a sigh before slowly fading away.

When Amelia awoke, she felt terribly guilty at shutting out someone who had been so good to her and was suffering mightily from not knowing what had happened or might happen next to her very own wife. She had to remind herself over and over that this secrecy was vital for the success of their plan. Only when Myriad was vanquished would Coral and Beatrice truly be safe, but it worried her all the same.

Her traveling companions weren't much better off. Click was full of nerves and chattered non-stop, excited about his apprenticeship and impatient to start his new life exploring space.

One-Eyed Jack was itching to move on too and hoped the sea witch was ready to send him home. He'd made the momentous decision to come back to life to join in the battle against the kraken when Beatrice first disappeared, but since then, he'd been of relatively little use other than making sure everything aboard the skyboat remained shipshape. His longing to return to his old life and command left him as antsy and discontented as Click.

Amelia attempted to cheer them both up, unsuccessfully, so gave up in disgust and spent her time petting Ome, who hopped around at her heels and slept on her bed, and talking to Moon and Star or Iggy. The skydragon had experienced much in their long life and Amelia got so lost in their winding tales, the time passed quickly for her at least.

All were relieved when the Kaleidoscope Lighthouse came into view once more. They were soon docked, met by Coral, who saw at once that the group was not entirely in sympathy with one another or themselves. She set aside her concern for Beatrice for a moment to quiz them.

"You all seem preoccupied," she observed. "Are you missing your brother already, Click?"

"Not a bit. He's a Blessed Baby, and he's off doing important things while I just hang around doing nothing."

"What would you like to do?"

"Travel with Jack. I want to see these other worlds he talks about. Planets out beyond our moons."

"And what do you think, Jack?" Coral asked.

"I'll admit to a most fearful hankering for home. I've me own responsibilities to tend to, and long-neglected they are, but I wouldn't mind having a new matey aboard whatever ship I can lay hands upon if *The Ghost* is no more."

"I don't see why that couldn't be arranged once our current situation is resolved," Coral reassured them. "Speaking of which, I think I've shown admirable self-restraint so far, but I believe I'm owed some sort of explanation or reassurances about my wife's fate."

Iggy circled around her head. "Congratulations to you for being such a pillar of patience and fortitude. Would you perhaps like us to pat you on the back or is that something you care to do yourself?"

Coral raised an eyebrow at the skydragon's wry comment as not many dare to scold a sea witch.

Iggy continued. "The lost button escaped once but has decided to return to the kraken. She is smitten with it."

Amelia paled at the lie. She understood they needed Coral to believe Beatrice was in love with the kraken so Myriad would believe it also, but it was hard to stand by while Coral was struck to the heart.

"You're lying! I understand my wife better than anyone. Her love for me is true. She would never want to live with such a monster. Besides, she can't even breathe underwater, so I know it's a lie."

"Myriad thoughtfully provided her with gills, something you neglected to do," Iggy pointed out. "And it endowed her with magic as powerful as any sea witch. Maybe more so. Why wouldn't she prefer to live with a being who has given her such precious gifts?"

Coral had known Iggy for eons and had never known them to lie before. She had no way of knowing the skydragon was quite content to lie on the rare occasion when it was truly called for. At their words, a rage and hurt such as she had never experienced rose up within her, calling forth lightning and thunder, hail and sheets of blinding rain.

A sea witch scorned has the power to create a cyclone of destruction that is awe-inspiring to behold. She flung this one far out over the churning waters as a message to Myriad deep in the sea so it might feel her rage and scorn and pain at her wife's betrayal.

Tears poured down Amelia's cheeks, but Iggy gently brushed them away with one of their leafy tentacles and spoke softly into her ear. "It had to be done. The only hope the button has is for the kraken to believe it has truly won her away from the sea witch."

Amelia nodded. She hated lies, especially ones that hurt someone she cared about, but sometimes they were the only weapon at hand. She only hoped it would be enough to keep Beatrice safe.

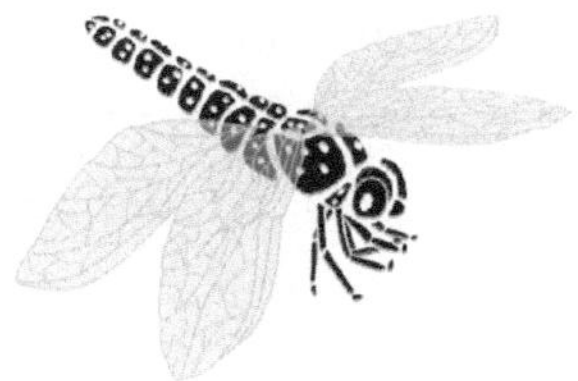

CHAPTER 25

BEATRICE IS VERY BRAVE

FEELING UNBALANCED FROM HER missing limb, Beatrice made the long swim back to the kraken alone, her thoughts twirling and spinning almost as much as the storm Coral unleashed overhead. How was she to pull off convincing a sea monster she was in love with it? That she would willingly return to the fiend who had kidnapped her and eaten her leg?

She decided one emotion she could genuinely project was excitement with the powerful magic and gills the kraken had bestowed upon her. She did have that to be grateful for, even if it came at too high a cost. Perhaps if she pretended to be cross that her own wife had never given her such tremendous gifts, Myriad would think it had won her over. Even imagining such a lie made Beatrice feel a traitor to the woman who owned her heart, but she hoped a creature who knew little about true love might believe such a motive.

But how could she be sure the kraken didn't just want her back to finish the job it had started? Stormy believed the gift of gills and strong magic and Myriad's lamentations at losing her meant it was infatuated with her, but what if the sea witch was wrong? Her return might end up being disastrous unless she could win the monster over quickly.

Maybe it would help if she was a more equal companion in size to the enormous creature. A wild idea, perhaps, but Beatrice wondered if she could use her magic to grow taller and thus be more of a match physically. Hoping fervently she would be able to return to her normal height once the kraken was conquered, she concentrated on stretching her arms and leg, fingers and toes. She didn't even realize it was working until she noticed her foot was now the same size as a large manta ray that passed by.

Next, she tried to summon memories of when she first met Coral so many years ago. If she could keep those warm and lovely emotions in mind, she might be able to project the feeling of devotion and attraction to Myriad. She remembered Coral's soft lips the first time they kissed and running her fingers through the sea witch's long blue hair. The sense of belonging and complete peace whenever she visited her wife at the lighthouse.

Recalling the terrible form of the kraken with its raspy tentacles and horrible, grasping suction cups, she tried comparing them to the delicate perfection of a baby cephalopod's suction cups on its tiny finger-length tentacles. Yes, Myriad was a terrifying beast, but there was beauty and fascination in its form too. She would do her best to keep these thoughts at the forefront of her mind and hope it was enough to deceive the kraken.

Beatrice knew she must finally be drawing near the monster when the sea, usually teeming with life, became emptied and still. Every creature that could had fled from Myriad's long arms, which had knocked about and damaged all of the vegetation and delicate corals within its reach. From out of the gloom ahead, a single piercing blue light, Myriad's eye, stared at her.

"You!" Myriad hissed with such force it sent Beatrice tumbling backwards.

"Wait! I've returned because I love you!" Bea cried.

The kraken pummeled her with its tentacles, half burying her in the sand. "We are supposed to believe you came back because you love us more than your sea witch?"

Beatrice spat out a mouthful of sand. "It was you who gave me my gills. True, it was also you who ate my leg, but when I skulked off to mourn the loss of it, I discovered you'd given me magic too and I adore you for it."

"You adore us?" Myriad wondered whether this was some trick of the sea witch and her wife. Its own thoughts were so confused, it had no way of knowing for sure, but it was intrigued and wrapped a tentacle around Beatrice's hair, pulling her out of the sand and dangling her in front of its baleful eye.

Beatrice swallowed her fear and pain and maintained a serene expression. "I shouldn't have left you alone so long," she said, with what she hoped was a convincingly affectionate tone.

"My dear," Myriad lisped. "We had hoped you would return but thought forces were at work to keep us apart. But you have changed your form. We like it. Never leave us again or we won't forgive you next time."

Beatrice made her eyes sparkle like they had for Coral the first time they met and gave the monster a forced smile. "Never! I used your magic to grow my body tenfold so that I might be a fitter companion for one as magnificent as yourself."

She did her best to bestow a look of utter adoration on the giant by pretending she was looking at Coral instead. Myriad's thrashing anger calmed as it became mesmerized by her. It loosed its grasp on her hair and drew her close with one tentacle tenderly encircling her waist. Beatrice's heart was pounding so fiercely, she was sure the kraken must feel it, but the monster mistook her racing pulse for passion and bent its head close to her for an attempt at a kiss with its horrific beak.

Beatrice stood her ground, repeating in her head the word *reveal* as Stormy had advised. Myriad's saliva mixed with her own. She felt a buzz as magic passed through her to the kraken and back again. The creature tried to withdraw, confused and alarmed, but Beatrice suddenly knew with all her heart that she mustn't break contact. Not yet. She stubbornly held fast to the beast even as Myriad rolled and writhed, striking her painfully as it tried everything it could to break her hold.

"What are you doing to us?!" it shrieked.

"I'm not sure," Beatrice murmured dreamily, feeling every bit of magical energy draining from her and into Myriad as her body shrank to its original size, "but I think we're losing our minds," she added.

She was convinced her eyes must be deceiving her or else she was hallucinating, for as she watched, the kraken's massive form exploded apart into billions of miniscule particles. Together they created a cloud in the water similar to a vast school of plankton. This wasn't at all what she'd expected the spell to do. Instead of vanquishing the creature, now there were even more of them.

Before she lost consciousness, a few of the things floated close enough for Beatrice to see. They looked like the tiniest fairy cap mushrooms she'd ever seen and were examining her as closely as she examined them. Had that immense creature been nothing more than a collection of fungi, held together by who knows what—a curse or a disease?

As the remains of the kraken drifted apart, a ring of observers swam close. Sea witches and shapeshifters, merpeople, and Stormy with young Bix, who wasted no time swimming into the fungal cloud, muttering some words only he could hear.

On the far side of the mushroom floaters, an object appeared. It was the Door of Lost Souls, the very door Myriad itself had created.

"Through this opening you entered our world. Now it is time to return to your own," called Bix, most commandingly for such a young child, but such is the power of a Blessed Baby that the mushrooms bowed their heads obediently to him and started a solemn march through the door.

There were so many, it seemed the parade would never end, but finally the last fungi crossed the threshold. The door slammed shut, vanishing from sight.

The seafolk clapped and slapped their tails and hooted and keened in relief that the menace that had threatened them for so long had been banished. Only Bix refrained from celebrating. He'd noticed Beatrice was floating in a strange position, almost like she was sleeping.

He shook her gently. "Miss Beatrice? Are you okay? Miss Beatrice?"

There was only silence.

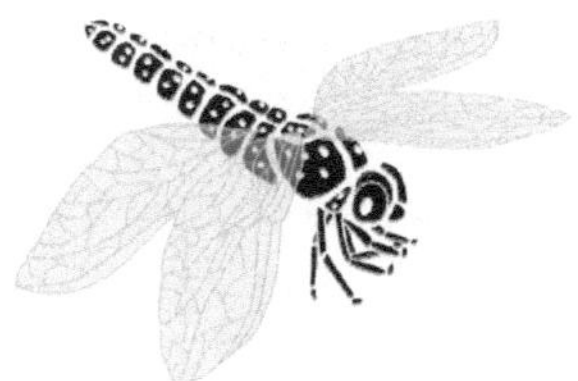

CHAPTER 26

STORMY IN THE LABYRINTH

WHEN BEATRICE DID NOT respond, a distressed Bix called Stormy over. The sea witch laid her hand gently on Beatrice's shoulder and a soft blue light enveloped her sleeping form.

"Coral, my sister," Stormy called out softly. "Your wife needs you and loves you as much as ever. We will return her to you, but you must believe me and cease this anger and your storm."

The turbulent waves and skies far above them instantly calmed. Stormy and the other sea witches laid hands upon Beatrice and Bix and brought them slowly up to the surface. The boy heard a whooshing noise in his ears and before he knew it, they were standing on the beach below the Kaleidoscope Lighthouse.

Coral, Jack, Amelia, and Click ran down the cliff steps. Coral was the first to reach her wife, who lay so still and pale on the sand. Amelia followed soon after, hands on heart in her dismay at seeing her friend looking like death.

"What's been happening? Who has done this to her?" Coral demanded of her eldest sister.

"It was necessary for Beatrice to pretend to be enamored of the kraken so she could get close enough to collect some part of it, as was foretold by the wise ones at Fungi Ridge. The being known as Myriad split into countless individual mushrooms that returned through the Door of Lost Souls summoned by Bix. This," Stormy said, pointing at Beatrice, "must be the result of the enormous power it took to break whatever spell had bewitched the kraken and bound its fungi into a diseased form."

Stormy bent over and gently scraped at Beatrice's arm with the dull side of a crystal knife. She waved her hand and a small cauldron appeared into which she placed the cells she'd collected. Next, she swirled in pewter gray, cerulean blue, and amethyst-colored smoke which she stirred while chanting low and peering intently into the pot.

Coral fidgeted impatiently but said nothing while her sister worked the spell.

Finally satisfied, Stormy looked up. "The mushrooms were a peaceful colony that became infected with a virus that bound them together and drove them slowly mad until they were unable to remember their former lives. They were in immense pain which is why they struck out as they did. The magic Beatrice imparted destroyed the virus and returned the organism to its original separate entities, but in so doing, her own mind has become fragmented. Think of it as a labyrinth with Beatrice lost somewhere deep within. To heal her, someone must enter, find her, and lead her out."

"I'll go," Coral insisted.

"Has the healing and banishment of the kraken ended your curse?"

"No," Coral admitted. "I can sense the tether to the lighthouse is as strong as ever."

"Then it is too risky. You are still bound here and must return each night. There's no telling how long it will take to find Beatrice, and we don't know what the consequence might be if you cannot return to the lighthouse by nightfall. It's possible you would both be lost in the labyrinth of her mind forever."

"Could I go?" asked Amelia. "I'm not magical, but I've learned a lot about Beatrice's mind since we first met."

"You are a devoted and loyal friend, Amelia Arrowheart, but this was caused by deep magic and I believe only deep magic can reverse it." Stormy caressed Coral's cheek gently. "Trust me, little sister. I am the eldest and strongest of us all. If I cannot accomplish this task, I doubt anyone can."

Stormy called all the witches gathered on the beach to attention. "I must enter the mind of Beatrice Buttons. I don't know how long it will take to find her and lead her out—if I even can—but the link I establish must not be severed unless one of us dies. As a precaution, I will tether my thoughts to Tern, she will tether hers to Turtle, and so on down the line so I can be pulled out if something goes wrong. We will have more of a chance with our combined strength than I would have alone. Let us begin."

One by one, the witches joined hands. A barely visible rope, twisted of silver and gold glowing threads, appeared between them. Bright halos, bolts of energy, ran back and forth along the connection between the sea witches. Stormy closed her eyes, gathering her strength and the strength of her sisters before laying a hand gently on Beatrice's brow.

The mind is a complicated place, twisting and turning like a maze, except every wall is lined with doors. Behind every door is a memory—some true, some imagined, some tainted by other people's remembrances, and some outright lies. Suppose you must pick a true memory to make progress. If you choose the wrong door, you might find yourself back at the start. Or worse, somewhere completely random that leaves you more lost than ever. Truth is a tricky thing, though. Often there isn't an absolute truth, so you have to pick the lie that is closest to reality.

The mind of Beatrice Buttons had more than its fair share of misdirection. There were not only her own adventures and memories, but also adventures she had heard about from others, stories she'd made up to amuse herself, and now, the pockets of magic the kraken had deposited into her memory when it kissed her. So much to sort through. So many doors. And at the center of it was Beatrice, lost and alone.

As Stormy stood at the entrance, buzzing with the power of the chain of witches stretching out behind her, she looked down the first corridor and wondered how best to proceed. A high, clear song caught her ear. She recognized the voice at once: her youngest sister, Coral.

It made sense Beatrice's mind would be full of thoughts and memories of her beloved wife. That might be the best place to start as love is a powerful magic all its own. Stormy walked down the hallway until she reached a door where the singing was loudest. Opening it, she saw a young Beatrice dancing to the tune while Coral sat perched on a rock like a mermaid serenading her.

The figure of Coral called out to Stormy: "You can't have her. This one wants me. Do not make me fight you for the right to make her mine."

"Little sister," Stormy replied, "You are nothing but a memory of the time when Beatrice first met you. You've been married for years and years. No one has her heart but you."

"She says yes?" the memory asked.

"Yes, and you've been very happy together. Only now, your wife has become trapped here in the labyrinth of her mind. I've come to find her and bring her to the real you, but there are so many doors, I don't know where to look."

This mere, insubstantial Thought of a Coral, ghost-like, considered this information, closing her eyes in concentration. "Hmmm, look for doors with glass knobs. You don't want any other kind. The glass comes in different colors so you will have to learn to decipher their meaning, but you definitely don't want anything but glass."

Stormy blinked in surprise at this unexpected advice but was grateful for the guidance. She stepped back out into the hallway and examined the knobs on the doors. Most were black cast iron or winking brass but, in the distance, she spied a brilliant blue glass knob.

As she turned this knob and entered, the door behind her disappeared and she found herself in the familiar waters of the deep ocean. She could feel it all around her though it was too dark to see. Then she heard a crack and a crunch and felt an excruciating pain in her leg. It was Myriad, taking a bite and slashing at her throat with razor-edged tentacles as she experienced Beatrice's memory of her first encounter with the creature.

She felt herself drop to the ocean floor, enduring searing pain but flush with the influx of magic Myriad had bestowed upon Beatrice. The kraken menaced her from above, its enormous maw vast and dark. The last thought that crossed her mind before she passed out was whether Beatrice could be hiding inside such a traumatic image of an injury and a foe too brutal to forget.

When Stormy awoke from this nightmare, her mouth dropped wide and she gasped, "Lichen wronged! So much suffering in your mind, little warrior."

She exited the room in a hurry and squinted down the hallway. All of the knobs had turned to glass of every color imaginable. There must be hundreds of them if not thousands. How to keep track of where she had already explored? Stormy bit her lip until it bled and, raising a webbed finger to her wound, used the blood to mark the door she had just exited.

Choosing another door at random, she entered to find a room rocking as though it was on a ship at sea. Lying down in the sailor's hammock before her, she shut her eyes, trying to imagine what this memory meant to Beatrice, but before she could formulate another thought, she was unceremoniously dumped onto the floor.

A furious bald man loomed over her. "Look what your witch did to me!" he shouted, running a hand across his smooth head.

And I'm guessing you deserved every last hair that was plucked, Sunshine, Stormy thought wryly as she gazed up at him from the floor.

The man faded away and Stormy exited into the hallway again, trying one door after another.

She spotted Bea on a mountain top. Then in the desert, in her granny's garden, in the Chimera Canyons. Bea in the soothing milky waters of Bathos talking with noops about Lichen only knew what. After a while, Stormy began to list in her own mind places that Bea hadn't been and there weren't many. Exhausted and wishing she too could bathe in the healing waters of Bathos, Stormy decided to try one more door before she rested.

Grasping a pale blue glass knob the color of ice and just as cold, she entered the next room to find a white and frozen world and a line of penguins, marching methodically forward. Tramping along beside them was Beatrice.

"My dear, is there anywhere you haven't explored?" Stormy asked the intrepid adventurer.

"Who are you?" Beatrice asked.

"I am the eldest of the sea witches and my name is Stormy. Am I familiar to you at all?"

Beatrice briefly glanced at Stormy and then trekked on. "Are you my wife? I think I lost her and I'm pretty sure that's what I'm doing out here. Trying to track her down."

"I'm your sister-in-law. Do you remember the kraken?"

A tremor shook Beatrice from head to toe and she collapsed onto the ground. "Did it kill me? Am I dead?"

"No, little witch, you cured it of a great sickness, but in so doing, it has sapped your own strength and broken your connection to reality. I've come to guide you back."

Beatrice shed a tear. "I've forgotten my wife. I can't remember her at all. Will she be angry with me?"

"No, on the contrary, she will celebrate your return with delight for she loves you deeply. Shall we go look for her?" Stormy asked. "We need to find a door."

"There aren't any doors out here in the Bitter Lands unless you count the entrance to the ice cave over there." Beatrice pointed to a sparkly gap in the towering snowbanks.

Stormy hoped with all her might this was the door they needed to walk through to escape the labyrinth. "Wouldn't hurt to look, would it?"

She held out a hand to Beatrice to help her up and gasped as she discovered the Beatrice standing before her was substantial and real, not a memory. "Beatrice, is that you?"

"Of course, it's me. Who else would it be?"

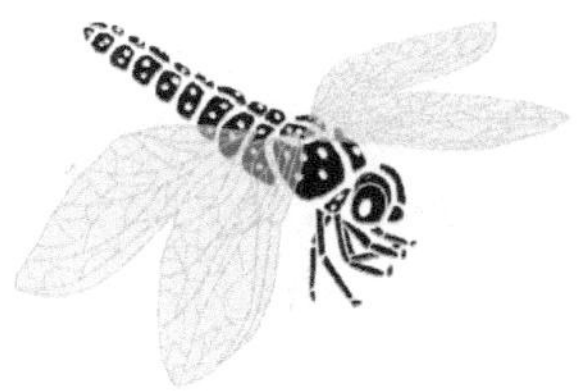

CHAPTER 27

BIX TO THE RESCUE

THE SEA WITCH HAD to laugh at Beatrice's bewilderment. "I was afraid you were only a memory, but now I've found the real you, we need to see if we can find our way out of here."

Stormy reached back in her thoughts to the chain of witches to lean on their strength for whatever might happen next. A swirl of silver and gold leaves appeared and circled like a cyclone above them. Beatrice reached up in wonder to touch the shining leaves and was drawn up into the air.

Stormy grabbed her foot to drag her back down. "Where are you going?"

Beatrice had no answer. Something was calling to her and she must obey. As she rose into the air, Stormy was pulled along also. She felt Tern's hands seeking to anchor her down to no avail as both witches began floating. Next, Turtle entered the scene in time to catch Tern's ankle only to be lifted from the ground herself.

One by one, the witches in the tether entered the labyrinth and attempted to stop the flight. One by one, they went sailing into the sky until there was a chain of witches like a kite's tail trailing after Beatrice. As they rose, the sky around them shifted from palest blue to azure to midnight to purple and finally to black. Stars materialized and a bone-chilling cold.

Stormy suspected Beatrice was astral projecting into the great beyond, a dangerous journey that was ripping her farther and farther away from Lichen. "Beatrice! Beatrice Buttons, come back. Coral is waiting for you. You're going the wrong way!"

Feeling torn in two at the mention of her wife, Beatrice became confused. She'd been so sure of the way, but now she lost faith. She looked down along the line of witches and saw the Kaleidoscope Lighthouse far in the distance, with Bix running around and waving wildly at her.

All of a sudden, she started falling. One by one, the sea witches fell also, losing their grips on one another. All awoke with a jolt and a shudder on the beach by the lighthouse where Stormy's journey into Beatrice's mind had begun.

Everyone looked on in anticipation and hope as Stormy awoke last. The look of disappointment on her face told the story. She had failed. Beatrice was still lost.

"No! I don't accept this!" Coral shouted, laying one hand across the brow of her still unconscious wife. "What happened?"

"Perhaps a mistake," replied Stormy, looking uncharacteristically uncertain. "Beatrice was being drawn through a tunnel of sorts into space and we couldn't stop her. I was afraid of where we might end up, so I called Beatrice back, but what if that was the way out for her after all?"

Frustration seethed throughout Coral's body and burst out as heat and vexation from the palm of her hand. Picturing herself and Beatrice standing nose to nose in her mind's eye, she shouted as loud as a sea witch can shout, which is very loud indeed.

"I've had more than enough of this, Beatrice Buttons! Come back to me right now, wife, or don't bother coming at all."

A visible burst of lavender-colored energy entered Beatrice's body.

"What did you do?" Stormy asked in dismay.

"I issued an ultimatum," Coral admitted quietly, no longer sure now that she'd done it if it was the right thing or not. She bowed her head in shame at this unusual loss of control.

Stormy shook her head. A witch in love could be so impulsive, but such a threat might only drive Beatrice into permanent madness. "Sisters, disperse. I will stay and keep watch. If there is any news, I'll send for you."

The crowded shoreline slowly cleared as the sea witches dove into the rough surf and swam away. Jack and Click returned to the lighthouse, but Amelia and Bix stayed behind to see what would happen next.

The eldest witch picked up a flat gray stone and skipped it across the waves with such force, it bounced a hundred times before being swallowed by the ocean.

Coral knew her sister was angry with her. She regretted her own impulsive action, but the thought of never being reunited with her love was unbearable. The two witches stood with their backs to each other and to Beatrice, so lost in their own thoughts that they forgot all about Bix and Amelia.

Now Bix was neither a witch nor a sorcerer, but he was a Blessed Baby, and often they couldn't be stopped from jumping in even when no one had thought of asking them to assist. As Amelia watched, he climbed atop Beatrice and hugged her with all his might. Beatrice's nose twitched twice.

"Miss Beatrice, would you like to borrow my handkerchief? I bet you've got an itchy booger that's gonna make you sneeze," he whispered to her.

Beatrice wiggled her nose again and turned her face away.

"Miss Beatrice," Bix whispered once more, convinced she only needed the right kind of coaxing to wake up, "if you don't want the fancy handkerchief, I could pick your nose for you."

Unobserved by the witches, Beatrice sat up and stared at Bix with eyes as wide open as wide can be. "Don't you dare!" she shrieked, thoroughly mortified and disgusted by the offer.

"Beatrice!" cried Coral, turning at the sound of her beloved's voice and rushing to her wife's side. "You're awake! However did you do it?" the sea witch asked Bix in amazement.

"It's my own magic and not for sharing or explaining. Just enjoy the results." He buried his face in Beatrice's neck and hugged her tightly.

"What a clever boy," said Stormy. "As a reward, you and I will camp out at a valley along the ocean floor where the sea leviathans gather to sing their secret songs. It's a sight no land dweller has ever seen, but you are a creature like us now, at home both in the sea and on land. We will give these two some time together to get reacquainted and return in the morning."

Though reluctant to leave, the thought of seeing something no other Lichen had seen was too tempting for Bix. He walked into the sea hand in hand with Stormy, swinging her arm with an uncontrolled enthusiasm that was comical to observe.

Amelia was bright red with excitement and relief but exhausted too. What a whirlwind it had all been! One surprise after another—some pleasant, but many far from it.

"I'm overjoyed to see you restored to yourself, my friend," she said, laying one hand on Beatrice's shoulder in that quiet way she had of showing affection, "but I, too, will see you in the morning. This time belongs to you and your wife."

Beatrice would have protested all these departures but was too weary herself to summon the energy. Coral carried her up the cliff to the outdoor bath, magically filling it and heating the water to the perfect temperature. She helped her wife undress and shampooed her hair.

"You don't have to do this," Beatrice said, even though it was blissful.

"Let me have this pleasure," said Coral. "Caring for you is another way to express my love and my delight that we are reunited. I was so afraid this moment would never come."

"You? Afraid? I thought you feared nothing."

"Nothing but losing you, my love, and now I never shall, for I sense that part and parcel of becoming a witch by way of the kraken's gift is immortality. We shall be together always now."

Beatrice settled back against her wife's tender ministrations with contentment. For all her restless soul might protest, this and no other place was where she belonged. But even as she thought it, she wondered if there would ever come a time when she and Coral might go adventuring together.

"It seems wrong," she said, "that after all of this you're still tethered to the lighthouse. Myriad is gone, why isn't the spell? I don't get it."

"I'm still bound to this place for the same reason you are still a witch even though the kraken has been dissolved and dispersed. We would have had to kill every last fungi of the collective to break their spell on us. That would have been impossible and also a pity, for they meant no harm. It was the virus that drove them to their raging misdeeds. And even if Myriad had been completely destroyed, I have known spells that far outlasted their makers."

After her bath, Beatrice asked her wife to show her the spot where the sea witch landed after Myriad threw her from the ocean when she was just a witchling.

There was a large dent there in the seawall that she had noticed many times but had no idea of the significance of until now.

"Which spot on your body was the first impact?"

"My spine," Coral said, pulling down the back of her dress to display a glittery patch of purple about the size of a cannonball. "It has borne the mark ever since."

"Why haven't I ever noticed this before?" Beatrice asked, sure that she had memorized every part of Coral's body.

"I've never liked discussing the curse, so I've always hidden it from prying eyes," Coral confessed.

"I wish you'd trusted me more, but at least I know now," Beatrice replied, blessing the kraken's mark with a light kiss before bestowing a more passionate one upon Coral's lips. "Let's go to bed, wife of mine."

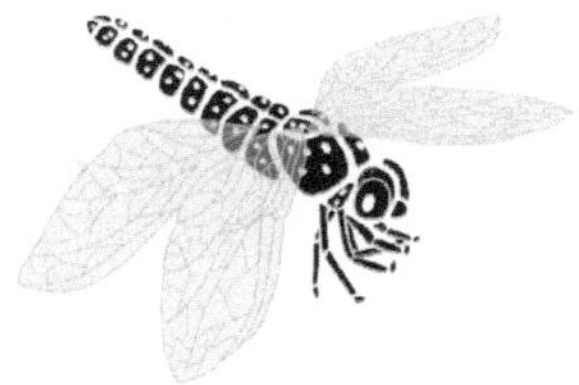

CHAPTER 28

ANOTHER DEPARTURE

THE NEXT MORNING, EVERYONE gathered in the skyboat's cabin so Moon and Star could participate in the discussion of what to do next. The kraken was vanquished and Beatrice recovered, but Coral was still tethered to the lighthouse.

"Myriad's spell is as strong as ever," Stormy observed, "and nothing we've ever tried before has worked. I must confess I'm not sure what else we can do."

Iggy floated over and perched on the sea witch's nose, leaning sideways to peer into one of her chocolate brown eyes. Amelia had to stifle a giggle at the comical sight.

"We recommend consulting the Pillars of the Deep," Iggy intoned solemnly. "They created the sea witches after all." Having made this pronouncement, they floated away, burrowing deep into Ome's luxurious fur, and promptly went to sleep. The black rabbit seemed not to mind in the least as it continued to munch on the limonberries that served as its breakfast contentedly.

"I've heard mention of these Pillars before," said Jack, "but what are they exactly?"

"They're the oldest fungi in Lichen, immensely tall and stately, and live in the deepest part of the ocean," Stormy replied. "They are an awe-inspiring sight even to our kind for they are our parents, I suppose you could say, though so much more to us than that. Our creators and our guides when we were first born."

"If the Pillars are fungi, perhaps I can help," said Amelia. "I could hear the thoughts of the pilgrims at Fungi Ridge, so maybe I can communicate with them too?"

"A bright notion, Amelia Arrowheart! It seems to me another journey is in order!"

Amelia sighed quietly. "Oh, dear."

"I don't want to waste any more time on these stupid quests," Click complained.

Star admonished her son. "Click! What a rude thing to say!"

"Why? Jack and I promised to stick around until Miss Beatrice was saved and we did. Why can't we go now?"

"I have an idea you're not the only one to feel that way," Coral said, looking at Jack. "I freed you from your prison of skin, but left you bound to this world just as I am bound to the lighthouse."

The pirate fingered his long braid thoughtfully, reluctant to admit his discontent when his companions had been so welcoming. "To tell true, every time I look up and see a night sky overhead, I long to lose me self in the inky black waves of space. There's nothing like sailing those vast distances with a trusty ship beneath yer boots and a faithful crew to command."

"But you can't leave before Coral is released from her curse! Don't you want to help? And we need time for a proper goodbye," Amelia protested.

Jack gave her a saucy wink with his one good eye. "I'm afraid a proper goodbye would take more time than either of us can spare, Captain. I've every faith ye'll solve this riddle without an assist from the likes of us. Besides, this lad's not getting any younger. In fact, he's growing older by the minute and had better start in on some proper training if he wants to master the secrets of the stars."

"How will you send them to Jack's home, wife?" Beatrice asked Coral. "Will your magic reach so far?"

"I think perhaps a ship will be the safest mode of transport, and there is one fit for purpose moored to the lighthouse. The oobble can be made spaceworthy with some sea witch ingenuity, but it will be up to Jack to navigate the way."

"That's not a problem," said Jack. "I've always been able to read the stars and guide me ship well and true no matter where we were."

"How very interesting," Moon commented. "We've only ever observed the Lichen sky through our telescope, but with a little modification, we might be able to see even farther. I don't suppose you could produce any sort of map of the stars for us to study?"

"I've no skill at drawing, but I'm willing to give it a go."

"Here," said Stormy, producing a sheet of black vellum so large that it covered the entire floor in front of the parents' photograph. A purple feather quill appeared in her hand as she chanted:

"Pen and ink, both wet and dry, fill up the spaces in our sky. Make the heavens come to life, so all concerns be joy, not strife."

Coral cocked her head at her sister.

"I suppose it's not the most prettily worded spell," Stormy acknowledged, shrugging her shoulders, "but it will work. Simply describe what you see in your mind's eye, Jack, and the pen will reproduce it."

To everyone's amazement (except the sea witches, who accepted the wonder of their magic very much as a matter of course), the quill pen moved of its own accord, scratching white ink quickly and efficiently against the dark piece of vellum as Jack described a map of the stars.

Star and Moon crouched down within the photograph so as to get a better look, and those outside of the frame gathered around with interest as the diagram came to life. Nobody noticed Beatrice slipping off by herself.

The idea of Jack and Click leaving them behind and traveling so far out of their reach was making her itchy and uncomfortable. Another goodbye was in the works and Buttons never say goodbye. They liked to pretend it's simply bad luck to do so, but deep in her heart, Bea knew it was a way of trying to avoid the inevitable heartache of separation.

She took off for a walk along the beach and, spying a lovely piece of driftwood, was inspired to make a parting gift for the travelers. She pulled the whittling knife she was never without from her pocket and began to carve more quickly than she ever had in her life.

From the wood, an excellent likeness appeared of Jack and Click, Coral, Stormy, and Bix, Star and Moon, and herself and Amelia, who had the tiny figure of Iggy perched upon her head and the black rabbit at her feet. When she was finished, words sprang into her mind:

"Magic fingers and magic toes, help the sand craft what the wood knows."

Pink sand swirled up off the beach and covered her carving. As Bea tried to brush it off, her hands emitted a fierce heat that melted the sand into glass as the driftwood burned away.

When all was said and done, she held a glass sculpture as light as a seagull's feather that twinkled in the sun.

"What do you know?" she said with a laugh. "This whole magic thing is going to take some getting used to!"

Beatrice returned to the skyboat's cabin and made an offering of her gift to Jack and Click. Everyone marveled over the beauty of the pink glass and the fineness of the details. Embarrassed by the fuss over the magical talent that was still so new to her and wishing to avoid the finality of witnessing their departure, she quickly retreated to the safety of the lighthouse cottage where she could process the parting in her own way.

Jack rolled up the finished star chart that included the route to his home planet and slipped it behind the photo's seashell frame to Star and Moon.

"Thank you, sir!" Moon said. "This will be an invaluable tool for us if we ever return to the observatory and are able to adapt our telescope. We will point it often in your direction, son," he added to Click, "and think of you."

In a rare sentimental gesture for him, Click ducked into the photo and hugged both his mother and father awkwardly before ducking back out again, red in the face. He reached toward Bix, perhaps to repeat the gesture, but his brother would have none of it.

"Why don't you leave already if you're going?" Bix said, digging a nasal nugget from his nose and flicking it at his brother.

Irritated, Click started to retaliate before remembering he was no longer a child but a mature adult.

"Bix!" Amelia scolded. "What did I tell you about using the handkerchief I gave you?"

"It's too pretty to dirty up," Bix said, pulling out the pristine linen and admiring it before tucking it back into his pocket and disappearing up the steps of the cabin.

"He's only upset that you're leaving, Click," Star said, "but he'll understand one day that we each must take our own journeys in life."

"Speaking of which, time is ticking away," said Stormy. "Come, sister, we will make their ship ready for flight and send these two on their way. Others here have their own journey to start and the sooner they leave the better."

With the sea witch sisters working together, the oobble was soon outfitted for its new purpose. Stormy, Coral, Amelia, and Iggy watched from the top of the lighthouse as Jack and Click disappeared within the vessel with a shouted "IN" and took off into the sky while Bix and Beatrice waited in the cottage below.

"I don't suppose we'll ever see them again," Amelia said, wiping tears from her cheeks as she waved goodbye to the fast-disappearing craft.

"We wouldn't say that," Iggy replied enigmatically, but as the skydragon refused to explain any further, there was nothing to do but prepare for the next step in their own adventure.

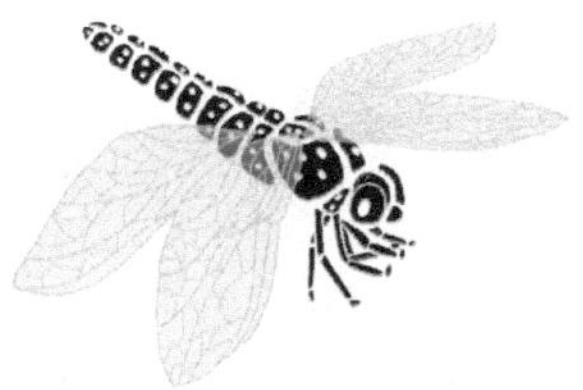

CHAPTER 29

THE PILLARS OF THE DEEP

"**I**T'S FINE BY ME that those two are gone," Beatrice said when they reconvened in the skyboat's cabin. "Amelia and I started this adventure together, so it's only proper we two should finish it."

"Quite right," Stormy agreed. "There is a pleasing symmetry in such a notion."

"Oh!" Amelia exclaimed. "I know Coral can't travel so far, but wouldn't it be better if you came with us? We might need your magical talents."

"You'll be traveling with a much more talented and powerful witch than I," Stormy said, laying her hand on Beatrice's shoulder. "My sister-in-law is only beginning to realize the extent of her new abilities, but she has a natural instinct for them that will carry her far. And do not underestimate the power of your friendship. Love and loyalty are a special kind of magic all their own."

"Can't I go too?" Bix asked. "I'd like to see the Pillars for myself and as a Blessed Baby, I could be of help, you know."

Star spoke up from the photograph. "I think you've had enough adventuring for now. I've already sent one son off into the unknown. I'd rather you stay behind, and we'll remain with you for company, if we may?"

"Of course, if you wish," Coral agreed, waving a hand.

The photograph and frame shrunk down to its original size and Bix picked it up. He had a rebellious look on his face but was still child enough to obey his parents' commands.

"Don't fret, little one," said Stormy. "Like all sea witches, I've visited the Pillars often and will take you there myself one day."

Bix perked up at this promise, carrying his parents away to show them the many wondrous sights of the Kaleidoscope Lighthouse.

Ever practical, Amelia had a pertinent question for her remaining company. "How will we travel under the sea?"

"On this very skyboat, of course!" Stormy replied. "Only we must make it seaworthy. Come along!"

The elder witch led them above. As Amelia watched from shore with Iggy perched on her head, the three witches worked together to create an aura like a giant soap bubble that encased the boat. This would serve both as a shield to protect the vessel as well as preserving a pocket of air for those on board without the gift of gills.

The skyboat's balloons were untethered and set aside for the time being. Their buoyancy would be unnecessary underwater and would even be a hindrance to diving deep below the surface. The beautiful dragonfly wings alone extended beyond the bubble to serve as both oars and rudder to propel and guide them.

Coral and Stormy were overwhelmed with how quickly Beatrice picked up the finer points of weaving such a complicated spell.

"You are a marvel, my love," Coral said. "You've always been a special being but from now on, I can't help but believe that you will be the teacher and I the pupil."

Such a startling idea made Beatrice so uncomfortable that she strove to quickly change the topic of conversation.

"Iggy! Amelia! Come see!" she called, eager to show off their craft. "The wings of our dragonfly will operate like fins underwater. We'll be able to swim and dart around as gracefully as any fish."

Amelia eyed the contraption warily, poking at the resilient bubble which sprang back under her touch. It would take an enormous leap of faith to trust her life to such a thing. "I hope you know what you're doing. If this should burst while we're diving, Iggy, Ome, and I would be goners."

"Don't be a silly!" Beatrice cried. "Sea witch magic is the best! And look, you say 'IN'..."

Beatrice disappeared and reappeared inside the bubble, waving at them from the deck of the boat.

"...and 'OUT'!" She reappeared at Amelia's side. "Just like the oobble! Isn't that clever?"

"I suppose so. Well, if we're doing this, let's get underway before I change my mind." Amelia picked up Ome in her arms and spoke a tentative, "IN!"

Iggy was left floating in the air without their perch. "We will not be left behind, we think. IN!"

Before Beatrice could follow her friends, Coral pulled her aside. "If you're unable to find a solution, don't take it too hard, dear heart. I've survived my imprisonment for hundreds of years already. I won't be disappointed in you but promise to come back to me."

A passionate kiss was the only reply Beatrice made as this was coming uncomfortably close to a goodbye.

Amelia and Iggy waved their own farewells at the witches as Beatrice resolutely turned her face seaward, commanding the boat to submerge. With a *BLOOP* and a *SLURP*, the dragonfly disappeared under the surface. Those left on shore could do nothing but bide their time in whatever patience they could muster.

Amelia had never even visited the seashore before she met Beatrice, so it was quite an experience to find herself sinking ever deeper below the surface of the ocean. Once she got over her initial fear that the bubble would burst at any moment, she spun in circles on the deck of the boat trying to take in the sights surrounding them.

Now that the kraken had been banished, the sea was teeming with life once more, joyous and shimmering in their new found freedom. Iridescent fish flashed by in schools. Cephalopods explored the strange bubble with their tentacles. Mermaids and shapeshifters gathered in pods, marveling at the vessel and waving in recognition as they saw it was Beatrice at the helm. She had become a celebrity to sea creatures everywhere for her part in freeing them from Myriad's wrath.

"Isn't it something, Bea?" Amelia cried, overwhelmed by the novelty of seeing in person things she'd only read about in books before.

Even Iggy was impressed and enjoying themself, floating around in the bubble erratically like a bumblebee, and the black rabbit hopped from side to side, holding out one paw as though it thought to catch one of the creatures just beyond its reach.

A small starfish tattoo peeled away from the side of Amelia's neck and flung itself at the barrier between it and the ocean.

"Oh, it wants to go home!" Amelia cried. "Do help it, Bea!"

Beatrice waved a hand and the starfish vanished in a puff of smoke, reappearing outside where it swam happily away.

"Do you think thisssss bug boat lookssss appetizzzzing to anything down here?" Amelia's snake tattoo asked, eyeing some of the larger creatures with apprehension.

"We are safe," the skydragon replied. "None shall harm the kraken-slayer."

"The kraken-slayer! Think of that, Bea," Amelia exclaimed. "You're like one of those heroes in the old Lichen myths."

"Don't be a silly, Melia. I'm just me, and I need to concentrate on navigating. It's not as easy to control our ship underwater as it is in the sky."

Regardless of Beatrice's protestations, the skyboat flitted gracefully, darting here and there rather than proceeding in a strictly straight line, but the bubble created a stable environment inside, so the lurching did not provoke any seasickness. As they continued down, the light from the surface grew dim. Amelia was swamped with disappointment as the waters darkened and her vision suffered.

"I can't see a foot in front of us. How are you steering, Bea?"

"Stormy gave me the gift of seeing in the dark. I remember how she did it." Beatrice beckoned Amelia closer, laying her hand across her friend's eyes and speaking the words of the spell. Amelia's jaw dropped as her vision widened out to view the amazingly weird deep-sea creatures she'd been missing out on.

"Oh, thank you! This is an experience I'll never forget no matter what happens!"

"Which do you like better, Melia? The sky or the sea?"

"How can I choose? Such amazing sights in both, things I never imagined seeing."

"Worth leaving your cozy house and garden?"

"Yes," Amelia admitted, "though I still yearn to be there again one day."

"Not long now, I hope. We just need to find out if the Pillars can grant our request."

The skyboat turned seaboat sank deeper and deeper into the farthest reaches of the ocean—trenches so cavernous, they seemed bottomless. The bizarre fish that lived there goggled at the sight of the bubbly dragonfly that flew among them.

Just when they despaired of ever reaching bottom, the Pillars of the Deep loomed ahead—enormous individual mushrooms, with flowing bells and thick stems. Hordes of fluorescent jellyfish made their homes in the gills, casting multi-colored light down into the chasm. It was a truly wondrous sight.

"There aren't even words in our language to describe them. How in the name of all things Lichen am I supposed to ask them how to free Coral?" Beatrice asked.

"That's what I'm here for," Amelia answered, seeming unusually confident she would be able to communicate with these sentinels of the sea. "During my tenure as Record Keeper, this appeared," she said, indicating a tattoo on the back of her left hand that Beatrice had never noticed before. It was a beautiful mushroom that mirrored the form of the magnificent edifices before them in every detail, down to the glowing jellyfish lights.

"You think it will allow you to hear them?" Beatrice asked.

"Let's find out."

Amelia ran one finger gently over her tattoo and felt the presence of the giants before them. Their thoughts were arcane and ponderously slow until she got used to the rhythm. They were curious about why a land creature such as herself would risk the depths of the sea to speak to them.

She explained the history of the kraken and Coral's tethering as best she could, while Beatrice watched curiously, unable to hear the silent conversation.

"The one who travels with you was given power by the fungi collective known as Myriad. She now contains all of that creature's magical knowledge, making her the most formidable witch of all. She should delve into her own mind to find the exact wording of the tethering spell. Only once she discovers this will she understand what to do," the Pillars intoned.

With trepidation, for it would mean a return to the labyrinth of her mind where Bea had been lost, Amelia reported this advice.

Covering her face with her hands, Beatrice cried out, "I can't do it. I won't!" and slumped to the ground in despair.

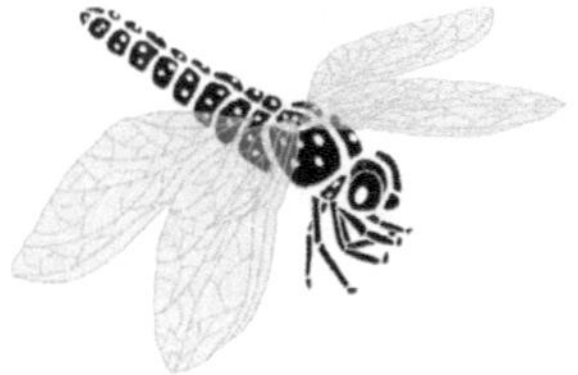

CHAPTER 30

RETURN TO THE LABYRINTH

AMELIA CROUCHED DOWN BESIDE her friend. "Don't be frightened, Bea. Remember you're a powerful witch now. Coral and Stormy said so, and the Pillars agree. I'm sure you'll be able to find out how to break the curse."

"Why? Do you think there's a neat and tidy box wrapped up with a pretty bow and a tag reading 'Coral's Curse' on it inside my brain?" Beatrice asked.

She honestly wasn't trying to be snarky, but after being trapped in her mind once already, she was afraid to try again. Searching through the memories left by the kraken was even more daunting since it had been a maddened thing, tormented by the virus that plagued it.

"I don't know, but we have faith in you, Beatrice Buttons. Don't we, Iggy?"

"We do. Why not? A button is a most useful thing," was that creature's typically cryptic reply.

Realizing that was the most she could expect from the enigmatic skydragon, Amelia continued. "Think of Coral. Wouldn't it be wonderful if she was free and you two could travel Lichen together? Isn't adventuring more fun with a companion than alone? I'd never have had the nerve to do all of this without you."

"You're right, and there isn't anything I wouldn't do for my wife, but I've never been this scared before. Not even when I had to confront the kraken. Will you stay beside me and hold my hand, Melia, while I enter my dreams?"

"Of course, I will! I'll never desert you, Beatrice. You're the best friend I've ever had and... and... I love you."

Spirits buoyed by this unexpected declaration of affection from the usually reserved Amelia, Bea took heart. They went below deck and Beatrice settled into her pea pod bed. Ome snuggled close while Amelia clasped one of Bea's hands in both of hers. Iggy hummed a quiet tune, like the softest lullaby ever heard. It filled the minds of their listeners with peace and courage.

"Goodnight, Melia."

"Goodnight, Beatrice. I won't say sweet dreams, because they may not all be so, but you can be assured that I will be waiting for you when you awake."

The labyrinth was very different this time around. Beatrice stood in the same hallway of doors as Stormy had experienced but it was infinitely longer than it had been and branched off into many additional byways. The kraken's memories were easier to spot than she had hoped, being of such foreign and complicated design that their entryways were just as complex. While Bea's memories mostly lurked behind plain wooden doors, Myriad's openings were elaborately carved with words in an unfamiliar language and made of a metal that gleamed with ever-changing lights and colors in the darkened space.

There was no question the organism they had known as Myriad was one of the most wondrous creations of the universe, Beatrice acknowledged. She hoped the fungi who had been returned to their point of origin were now healthy and benign again. Such power as they possessed when united should not be at the beck and call of madness, pain, and rage.

While locating the kraken's thoughts was straightforward, she was overwhelmed by the sheer volume. Thousands upon thousands of years of the lives of so many individuals would take an eternity to sort through. So many rooms to explore.

Gathering her courage, she opened the door nearest to her. What awaited inside was so overwhelming that she backed out again as quickly as she could, slamming the door shut. She would never be able to describe what she had seen to anyone who had not melded with the kraken in the way she had. She burst into tears at the idea of opening one door after another to face such sights.

Beatrice was startled awake by one of the weirdest sensations she'd ever experienced.

"What in the name of Lichen!?" she cried, sitting up in bed.

"We would wake the button," said Iggy, "so we stuck our tail in your ear."

"Well, don't ever do it again!" Beatrice shook her head as though trying to empty her ears of water after a shower. She wiggled a finger in each one to get rid of the tickling sensation that lingered and sent shivers traveling up and down her spine. "It felt like an icy breeze blowing in one ear and out the other. Not pleasant at all!"

"If you felt it go out the other ear, there must not be much of substance between the entrance and exit."

Beatrice glared at the skydragon's witticism.

"Buttons have no sense of humor," Iggy observed, floating away to curl up on Amelia's head.

"I'm sorry, Beatrice. It was my idea for Iggy to try and wake you. You started weeping and flailing around on the bed. I was worried about you. What did you see in there? Is it worse than you thought it would be?"

"It's too much. Too many rooms to explore, and the first one I tried freaked me out so bad, I'm afraid to go back."

"Why don't you take a break and calm down. I made you some tea. And here's a bar of your favorite chocolate. We'll figure something out."

Sucking on the chocolate bar did soothe Bea's shattered nerves somewhat as chocolate has been known to do.

"It's such an immense amount of information, Melia. There's weird writing on the doors that I can't read and the energy that radiates from them feels like standing in front of a roaring fire. Myriad had power beyond what any of us can imagine."

"Just think, Bea, if you can learn to tap into it, there might be no limit to your magic! What if you could use that ability for building and healing and helping rather than the fear and destruction the kraken brought to Lichen."

"To be fair, the fungi collective was diseased. I can't believe they were like that at heart. Who ever heard of an evil mushroom? Can you imagine what such a villain would say?" Beatrice dropped her voice an octave and whispered, "Do as I say or I shall slime you again and send nasty spores up your nose!"

Amelia was inclined to giggle at the image that popped into her mind at Bea's words, but it also gave her an idea. "What if I went with you?"

"Hmm, went with me where?" Beatrice asked, distracted by a large mouthful of chocolate.

"Into your mind, of course. I've been given the gift of understanding fungi. Maybe I can read what's written on the doors and help you narrow down your search?"

"Would you really do that for me and Coral? It might be dangerous for you. Far more dangerous than anything else you've faced since I dragged you on this adventure. What if we both get stuck in there? We could be floating along in this boat forever while our bodies waste away from lack of food."

"I'm not worried. Iggy will warn Stormy and Coral if we're in trouble. They can call on all of the sea witches and other seafolk to help us, can't they, Iggy?"

The skydragon floated down to the head of the pea pod bed and promised, "We will keep watch."

"Let me do this for you, Bea," Amelia pleaded. "I may not be as powerful as you, but I'd never forgive myself if I didn't do everything I could. Isn't it worth a try?"

"Okay, but you'd better rescue us if we need it," Beatrice said to Iggy. "Or Coral will have some very stern words for you when you see her again."

"Phoo," said Iggy, and with that they had to be content.

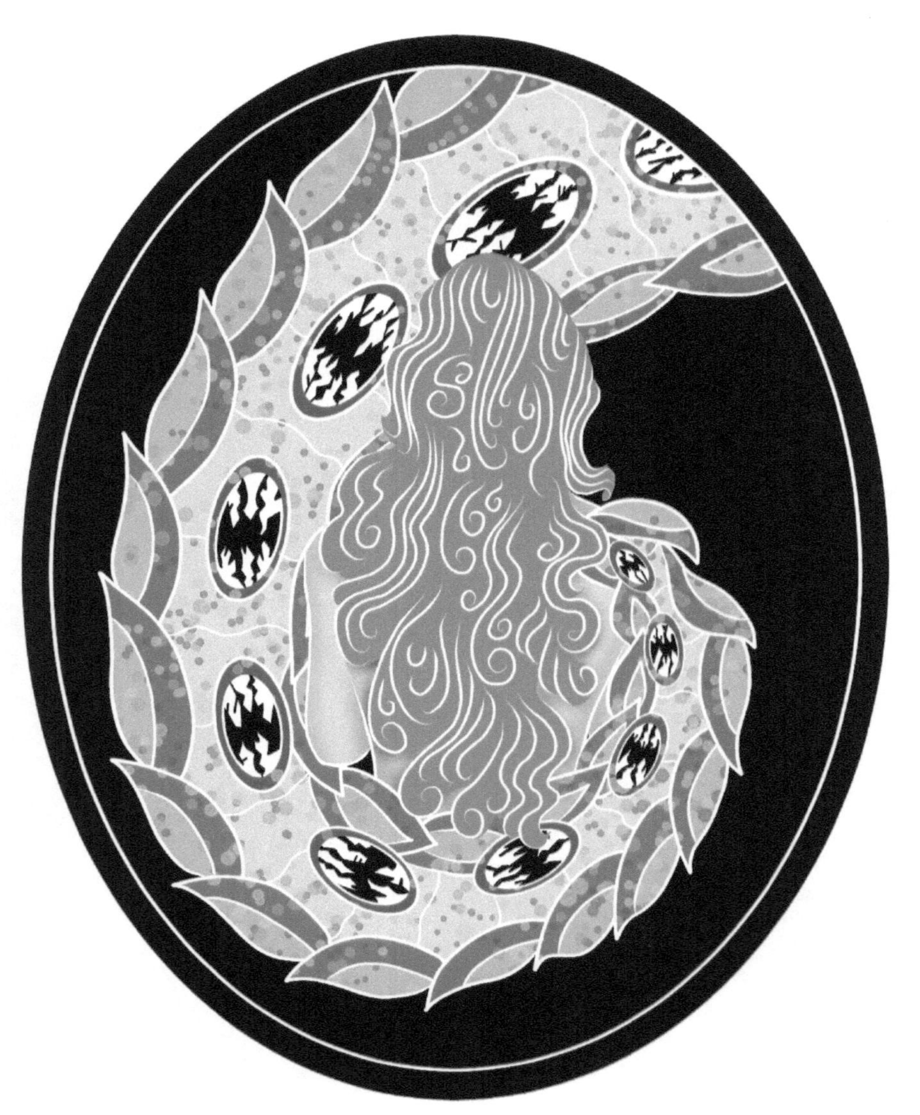

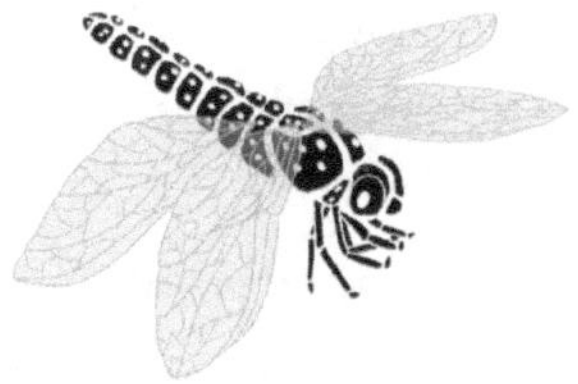

CHAPTER 31

BREAKING THE CURSE

"BEATRICE! ISN'T THIS ASTOUNDING?" Amelia said as they stood in the corridors of the maze that was her friend's mind and memories. "I can't wait to make some sketches of this once we get back."

"I like your confidence that we will get back," Beatrice replied. "You see what I mean about this being an impossible task. Look at all these doors!"

Amelia ran her hands along the peculiar writing on the nearest door. "I can understand it! The meaning runs through my mind just like when the fungi talk to me!"

"What does it say?"

"This one is about you! Myriad's memory of your birth that it pulled from your mind. You'll never believe this, but you weren't conceived in the ordinary Lichen way. A stray space spore landed on your mother and you're the result."

"Are you calling me a mushroom?" Beatrice asked indignantly.

"Fungi. A new species similar to the Pillars of the Deep, but one that took on a Lichen form. That's why the kraken collective was so attracted to you. Myriad only meant to give you long life and healing powers so it might never lose you, but instead, once it opened its mind, you were able to easily absorb its thoughts and power in a way no ordinary Lichen could have because of your fungal nature. Bea, you are the most unique being in all of Lichen!"

Beatrice's first reaction to Amelia's shocking news was a panicked fear that left her hyperventilating, shivering, and sweating. She wasn't simply another Buttons in a long line of them after all. She was a foreign object—a kind of invader from beyond just like the kraken. Her life was built not upon a firm foundation as she'd always believed, but quicksand, and everything about it felt like a lie.

A buzzing in her mind increased in volume and intensity as she mulled over this revelation, until suddenly all thought fled, leaving a hole, a quiet emptiness, white and vast. She felt more alone than she ever had in her life and as lost as she'd ever been.

But then she heard a gentle thrumming sound. It was Iggy, humming their lullaby into her ear, full of a harmony that spoke to Beatrice's innermost soul.

All at once, she felt her cells align. Her mind burst with streaming fireworks of knowledge. Instead of being bewildered and overwhelmed, she understood the pattern of the labyrinth as a whole and was sure without a sliver of doubt that she could pluck any piece of information out for use at any time. She'd never been so attuned or so at peace with herself.

She was Beatrice Buttons. A new kind of being, a new kind of fungi, and a new kind of witch. She reached into the pool of magic swirling in her head, caught the curse that had trapped Coral, and knew at once how to end it. She must take the form of the kraken, pluck Coral from the shore, drag her into the depths of the ocean, and repeat the words of the spell backwards. By reversing the sequence of events, the curse would be broken.

The old Beatrice would have been completely undone at the idea of doing such a thing, but that Beatrice was no more. The new one closed her eyes, centering herself until she was as one with every fiber of her being. Calm and collected, and feeling far wiser than she'd ever believed possible, she reached out for Amelia's hand.

"I know what to do. Thank you, my friend. I'll never forget what you've done for me. Now let's wake up and rescue my wife!"

Such was the strength of Beatrice's new-found magic, she was able to wish them back to the lighthouse in the blink of an eye. As the dragonfly boat emerged from the waves onto the beach, its bubble burst as it grounded itself safely in the soft pink sand.

The sea witch sisters were waiting there for them, drawn to Beatrice's surge of power.

Coral ran to her wife and embraced her. "I've been so worried about you. I never should have let you go. I'd prefer to be tethered here forever than to risk losing you."

Beatrice silenced her with a kiss. "Shhh, don't fuss. I've discovered the secret of breaking the curse and much else besides."

"Bea is a mushroom!" Amelia blurted out, unable to suppress a giggle that was half hysterical at the notion. It was still hard to reconcile the idea with what she knew of her friend.

"What?" cried Coral.

"What do you mean? Are you a sea witch or a kind of fungi?" Stormy asked Beatrice.

"Both and neither exactly, I suppose, but I'd prefer you still think of me as your sister-in-law and little sister. You are the eldest witch after all."

"But one with much to learn from you now, I think. The kraken's power and knowledge far outweighs those of any sea witch living. You will be a blessing for our kind and for all of Lichen."

"Perhaps you won't want to be tied to me now that you have magic so much greater than my own," Coral said.

Beatrice gave her wife an extra hard squeeze. "Don't be a silly! I didn't fall in love with you for your magic. You'll always be my one true love. But I'd rather you weren't tied to this place anymore. I've discovered how to break the curse. I have to take the form of the kraken and drag you from the shore back into the sea, chanting the spell it wove backwards. If I can do it correctly, it will reverse the curse laid upon you. We'll be able to roam Lichen, and maybe even beyond, together."

Coral kissed her wife passionately. "I believe in you and trust you implicitly."

"Then wait here for me at the exact spot where you landed when Myriad threw you from the ocean as a witchling. I'll return for you and do what I must. Don't be afraid of me. Even though I'll look like that monster, I'll always be your own faithful wife."

With that, Beatrice turned her back on the beach and strode out to sea, still awkward on her crutches, but those were soon discarded as her form changed. Tentacles shot out and grew to immense length as she took on the form of the kraken and swam out of sight.

Coral went to stand by the dent in the seawall where she had so rudely and abruptly arrived from the sea when she was no more than a witchling. Amelia and Stormy withdrew to the top of the cliff where they were joined by Bix and his parents in their frame. Everyone waited anxiously to see what would happen next.

A tremor shook the shoreline, knocking loose rocks from the cliff and causing those waiting to stumble on their feet. Coral suddenly flew up into the air in an arching swoop before being plunged into the water and disappearing.

"Beatrice has drawn Coral to her along the original path the kraken threw my sister," Stormy said. "If she can repeat the words of the curse backwards correctly, it should be broken."

Far beneath the surface and far from shore, Coral and her wife were reunited.

Coral comforted herself as she was drawn closer to the monster's maw, and tentacles as strong and cold as iron bands wrapped around her. "It is only my very own Beatrice Buttons."

As she closed her eyes in involuntary fear and listened to the harsh voice of the kraken, she sensed a change happening, like a rope being unwound slowly, strand by strand. With a *snap* the tether to the lighthouse was broken. Little by little, the creature before her shrunk and changed until Coral found herself wrapped in the familiar and loving arms of her wife.

Beatrice whispered in her ear. "You are free, my love."

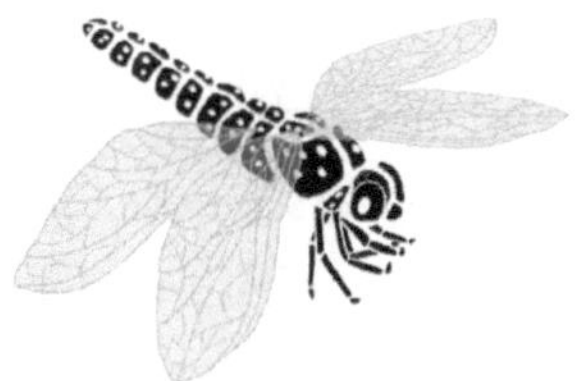

CHAPTER 32

GOING HOME

"**I**'M FREEEEEEEEEE!!!!"

Coral darted and danced beneath the waves, feeling at home in the deep, distant ocean now that her leash had been destroyed. She was safe. The sea was safe. She was with Beatrice and this time it wasn't a dream. She was really with her wife, far from the lighthouse and the prison it represented and need never return unless she wanted to.

She shot to the bottom of the sea and wiggled her webbed toes in the pink sand then torpedoed up, breaching the surface of the water like a dolphin, twirling through the air before plunging below again.

Beatrice watched her wife with a grin so big she worried her cheeks might split. After all the many magical gifts Coral had given her, she at last had been able to return the favor. Although she'd never felt the sea witch's inferior, there was no doubt having her own power would put their relationship on a different footing. It would take some getting used to, but she had no fears it would come between them. True love, after all, is the strongest magic of all.

The reunion back on shore was the most raucous and ecstatic one yet. Stormy decreed a proper celebration was in order and conjured up a table set with rainbow-colored linens and seashell platters weighed down with every delicacy imaginable, and beetroot wine flowed like water. Even the boys' parents got in on the action when Beatrice supplied them their own feast within their frame with just a wave of her little finger.

The stars and moons were bright overhead by the time they'd exhausted their excitement and went their separate ways for the night. As was their habit when Beatrice was at home, Coral ran her a bath under the stars and brushed and braided her hair into the crown that she loved to see on her wife's head.

Beatrice winced as her stump hit the side of the bath.

"Does it pain you much, my love?" Coral asked.

"Not as much as at first, but I could swear that foot was itching even though it's no longer there."

"Your body remembers. I would give anything for you not to have endured such trauma and shock because of the kraken's hatred of me. Is there anything in its memories that indicates a way to regrow your leg? Surely that isn't beyond the reach of the power you now hold?"

"I've searched but found nothing. Maybe it's the price I have to pay for the other gifts Myriad gave me. I could magic up a replacement so I don't have to rely on my crutches all the time, but I'd kind of rather you did. That would make it more special."

"My precious, precious love." Coral kissed the tips of each of Beatrice's fingers and lost herself in the depths of her wife's celadon green eyes. "Because you will never experience the beauty that was the omes' existence first-hand, I shall craft you a leg from their bones, collected by my sisters from the bottom of the sea where Myriad cast them aside. You alone shall carry their weight and share the stories they whisper. In that way, the memory of them will live on."

"What a lovely idea," Beatrice said, pleased with the responsibility Coral was offering her. She had not forgotten the agony of the omes' extinction and did not want their existence to ever be forgotten. "Just as I expected from one as lovely as you."

While Coral crafted the new limb, Beatrice cut all of her trousers off at one knee so she could expose the ome bone limb in all its rare beauty. She also decided she wanted a pair of crutches as special as her new leg for the times when she needed extra support.

Growing along the coastline, there was an abundance of winkwood trees, bare hardwood trunks that support branches fanning out at the top like giant eyelashes, dancing and blinking in the sea breezes. Bea picked two stout branches which had fallen and carved an elaborate design of fungi all down them with smooth handles that fit her grip and height exactly.

Amelia painted each mushroom with bright colors, and they varnished the wood with a potion Coral made from their tears to protect it from wear and tear. Finally, Beatrice shrunk them down and tucked them into the nest of her thick hair so they would always be at hand when she needed them.

The shock and pain of her first encounter with the kraken would never fade completely, but the splendor and meaning behind her new aids did much to reconcile Beatrice to a loss as profound as the one she had suffered.

Finally, everyone gathered together for a farewell supper in the lighthouse cottage. It was time for all of them to start the next chapter of their lives.

"A simple 'thank you' is insufficient to express the gratitude I'm feeling to everyone here for my freedom," Coral said as she looked around the table. "What a fortunate day when Beatrice moved next door to you, Amelia Arrowheart, for it was that which set in motion the events that have led us to this happy occasion. I cannot wait to see this pink palace with all the turrets."

"It most certainly is not a palace," Beatrice protested. "I see Melia has been teasing you with descriptions of my house. She always thought it too large and ostentatious for one person."

"It's a good thing then that now there will be two," Coral crowed. "I'll be leaving the lighthouse in the capable hands of a retired fisherfolk couple, and though I long to travel Lichen with my wife, it is always good to have a base to return to from time to time to rest and regroup. And I want a place to entertain any of my sisters who wish to vacation inland for the novelty of the experience."

"That would make me very happy," said Beatrice. "They'll always be welcome wherever we are. I can't wait to meet more of my sisters. After being an only child all my life, it makes quite a change!"

Stormy laughed. "You have more siblings now than you will ever know what to do with, and more will be on the way when the next wave of witches arrives next century. The sisterhood of sea witches claims you as its own though you may consider yourself above us."

"Of course not. I'm honored to be part of such a large family."

"Speaking of family," said Coral. "Before we part, we must decide what to do about Bix and his parents. I've been hesitant to attempt to free them. Stormy and I have discussed it and neither of us can be sure of what the result will be. What do you think, my love? Does the kraken's magic hold a solution for this?"

Beatrice closed her eyes and meditated while the others watched anxiously. After what felt like an uncomfortably long time, she opened them again, shaking her head. "From what I can tell, it would be too dangerous to attempt. I think it likely they would crumble to dust if they were freed. But I have another idea. If you make the frame life-size again, Coral, I can create an exact replica of the observatory and its surrounding grounds inside the frame. That way Moon and Star can carry on with their research, and Bix can go back and forth between the real observatory and the photograph as much as he likes. It's not a perfect solution, but it may be the best we can do. For now, at least."

"That's not fair!" cried Bix. "I want them to be real again. We never meant for them to be a photograph forever!"

"Don't cry, dear," Star said from the picture frame. "It's a better future than we'd hoped for and means we can take care of each other and live as a family again. Who knows? Maybe someday, the means to be freed will be found. In the meantime, I'm content."

"As am I," said Moon. "I'm eager to get back and start studying the map Jack gave us. I've a number of ideas for improvements to our telescope. Wouldn't it be something if we could see beyond the moons. Click may be surprised one day to find we have found a way to keep an eye on him after all!"

And so it was agreed. Bix and his parents returned to the observatory proper and its mirror image within the photograph. Beatrice offered to bring their floating dwelling down to the ground, but they decided they preferred their sky views. Bix could always use his magic leviathan necklace to float down and visit with Beatrice, Coral, and Amelia as often as he liked. Bea even lent Bix the use of Sir Walks-a-lot so he could explore the countryside in comfort. Stormy visited her sisters often and kept her promise to take Bix to visit the Pillars of the Deep and many other ocean landmarks whenever he grew bored of land.

The novelty of living far from the inescapable roar of the ocean and being able to embrace and hold her wife in the flesh whenever she wanted contented Coral. However, she knew it was only a matter of time before Bea's roving feet would have them on the move again. Her restlessness was one thing about Beatrice that hadn't changed with her new powers and never would. The dragonfly skyboat, now stored safely away again in the conservatory, was kept in ship-shape fashion for just such an occasion.

And as for Amelia, the thought of returning alone to her empty house had somehow not been as satisfying as she had expected when the subject was first brought up back at the lighthouse.

"You might invite someone over," suggested Iggy as though they could read her thoughts.

"A guest? Like who?"

Iggy hovered in front of her face, huffing little puffs of air that tickled her nose. "Anyone you had the sense to ask, we suppose. It would be rude to invite ourself."

"Oh, Iggy!" Amelia asked tentatively, more afraid of a rejection than she liked to admit. "Would you come and stay with me?"

"About time you asked," they replied, curling themself up in her short silver locks for the trip.

Amelia glowed with delight. While the adventuring with Beatrice had gotten entirely out of hand, she'd grown more used to company than she would ever have thought possible once upon a time, but she still wasn't fond of crowds. The tiny skydragon was the sort of undemanding companion that would suit her.

She tsked, tsked over the state of her flower beds when they arrived back at her house. Weeds had run wild in her absence, and it seemed an impossible task to tidy them, but Iggy surprised her by inviting thousands of their many children to help. The small creatures darted and flew here and there, whispering and humming their arcane songs to the plants. Before long the garden grew tame and lush again.

The wild rabbit that dwelled there was happy to make Ome's acquaintance, and before too long, there was a clutch of tiny black bunnies running around, much to Amelia's delight and dismay. Dismay because they nibbled her plants but delight because they were too adorable for her to get truly upset about it.

The last few of her tattoos fled now that her traveling days were over, but the scarlet snake declared it was happy where it was, "thank you sssssssso much," and had no intention of leaving. Amelia was grateful. She always felt a push and pull between wanting to be left alone but not wanting to be all alone in the world.

As she stood one day among the busy insects and nodding blooms in her garden, she ran her fingers over the carved wooden figures of the penguin and snow cub that Beatrice had given her near the start of their journey. She knew it was only a matter of time before Beatrice's irrepressible spirit would lead to another adventure. She wondered if she would be invited along next time.

A small, quiet part of her hoped the answer was yes.

ACKNOWLEDGEMENTS

The authors would like to thank our friends and family in online and real life spaces who have provided support and encouragement.

Extra special gratitude to Ian, AJ, Carol Beth, Jacob, Kim, and LA for their thoughtful beta reading and feedback.

And thank you to our readers and fans! You make it all worthwhile.

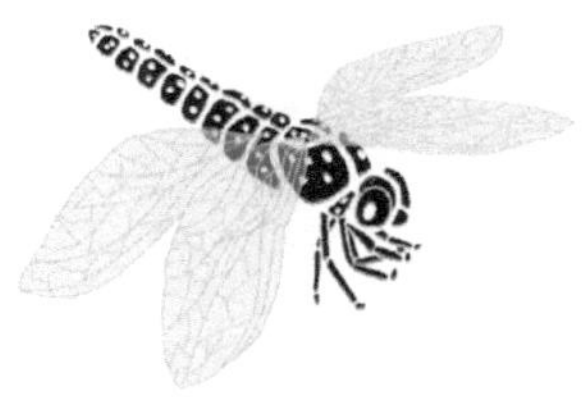

ABOUT THE AUTHORS

Eli Belt (she/they) is an indie writer and nature photographer most often found in the wilds. They have contributed a short story and several poems to various anthologies with themes exploring her autism, life and death, disability, and nature.

Helen Whistberry (they/she) is the pen name for an indie author and artist who began writing after retiring from a long career working in libraries. They have published numerous books as well as contributing horror and fantasy stories to anthologies. Helen's writing often explores their own experiences with gender, asexuality, alienation, and autism. Their whimsical digital artwork focuses on the natural world. Helen also loves to read and review books by fellow indie and small press authors. You can find out more by visiting their website for a complete list of publications and links: https://www.helenwhistberry.com/